PENGUIN ESSENTIALS

The Road to Lichfield

Penelope Lively is the author of many prize-winning novels and short-story collections for both adults and children. She was shortlisted for the Booker Prize for *The Road to Lichfield* in 1977 and *According to Mark* in 1984, and she later won the Booker Prize in 1987 for her highly acclaimed novel *Moon Tiger*. She was appointed CBE in the 2001 New Year's Honours List, and DBE in 2012.

Angie Lewin grew up in Cheshire and studied Fine Art Printmaking at Central Saint Martins and Camberwell School of Arts and Crafts. Her prints, watercolours and collages depict the native plants of the Scottish Highlands and Islands and the saltmarshes and clifftops of the north Norfolk coast. She also designs fabrics and wallpapers for St Jude's, which she co-founded in 2005. Her website is: www.angielewin.co.uk

The Road to Lichfield

PENELOPE LIVELY

PENGUIN BOOKS

PENGUIN ESSENTIALS

UK | USA | Canada | Ireland | Australia
India | New Zealand | South Africa

Penguin Books is part of the Penguin Random House group of companies whose addresses can be found at global.penguinrandomhouse.com.

First published by William Heinemann Ltd 1977
Published in Penguin Books 1983
This Penguin Essentials edition published 2017
001

Printed in Great Britain by Clays Ltd, St Ives plc

A CIP catalogue record for this book is available from the British Library

ISBN: 978–0–241–98140–5

www.greenpenguin.co.uk

For JACK

One

Anne Linton drove north to Lichfield through the morning. Berkshire gave way to Oxfordshire, Oxfordshire to Warwickshire, and Warwickshire to Staffordshire. A scum of insects gathered at the edge of the windscreen; the landscape lay misty and unreal at either side of the car, the road slicing through fields and villages as though it were of a different dimension, a different order of things. From time to time towns offered themselves on signposts – Daventry 12, Stratford 8, Birmingham 17. They seemed like actors in the wings, and the landscape itself a palimpsest, suggesting another time, another place. Edgehill recalled the Civil War; Tamworth, lurking over to the right, had something Saxon about it, she seemed to remember. Her own past, too, waved a cheery hand from over the horizon, or the other side of a motorway interchange. In Stratford, once, on a wedding anniversary outing to a production of *Much Ado* she and Don had discussed on the banks of the Avon whether or not to conceive another child. And in Oxford – well, in Oxford of course a great deal more than that had happened. She had thought of that last night, planning her journey. Private and public memory, it seemed, were fused on the R.A.C. Route Guide.

'I could go through Oxford.'

'Trafficwise,' her husband had said, 'You would do better not to.'

And so her intended route had lain neatly to the left, obedient to bypasses and ring-roads, and so also, when the city had appeared, shining in the sun like a mirage, she had obeyed instead some whim, and swung off in pursuit of the City Centre signs. And had sat then trapped in a traffic jam somewhere down by the station, remembering Don's advice and wondering why this place did not inspire more feeling. She had fallen in love here, taken irrevocable decisions here, but it seemed in no way personal. Living a bare twenty miles away, they seldom visited it, were never inclined to home on it for reunions or brandish it before their children like a possession. She thought of stopping for a cup of coffee, vacillated in confusion before an unfamiliar system of one-way streets, and picked her way up through the town towards Leckford Road. Let us see, she thought, what this will do.

And, turning into it, there came indeed the obedient ghost of an emotion, the relic of joy as that particular window came into view. At this point, by this particular lamp-post, once upon a time, she would walk more slowly, prolonging the approach, because however glorious the seeing him, the being-about-to-see-him had to be savoured to the full, drawn out step by step along this enchanted street of sour brick and shabby privet hedges. At that corner, time was, she could expect to see his duffle-coated figure coming towards her, wheeling a bicycle whose loose spoke clicked with each turn of the wheel, the background music of happiness. Which window? she thought, muddled – that one? Or that? A curtain was pulled back, and she found herself staring for a moment into the eyes of a strange young man. Behind her, someone hooted impatiently (no parking spaces in this road, cars glittering bumper to bumper along the kerb, how right Don was, what have they done to this place?) and ahead lay a long road yet to Lichfield, and the time already nearly twelve. She put her foot on the accelerator. No more of this, whatever it may have been.

And now, an hour later, stopped again, but more advisedly this time, to fill up with petrol, she checked the route. She had begun there, at that dot, and now was here, at this: a mere hand-span on the map. From Cuxing to Lichfield, a hundred odd miles, measured perfunctorily in finger-lengths last night, at the kitchen table.

'At a conservative estimate, I should think you're about twenty miles out, with that method. Here, let me.'

And of course there is a gadget with which such reckonings are made, a little thing that runs on a wheel along the map and comes up with what you want. 'And here,' he says, 'I'll do a route out for you, give me a bit of paper, pass the map over.' And presently there it all is, planned out leg by leg with the distance roundly stated at the end.

'Thank you, darling.'

But, somehow, she left it behind, the bit of paper, along with the other bit of paper she had parked on the kitchen table issuing instructions about meals (supper tonight in fridge, buns for tea in bin) and reminders (dinner money on shelf, 'phone me tonight). By the day after tomorrow it would be lost or forgotten and in any case few men, not even prudent and organized men like Don, are going to reproach a wife returning from a visit to her dying father for not going the way she had been told to go.

Lichfield, of course, is the ultimate fusion of private and public memory. Lichfield belongs once and for all to Samuel Johnson, and is also where my father has lived – or just outside which my father has lived – for the last twenty years. Samuel Johnson, she thought, paying the garage attendant without seeing him or hearing what he said, so that only his finger tapping the closed window recalled her sufficiently to take the proffered change, Samuel Johnson once said a formal farewell to a dying old woman. He sat beside her bed and prayed with her and said goodbye for ever. Nowadays we do not do that. I haven't, she thought, the slightest idea what I am going to say to father, or even what, if anything, he will be able to say to me. Confused, this Matron person had said, confused and going downhill rapidly, I'm afraid. And Anne had wanted to say: but it is I who am confused, who are you and what are you doing with my father?

She had said to Don, later 'It's just like him. Just like him to be getting ill and not tell anyone and then up and dump himself in some nursing-home, with everything arranged and sorted out. It's only three months since we were there. He seemed perfectly all right then.'

'He's eighty, remember.'

'I know that.'

'You sound as though he's done you an injury. He was trying to save you trouble, presumably, and preserve his own independence.'

Oh, do be quiet, she thought, you don't understand at all, and when he ploughed on with, 'Hadn't you better get hold of Graham?' she had snapped, 'Look, do leave that to me,' and the disagreement might have blossomed and run its proper course except that reasonable people do not quarrel at such a time. Or, indeed, much at all.

She was, now, on the outskirts of Lichfield and must devote herself to finding this place which she did not know in some unfamiliar suburb. When had her father tracked it down? In what cool moment had he said yes, that will do, I will take myself there? Perhaps, she thought, running it to earth at last, solid and sombre and nineteenth century amid its institutional garden and gravelled drives, perhaps it made him think of schools. It might have been one once. He must have inspected many such places, approving or disapproving of dubious private establishments on behalf of the Ministry.

But no, getting closer, leaving her car beyond the notice that tidily segregated Visitors from Staff, passing through an open door into a black and white tiled entrance hall, she could see the place had had a more domestic past. This must originally have been the home of some prosperous Victorian. The marble frieze above the fireplace was surely a legacy of someone's personal taste (albeit most discreetly of its time); the stained glass fanlight above the door displayed a proper civic pride, with the cathedral crudely rendered in green and red. Some local manufacturer on the way up, presumably.

'Will you come this way, Mrs Linton.'

The nurse tapped ahead down linoed corridors, talking cheerfully of weather and distances.

'How is he?'

'Very up and down, you know. Rather confused. But he knows you're coming. He's expecting you.'

Her father, propped high on pillows that seemed to devour him, their plumpness engulfing his thin face and body, turned his head as they came in, peering.

'Who is it?'

'It's me, father.' She bent to kiss him and he said doubtfully, 'Anne?'

'Yes. Anne.' How could illness make a person appear literally to have shrunk? His eyes were filmy – how much could he see?

The nurse said, 'I'll leave you with him, Mrs Linton. They'll be bringing him his lunch soon. Would you like something yourself?'

'I'd love a cup of coffee.'

'I'll tell them.'

Anne pulled a chair up beside the bed. Now sound normal and ordinary, the last thing he wants (or ever wanted) is fuss, a performance (distantly, in her childhood, a crisp voice saying, 'That'll do, Anne, we're not having a performance . . .').

'Everybody sends their love' – yes, her voice was coming out loud and overbright – 'Don was sorry he couldn't get away just now but it's a bit of a bad time at the office. Paul's got O-levels coming up, you know, this year, so he's actually doing a bit of work I'm glad to say. Judy's having riding lessons, I didn't want her getting involved in all that kind of thing but it's hopeless, living where we do. . . .'

And he was not, she could see, taking in a word. He smiled and blinked with the half-comprehension of the deaf (yes, he was a lot deafer last time we were up, that I did notice). Start again, more slowly, more clearly; what could be more tiresome when you are old and ill than someone, albeit someone you love, yapping at you things that you cannot understand. And yes, that's better, now he's remembered who Judy is, now we're getting somewhere.

The old man's speech was laboured, backed with a dry whistling of his breath. She, too, strained to follow. 'How long do I what? Stay? Oh, I'm staying a couple of days this time, and then I'll be up again soon.'

A nurse brought a tray and set it on the bedside table. 'There, dear. Are you going to sit up a bit more?' She said to Anne, 'He manages fairly well on his own, but he may need a hand when it comes to the tea.'

The food was pappy stuff in bowls. The old man ate slowly, each spoonful a new difficulty; he was absorbed in what he was doing. When his hand shook uncontrollably and food dribbled down his chin Anne found herself reaching forward to take the spoon from him and retrieve the mess with the familiar deft movement she had used in feeding her own young children. Her father appeared quite unaware of her. She sat drinking her own coffee. Her ears buzzed still with travel motion; she felt both depressed and charged with energy. I must go out to the house and see what needs doing, it must need airing, cleaning perhaps – does that Mrs Ransome still come? – I could bring him flowers from the garden.

'We thought we'd go to Scotland this year, father, for our holiday. Just Judy and us – Paul has something fixed up with a school party.'

'Southwold' the old man said, with sudden clarity.

'Not Southwold, Scotland.'

'We took you to Southwold when you were a child, your mother and I.'

'Southwold in Suffolk? Yes, I remember.'

'You remember?' He seemed pleased.

'You bought me a red spade. And there were sea-birds running in and out of the water at low tide – I can see them now. Little spindly legs skittering about.'

'That was just after the Great War.'

'No, no, father,' she laughed. 'I wasn't born then. Don't make me feel older than I am. It would have been about 1939 – the last war, not the one before.'

'Eh?' He stared stupidly at her and said again 'You remember Southwold?'

There was a knock at the door. 'May I come in, Mr Stanway?'

The speaker came into the room, saw Anne and hesitated. 'I'm so sorry. I didn't realize you already had a visitor. I'll come back later.' The old man, peering, said something inaudible: he was trying to smile.

Anne said, 'No. Please don't. I shall have to go in a little while anyway.' They looked from each other, awkwardly, to the old man in the bed, the link who might explain each to the other, but he merely blinked and muttered. Anne said 'I'm Anne Linton. His daughter.'

'Oh – yes, of course. I should have realized. My name's Fielding, David Fielding. I used to be a neighbour of your father's out at Starbridge, and we've kept in touch over the last year or two.'

The old man said suddenly, 'Mr Fielding runs that school. He's the headmaster. You know, that school . . .' He looked from one to the other of them for help, his voice trailing away.

David Fielding said, 'The boys' school. Your father took rather an interest at one time.'

She said, 'I'm sure. He didn't like retiring – he never could keep away from schools.' They both looked towards the bed again, smiling.

Benign smiles, Anne thought, at least mine is. Benign understanding smiles, as to a child. He shouldn't be talked of like this, as if he weren't here, or was too stupid to understand. And David Fielding, seeming to share her feelings, pulled up a chair and sat by the bed. He talked to her father, waiting patiently through his laboured responses, and making his own remarks clear and careful. Anne thought: what a nice man, why did father never mention him I wonder, but he always liked to shut off bits of his life, even when mother was alive. She always complained she never knew his friends.

After a while she said, 'I'll go now, I think, father, I want to have a word with the Matron. I'll see you again this evening.' David Fielding got up, 'Look, I don't want to be in the way . . .'

'You aren't in the least. There's a lot I must do today. Goodbye – it was nice meeting you.'

'Goodbye.'

Sitting in the Matron's chintzy office, looking out onto neat lawns swept by a huge Cedar of Lebanon, beneath which old people were tidily disposed on benches and wheelchairs in the early spring sunshine, she said 'What exactly is wrong with him?'

The Matron smoothed her hand across a card in front of her, hesitated a moment, 'Parkinson's, of course, but that can be controlled nowadays – there is this new drug. His heart is weak. Incontinence.' She looked across the desk at Anne. 'Old age, in the end. The body running down, you know.'

For a moment Anne thought again of Southwold, revived just now for the first time in many years; she saw that same body, upright in a pewter sea, urging her towards it with outstretched hands. She said, 'Yes, I suppose so.' And then, 'He seems quite comfortable.'

'He is quite comfortable. We can see to that. But he will go downhill from now on, I'm afraid.' The Matron paused and went on, delicately. 'I think that if you feel – if you wanted to make arrangements about his house, that kind of thing, it might be wise.'

'He can't ever go back there? Even – even with nursing arrangements or something? If he improved?'

'He won't, I'm very much afraid, ever improve that much.'
Anne said 'I suppose he knew that?'

'One rather had that impression. He was more lucid – much more – when he first came to us.'

There was the faintest creak from the Matron's chair; a minute shift of stance indicating perhaps the passage of time, other patients, other matters to be seen to. . . . Anne said, 'Yes, I see. I thought in fact I'd use the house myself while I'm coming up to see him.' She got up. 'You will let me know how he is?'

The Matron smoothed her notes again. She said, 'Of course. We must think in terms of months, or possibly weeks. It's very unpredictable, though. He might rally – but I would be surprised. Your visits will be the greatest help. Some of my old people have no visitors – no telephone calls; that I find very sad.' She smiled with sudden sweetness and Anne thought: she is a nice person, kind, good. Or am I in such a state of susceptibility that everyone I meet seems nice?

She walked through the building and out towards the car park. A nurse came out and toured the benches and wheelchairs, adjusting a rug, trundling someone into the sun. Inside the building, there had been a room in which, through an open door, two old men could be seen sleeping in front of a television screen on which a woman briskly demonstrated the icing of a cake. This place must be expensive. How much? And had her father been clear-headed enough to work out that he could afford it? I should have asked the Matron, she thought, how stupid, I can't go back now. And her head began to ache with this new concern. Perhaps there'll be something at the house that'll help. No, better perhaps go to his bank, talk to the manager. Blast, which is his bank?

She said 'Midland' out loud, at the same moment as someone came up alongside, saw that it was David Fielding and said, embarrassed, 'Oh, hello. I seem to be a bit deranged – talking to myself. I'd just remembered something I was trying to think of.'

They walked together towards the cars. He said, 'Have you come far?'

'Berkshire. Not all that far but I'm not used to long drives, I suppose – my husband usually does the driving.'

They stopped. Anne felt all at once dulled by tiredness, and something else – shock, perhaps – detached from herself so that sights and sounds were magnified, but all sensations gone. She stood staring at this man, who was talking for some reason about fishing, and saw that he had a thin face with hair slightly greying at the sides and lashes curiously noticeable for a man and a spectacle mark at either side of his nose (he must wear them for reading). 'Yes,' she said. 'Yes, I see.' Someone was riding a grass-cutter up and down the lawn, and rooks swirled around a stand of chestnuts, so that the moment was tethered, and for ever would be, to its own backdrop of those particular sounds. Sunlight snapped from a car windscreen and David Fielding was saying, 'Look, are you all right?'

'What? Yes, I am. Sorry – I suppose I'm a bit tired, in fact.'

There was a pause. The grass-cutter came closer, turned, and set about its return crawl up the lawn. The rooks planed in the wind. Anne groped in her pocket for the car keys, found them, stared down at them, and said to this stranger, 'My father's going to die.'

'Yes,' said David Fielding. 'Yes, I'm afraid he is.' And he laid his hand for an instant on her arm, removing it almost at once so that it was only later, at another time, that she felt his touch, in the way in which recollection can sometimes be more real than experience itself.

'Look,' he said, 'Are you sure you're all right? Would you like to come and have a cup of coffee or something?'

'No, really, I'm fine.' She smiled, to demonstrate, and indeed as she said it a new wave of this lurking energy came back. Bank, shopping – there'll be no food out at the house – then start sorting out. 'I'm fine. It was just the drive and everything. Goodbye again. And thank you fo being so kind to my father, visiting him.'

'It's he who has been kind to me in many ways. He was a very agreeable neighbour. I'll drop the rod in sometime.'

'What?' But he was already getting into his car (not very new, rather grubby, the back shelf littered with the bits and pieces of family life, Kleenex and a thermos and a slithering pile of exercise books). Rod? He must have thought me very off-hand. And suddenly the pressure of his fingers on her arm came back. She sat still in the driving-seat for a moment before starting the car

* * *

Old Mr Stanway lay propped up in bed and wondered what time of day it was. At some point recently, he knew, there had been people in the room, talking. One of them, he was almost certain, was his daughter Anne. The other, a man, he had recognized but now could no longer identify; perhaps it had been her husband. In the corner of the window there was an outline he could not quite make out. He screwed up his eyes, peering, and thought that it was possibly an aeroplane, or some very large bird. While he was in the middle of this a strong, competent arm came round behind him, hoisted him higher on the pillow and gave him a cup of tea. Since the cup of tea required all his concentration he abandoned the matter of the aeroplane, or bird, but it came to him as he drank that if the window was light it must, at any rate, be daytime. He smiled in silent triumph and someone he had not known was in the room said, 'There, nice to see you feeling cheerful, Mr Stanway.' The tea was hot, but not sweet enough.

* * *

The bank manager said 'He's not in BUPA or anything like that?'

'I don't think so.'

'We can make sure, of course. I need,' he went on, with a trace of awkwardness, 'a certificate from the doctor confirming his – the failure of his mental powers – and then I can discuss the state of the account with you, Mrs Linton.'

'Oh, should I . . .'

'I'll telephone them. I'm sure you have plenty to do this afternoon. And then I'll go over the figures again, and check some share prices, and perhaps tomorrow I can give you a ring with a clearer picture of how we stand?'

Anne said, 'Thank you.' She watched the bank manager draw a neat black circle round a figure he had jotted down on his pad and thought: he doesn't know what to divide it by. She said, 'Apparently we should think in terms of months, or even weeks.'

'Ah. I don't really imagine, Mrs Linton, that there is anything to worry about. The pension and securities should cover it perfectly well.

But I will go over everything.'

She drove out to Starbridge along quiet lanes, quite unlike the busy roads – dual carriage-ways and snatches of motorway – on which she had travelled from Cuxing. She saw, for the first time today, the landscape gleaming with spring; dandelions at the roadsides, the sheen on a field of grass, the plumper outline of trees. A thin sunshine reddened the bare earth of the fields; flights of small birds showered from the hedgerows at the car's approach. The road reached out ahead of her, empty of traffic, darkly grey between the green verges, its width neatly defined at every bend by a run of white lines in the centre. She could have been quite alone on it, as though it were there for her only. Behind her, clear in the driving-mirror and yet curiously diminished, it reached away again in reverse. She drove watching the road ahead and with one eye at the same time on the mirror, to keep this double image of advance and retreat. She passed a cyclist, and the anonymous, androgynous backview became in the mirror a tow-haired boy, red with exertion, bent over the handlebars, dropping further and further behind until a bend in the road took him away altogether. He might have been Graham, in their shared childhood, off on his private male pursuits, already exclusive and faintly improper. It was all brothers and sisters did share, she thought – time, and a humdrum assortment of memories. And then time-with-parents-and-brother became time-with-husband-and-children. Places shared with one lot were overlaid by places shared with the other. In between, a slice of solitude.

I hardly ever, she thought, go anywhere alone. Travel. You are alone in days, for bits of days, nights even, seldom is moving from one place to another done alone. Not for a long time, not since before we were married. And she felt, driving this road, as though the sequence of her own life had been tampered with, as though she were again the young woman who used to come up here to visit her parents. The edge of her own face in the driving mirror, eye and swatch of hair, was not, fleetingly seen, so very different after all from the face of twenty years ago. That eye, though, that eye of 1955, knew nothing of Don, nor Paul, nor Judy. Nor of things like this housing estate on the edge of the village or that supermarket so grossly set down between the pub and the church. They've ruined this place, it used to be lovely when mother and father first came here, just old brick and half-timbered things.

Except, of course, her father's house, itself an intrusion of the nineteen twenties. Why this, father, why not a nice old cottage? And he'd scoffed at her for a romantic: all very fine, but I want a roof over my head that doesn't need propping up every few years.

It's an ugly house, she thought, staring at it for a moment before getting out of the car. But of course he came here for the river, the fishing, the house was neither here nor there. And mother had to take it or leave it, I suppose, but she always seemed happy enough.

She carried her things inside. As she stood in the dank-smelling kitchen the leaden stillness of the house seemed callous, so empty of those two familiar presences. But her mother had been dead ten years now: the image of her aproned figure washing dishes at the sink was dimmed by that stretch of time, and fossilized by it too, leaving her, forever now, younger than her husband, more spry, not deaf nor bent. Not diminished in stages, a little more each week, each month.

Anne went round the house, flinging windows open. In the spare bedroom, where she would sleep, her own past proffered itself in concrete form: a row of her old books on the mantelpiece, a spurned wedding-present vase on the windowsill, a pair of her shoes in the wardrobe. She set about finding sheets and blankets, lighting a fire in the sitting-room. She went out into the garden and picked the last of the daffodils and some branches of flowering currant. Presently, sitting by the fire over a cup of tea she felt a small satisfaction at having rescued the place from its indifference. Just now, coming in, it had felt as though her father had never been here, even his familiar tobacco-smell driven out by the damp and cold. In the garden, though, the flower-beds were blurred with weed and the grass long. Perhaps there would be time to do something about that, too.

Mrs Ransome had, evidently, been coming in to clean and tidy. The kitchen was spotless, all scraps of perishable food cleared away, the fridge turned off. Anne opened a cupboard and thought: heavens! I never knew he went in for this kind of thing. The collection of tins and packets was like a schoolboy's tuckbox hoard; exotic soups, a magpie store of biscuits, pâtés, expensive jams. She thought of her mother's sensible, unadorned cooking. The contents of these kitchen cupboards seemed like a belated protest. She ferretted further, curious now, and found tucked away in another cupboard, thick with dust, the nineteenth century Staffordshire plates that her mother had collected over the years and that had previously been ranged on the dresser. The dresser held now a functional assortment of crockery. Had he always disliked those plates? She started to take them out, and then, muddled by the vague conflict they suggested, closed the cupboard again and continued her investigation of the kitchen. She had forgotten to buy any food for herself but there would be no need. She could feed off those motley tins.

The study was clean and tidy too, the familiar litter of papers on the desk trimmed into neat but arbitrary piles. There were a few unopened letters. Reluctantly – what deep-seated taboo forbade you to invade a parent's privacy? – she sorted through them. A couple of circulars (throw away), the electricity bill (pay that), a curt note from the telephone people threatening to disconnect (pay that quickly). Something private, in an unknown handwriting. That must be taken to him and read aloud, perhaps. A postcard of some Italian resort from Graham, several weeks old ('A couple of days here as a perk at the end of a filming assignment, hoping to get up to see you soon . . .'). She glanced at the top paper in one of Mrs Ransome's random piles and saw that it was a renewal reminder from an insurance company, a couple of months old – the house insurance. Under it was a letter from her father's stockbroker, asking apparently for the second time, for some instruction. She realized, sifting quickly through the pile, that her father had ignored these. His systematic red ticks at the foot of correspondence dealt with had ceased a couple of months back. She sat at the desk, chilled by this suggestion of the old man's solitary decline, and thought: I'll have to do something about all this, there may be other urgent things like the insurance. She felt again a sense of intrusion. But it's no good, someone's got to, me or Graham, and Graham can jolly well come up and do his bit. I'll have to ring him, blast it, and go through all the business of how he's a bit pushed at the moment but he'll try to get up, and listen to him trying to remember how old the children are and what Paul's name is. And there'll be people noises in the background; talking and glasses chinking. And anyway in the end, eventually, all this stuff has got to be cleared out, we might as well start now, there's no point in being squeamish!

She had a meal and then went back to the nursing-home. Her father was more confused than in the morning and hardly responded to her. She read his letter to him – from a former colleague, oddly impersonal, talking of the economic situation, Ireland, as though retirement and old age removed the right to private preoccupations. Or was it the opposite – a determination to be involved with the public world? But her father had dozed off before she reached the end of the letter: she left it by his bedside.

It was still early when she got back to Starbridge. She was brought out of a bath by the sound of the telephone and went to it expecting to hear Don's voice.

'Anne?'

'Graham!'

'How are things?' His voice, muted by distance, sounded thin and sober.

'Not too good,' she explained. Ending, her own voice fell away into silence. 'Hello? Are you still there?'

'Yes. Look – I'll try to get up at the end of the week, or early next. I daresay I can scrap something.'

'I think you should.'

'Right-o. Will do. How's Don?'

'Fine.'

'And the kids? Far too long since I saw them. Judy and, er . .'

'Paul.'

'Growing up, I suppose?'

'They're thirteen and fifteen,' Anne said. 'Yes, they're growing up. Children do.'

'True enough. You sound a bit stroppy. Anything wrong?'

'I'm tired, that's all.'

'It was bound to come, you know, Annie, sooner or later – Dad.'

'Yes, I know.'

'Are things O.K. financially?'

'I think so. The bank manager's being very helpful.'

'Let me know otherwise – I can always chip in.'

'Yes, I will.'

When she had rung off she picked up the phone again and dialled her own number. Waiting for Don to answer, she pictured the empty hall in which it rang. It seemed removed from her by more than the road to Lichfield, momentarily inaccessible as though it were in a different sphere of time, not space. For reassurance, she toured it in her mind's eye, moving from door to window to the print of York Minster above the radiator. And then Don's voice broke in and they talked of her father, and of an arrangement for the weekend, and of Anne's journey.

'Car behave all right? Did you get that indicator seen to?'

'Yes. No, I will do – I meant to. I'll go to bed now, darling, I'm dead tired. Oh, Graham rang just now.'

'You do surprise me.'

She lay in bed, reading a copy of *Brideshead Revisited* that carried her own unmarried name on the flyleaf, written in angular, schoolgirl script. She felt cold in the unaccustomed emptiness of a single bed, no warm flank against hers. Once, a long time ago, shared nights had been translated from furtive hours to the amazing rapture of security. And thence to unconsidered acceptance. I am no more used to sleeping alone than to travelling alone, she thought. And, despite her tiredness, a great surge of sexual desire swept through her, latent in her body, she realized, all that day, and somehow prompted by the touch of that schoolmaster's hand laid in passing sympathy on her arm. She heard again rooks and lawnmower as she switched the light out and turned to go to sleep.

* * *

Graham Stanway telephoned the divorced lady with whom he was, on two or three nights of every week, sleeping. 'Look,' he said, 'I shan't be able to make Friday. I'm most frightfully sorry, love, something's cropped up.' The divorced lady, who had a second, back-up arrangement available for such an eventuality, made some outline plans (to herself) and noises of protest and regret (to Graham). Then she said, 'Why?'

'My father's not so good, up in Lichfield. Matter of fact, I'm rather afraid he's going to pop off before too long.'

The divorced lady said, 'Oh darling, how wretched for you, I am sorry. Are you terribly fond of him?'

Graham said something about always getting along all right. The divorced lady said again how wretched and then launched into a rather scabrous story about a mutual acquaintance of theirs (older, and female) at which Graham laughed quite a lot. During the course of the tale she let it drop that she had been out, recently, with another mutual acquaintance of theirs (younger, and male). They then exchanged some further remarks of affection and anticipation and hung up. The divorced lady, in her flat, picked up the telephone again almost at once. Graham, in his, poured himself some whisky and went to stand by the uncurtained window; five storeys below, the tail-lights of cars blinked in a traffic-jam and reminded him, unaccountably, of a fun-fair. Once long ago, he had ridden on a dodgem or some such thing at a fun-fair and red lights had glittered, thus, against a backdrop of water, as, now, the Thames shone black beyond the Embankment (Graham's was an extremely choice and expensive view). He was nagged, irritatingly, by this fitful memory until all of a sudden it clarified itself. In Southwold, once, on holiday when he and Anne were kids, there had been such a fun-fair on the promenade; the lights, the sea. Christ, he thought, whatever brought that back? He was not a man much given to recollection. He finished his whisky and went to bed, alone.

Two

'And there's this monthly payment to Mrs Barron,' said the bank manager. 'Is that to continue?'

Anne said, 'Mrs Barron?' Behind the manager's voice on the telephone she could hear the click of a typewriter.

'Mrs S. Barron of Gloucester. 16 Ellesmere Road. Paid into the Gloucester branch of the Midland.'

'I'm sorry. It's just I can't quite think for the moment what that can be . . .'

'It goes back a long way,' said the manager. The typewriter was overlaid by the rustle of papers. 'Since – oh, ever since he's had his account with us. Ten pounds a month. He put it up to fifteen the year before last.'

'I see,' said Anne. 'I – I'll have to look into that. Can you just leave it for the moment. But I think cancel the club subscriptions, if you would.'

She put the receiver down in bewilderment. Ten pounds a month – fifteen? Out of her father's far from lavish pension? For a moment she was visited with the idea of some enormous, continuing mistake on the part of the bank, and then knew that her father would never have overlooked such a thing. Ten pounds could only be ten deliberate pounds. I don't know – how extraordinary. Could he have borrowed money from someone, once? Surely not – not father. Is it someone who worked for them? But they never had anyone. I'll have to ask Graham, she thought, or even father himself if he's a bit clearer before I go.

Having decided to visit the nursing-home in the afternoon and devote the morning to sorting things out in the house, she set off into the village to call on Mrs Ransome and thank her for all she had done. It was probable, too, that she was owed money.

The day was fine, the landscape aching under a cold spring wind that poured though the scanty trees and sent the last leaves of autumn spinning round her feet. Here, the season was as yet only a faint green mist lying over fields and hedges; down in Berkshire the leaves already offered rumpled shapes. It was as though, moving upwards on the map, you moved backwards, by a week or so, in time, as though too in the conservatism of the climate regional idiosyncracies made their last stand. You could read the same newspaper everywhere, but must travel to look again at last week's flowers. And I should move about more, Anne thought vaguely, by myself like this, you see things differently.

Mrs Ransome lived in one of a pair of brick cottages beyond the Post Office. She offered tea, switched off a chattering radio, and asked diffidently if Mr Stanway was likely to come home.

'I'm afraid not.'

'I thought that. He'd got like my mum was, towards the end. You know, don't you, when a person's bound to go. Is he comfortable enough?'

'I think so,' Anne said. She saw again her father's face on the pillow, with its strange quality of removal, inscrutability, emptied of the kaleidoscopic responses of other faces. The woman, as though picking up the thought, said, 'It's hard to tell, isn't it, when they can't really say any more. It's like with a baby.' They sat in silence for a moment, looking out of the window to where, in the primary school playground, children wheeled and shrieked on the tarmac.

'He was always a nice person to work for. We let each other alone.' Mrs Ransome laughed, suddenly. 'More tea, Mrs – er . . . ? To tell you the truth, I don't think he noticed much what the place was like. A man gets like that, living alone, doesn't he?'

'I suppose so.'

'Mind, I can't think of him as a family man, somehow. I was ever so surprised when he first mentioned you and your brother. I'd thought of him as, well, a bachelor type.' She looked attentively at Anne. 'I hope you don't mind my saying that. It was there being no photos about, that kind of thing.'

'They're all in drawers, I suppose. Yes, I see what you mean.'

It surprised her that her father, so welded to her own past, could suggest to a stranger someone entirely different – a man untethered by commitment and obligation. She remembered how one of her own children when very small had gazed up at her in curiosity once, returning from school, and said, 'When I'm not here all day where are you, what happens to you, are you here, in the house?' Mrs Ransome's remark had discovered in her the same self-absorption, the same assumption of those we know best as extensions of ourselves.

'He didn't mind being on his own, I'd say. Not like some people would.'

'Yes, I think perhaps that's true.' Mother did, though – she always hated him being away so much. And us going, when we did. She kept our possessions like anchors, it was always her who answered the phone, wrote every week, tried – too hard – to keep up with our friends. She remembered her mother making a fuss of Graham's Cambridge girl-friends – slick glossy creatures who thought his parents drab. And patronized me, she thought – the earnest little sister.

She said to Mrs Ransome, 'I imagine we must owe you something – I'd like to settle up, if you could just tell me how much.'

The money lay awkwardly among the tea-cups. Seeing Anne to the door, Mrs Ransome said, 'I'd go to see him, but I'm not that often in Lichfield, and I daresay . . . Well, I don't want to disturb him.'

'It's nice of you, but he's very confused – he might not know you. He did have a visitor yesterday, in fact – a Mr – Mr Fielding. He used to live here.'

'That's right,' said Mrs Ransome, 'in the cottage down the lane from your father. He was often in for a chat. They'd go fishing together, too.' For an instant she seemed about to add to this, and then said merely, 'He was glad of the company, I'd say, Mr Fielding.'

* * *

In Berkshire, the car radio warned Donald Linton that there would be hold-ups on the A329, a lorry having spilled its load. That done, it reverted to the music programme (the same that Mrs Ransome, in Starbridge, now switched on again) while Donald took an expedient turn to the right and then left which would avoid the A329, he being already five minutes late. The music programme, steering a diplomatic course between light and classical, played him a selection from an American theatrical extravaganza of twenty years ago to which, he seemed to remember, he had taken Anne in their courting days. In three years' time, he thought, I will be forty-five, by which time undoubtedly Thwaites will have retired and I shall be senior partner and on, presumably, nine or ten thousand. At that point, he thought, it might well be wise to sell the house and get something a bit more appropriate from an investment point of view. Like that, for instance. Sitting in a traffic-jam (unheralded by the radio, which was now moving into the overture to *The Magic Flute*) he contemplated a spruce Georgian building with garden running down to the Thames. Like that, or possibly something with a bit more land. Anne, of course, will take a bit of budging, us having lived in the same place for sometime now and her being inclined to cling to things a bit, but no doubt reason will prevail. The lights changed and he moved off. I wonder, he thought, if Annie got that car seen to, just a wiring job, it wouldn't take a minute. He travelled in his mind to Starbridge, to review the garage situation there, thought he located one near the pub, and saw, unexpectedly, his father-in-law turn to hand him a drink in that same pub, years ago. 'Well, Donald, all the best to you both. She's not a bad girl, my daughter, though I say it myself. A bit intense, occasionally, but I daresay that won't bother you. Look after her.' Poor old chap, Don thought, let's hope it doesn't drag on too long.

* * *

They had got him out of bed and into an armchair. Anne arrived to find a nurse packing cushions around him and arranging a rug over his shoulders. 'He's not too bad in himself today, so we've sat him up for a bit, but he's not very clear in his head, I'm afraid.' She bent to the old man and said, 'Here's your daughter, dear, come to see you.'

Anne sat reading the newspaper. Her father was silent, his head nodding, his hands plucking and scrabbling at the rug across his knees. Once he muttered to himself, and chuckled, but when she tried to speak to him he stared at her vacantly: for the most part he seemed quite unaware of her presence. She was surprised when he said suddenly, 'Are they bringing my dinner now?'

'No, father, not just yet.' She pulled her chair closer to him and put her hand on his. 'How are you feeling?'

He grunted. 'Who's that woman there?'

She followed his stare into the corner of the room. 'There's no one but me, father. Nobody over there.'

'Eh?' His eyes seemed to follow movement, and stop again. 'Tell her I can't see her now. She can't come here, it won't do.'

'Father, I promise you there's no one.' But he had gone back into himself again, apparently half-asleep, his breath rasping.

When the nurse returned Anne mentioned the hallucination.

'A lot of them do that. Oh, they see all sorts of things – flowers, ships, people. They're never alone. It's uncanny sometimes – you don't know what's going on in their heads. Now, are you going to help me lift him back into bed? Ready, Mr Stanway? We're just going to put you back. Lock your hand with mine under his knees, can you, and the other one behind his back. Then lift when I say and swing round as you get his legs up on the bed.' She was a girl of twenty or so, thin and wiry, her hair scraped back into a pony-tail under her cap, a cheap crucifix pinned to her apron.

His pyjamas gaped open over skin as pellucid and soft as a baby's. They lifted him onto the bed to an ammoniac reek and the nurse said 'Just a tick while I get him a clean pair of trousers. Hold him on one side for a minute, please.' Her actions were an economy of effort, no movement wasted, the soiled garment replaced by the fresh in one sequence of liftings and lowerings. Anne, her hand against the old man's back, turned awkwardly from the withered bare thighs and genitals. He muttered and grumbled against the pillows, slumped helplessly between them.

'It's disappointing for you,' said the nurse, 'him being like this, when you've come up specially.'

Anne said, 'He knew who I was yesterday.'

'They have their ups and downs. That's what's interesting about geriatrics.'

'Don't you find it – depressing?'

'Oh, no,' said the girl vaguely. She arranged the old man in the bed with the kindly detachment of a child tucking up a doll and he lay with compliant orderliness against the pillows, the sheet turned back under his folded hands. Anne thought: how he would hate this if he knew.

'Mind,' the girl went on 'I'd really like to do psychiatric. I'm going to do the course next year, with any luck. There – he's ready for his dinner now. Are you staying?'

'No, I'll look in later.'

* * *

James Stanway said, 'You must go away. I've told you before, Betty, you cannot come here, it won't do.'

But she sat there, smiling and saying nothing, wearing the blue spotted dress she had that summer at Lyme, smiling and smoothing the silk across her knees. It's not that I don't want to see you, my dear, he said to her, you know that, but you must realize that it won't do, that has always been understood between us.

And presently she did indeed go away, though he did not see her go. People jostled and manhandled him in some crowded place: leave me alone, he said, leave me alone, but they were so much stronger and after a while he lay exhausted. The sound of the river was in his head now, running over stones.

* * *

Anne ate biscuits and cheese at the kitchen table and thought: this afternoon I must really get down to it, and then I can be off first thing tomorrow. Go through his desk and see what has to be done, and ring the bank manager again. And if there is time I will get out into the garden and do a bit there. She pushed the dirty things into the sink and went through to the study.

The papers on the desk were fairly quickly dealt with. A couple more unpaid bills, an unanswered letter from her cousin, an acrimonious correspondence with the local Water Board (they would have the last word now, and probably never wonder why). She sorted them into piles and made a list of what must be done. Opening the drawers of the desk, though, she found herself reaching back into a disorderly past – five, three, ten years. Letters; receipted bills; membership cards. The pieces of paper charting a lifetime. If, she thought, if I were a stranger, if I didn't know father – what would all this tell me? Here is a member of the A.A., a householder whose mortgage was paid up fifteen years ago, father of two, husband, subscriber to the *Times Educational Supplement*, occasional visitor to Trust House hotels. A man who shopped by post for esoteric foods, supported the Preservation of Rural England, and once, when younger, stood at the side of a young woman whose hair was blown across her face by the wind.

Mother, presumably, Anne thought, laying the photograph on the blotter in front of her, in 1940 or thereabouts. I wonder where we were – Graham and I? They must have had a leave somewhere without us. She turned the picture over and in the corner, in her father's handwriting, saw pencilled 'Dorset'.

Throughout the afternoon she travelled with the contents of her father's drawers and files into her own girlhood and childhood. Here were photographs and childish letters and swimming certificates. Here was her mother's recipe book and her own sixth form prize essay and Graham's school reports ('Stanway has a good mind which he uses when he thinks fit or when it suits his purposes'). She began to divide up what she found, thinking that it must be done in the end, eventually, and she might as well make a start. The recovery of forgotten places and events detained her so that only slowly did the piles of papers grow in the grocery boxes she brought through from the larder and labelled 'A.S.', 'G.S.', 'Father', and 'Throw away?' Sunlight moved round the room, splashing in turn the desk, the glass front of the bookcase, the trodden-out pattern on the Persian rug. She moved from childhood during the war to time at Oxford and back again through the unending school years. She and Don smiled glassily as bride and groom. From an envelope there slithered another clutch of photographs – the irretrievable faces of her own children in infancy.

Once, before her marriage, she had worked for a short time in the manuscript room of a museum. Sitting now on the floor of her father's study it seemed to her that this random archive of paper in his desk was the same kind of fitful evidence about people's lives as those miraculously surviving scraps of Saxon writs and medieval tax returns. They told you facts, but facts stripped of the whole truth. She looked at her wedding photos and thought: mother looks glum but in fact she was the only one who really enjoyed it, and Graham I daresay, pawing that girl I never said he could bring; that day at Poppet Sands was when Paul cut his foot on some glass, just before Don got his new job and we moved to Cuxing.

This was the easiest part, the extraction of what was hers and what was Graham's, and what could probably be thrown away. The rest, her father's personal things, she assessed with apprehension and thought: all that must wait, in time I will come to all that. One file only, a box of bank statements, she did open, remembering again that curious standing order, and found the monthly payments, just as the manager had said, leapfrogging backwards over sheets of paper that covered years and years. She could not find when they began, jumbled as the statements were, and put the file to one side. I cannot leave this, she thought, I have to find out what this means.

It was nearly evening. In the garden a blackbird chattered. She went out into the tool-shed and took down a spade and fork from the tidy row of garden implements, each hung in its own place and wiped clean of dirt. The rose-beds were full of groundsel and dandelion seedlings and she set to work there, sifting greenery from the loose damp soil with the fork, working energetically, pausing now and then to admire the scoured bed that she left in her wake, and the roses putting out minute fists of new growth. They had been pruned. Her father must have done that in the autumn or winter, knowing, perhaps, that he would not see next summer's blooms.

The garden sloped down to a field – rough pasture speckled with grazing cows. Its far end was defined by the line of willows and alders on the river bank. Her father was a member of a syndicate that had fishing rights along this stretch and he had bought the house for its nearness to the river. Wandering down to the fence at the far end of the lawn she could just hear, in the stillness of the evening, the rush of the water round some obstacle. Out of sight, a tractor coughed, started up, and throbbed away out of earshot. At the far right hand side of the field a man came along the river bank, walking slowly, and struck out across the grass.

She went back to the rose-bed and began to dig out an ancient woody plant with little new growth. It mandrake roots, though, plunged deep down into the ground and defied her efforts to drag it out. She had put down the spade and had the stem clutched in her bare hands as she wrestled with it when a sense that she was not alone made her look up. The man who had been walking across the field had reached the fence at the bottom of the garden and as he ducked under it and then stood again she saw that it was David Fielding. He carried a fishing rod and waders.

'Don't let me interrupt you. I just thought that while you were here I'd better return your father's rod.'

Anne said, 'This bush was defeating me anyway.' She straightened, and thought: that was what he was talking about yesterday, something about a rod, father must have lent him his. 'I'm sure my father would prefer you to keep the rod, you know.'

'Wouldn't your husband use it? Or your brother?'

'Heavens, no. They neither of them fish.'

'It's a fairly lunatic occupation,' he said. 'I seldom catch anything much. Your father could at least be pretty sure of his supper – he was a good fisherman.'

'But rivers are nice . . .'

'Precisely. Rivers are nice.' Across Anne's weeded bed, its brown earth as clean and crisp as cake-crumbs, they smiled at each other.

'Do keep it. None of us has any use for it.'

'Well, for the summer anyway . . . I'd like to. It's a very good rod, you know, worth a lot now.' He looked down at the mangled rose-bush. 'Shall I have a go at that for you?'

'I wish you would.'

He could not move it. Anne laughed. 'It's like the World Tree or something – I think its roots go on for ever. I shall have to see if there's a saw anywhere.'

'Don't bother. I've got a knife. I'll hack it off as far down as I can. I shouldn't imagine it'll start sprouting underground.'

He reached down into the hole around the root, fumbling with one hand while he held the stem in the other, and as Anne started to say, 'I'm afraid you must have thought me very off-hand yesterday, the fact is I . . .' he brought his hand up sharply.

'Bugger! Sorry!'

Blood welled up through the crust of earth on the ball of his thumb. He groped in his pocket with the other hand and said, with sudden helplessness, like a boy, 'I haven't got a handkerchief.'

Anne said, 'That looks rather deep. You'd better come in and put it under the tap.'

He followed her into the kitchen and sat at the table. She ran water into a basin, hunting in the cupboards for Dettol and cottonwool, and when she turned to him again saying, 'Here, let me . . .' saw that he was white and sweating, his head turned from the thumb which dripped earth and blood onto the floor.

'Are you all right? Here – put your head between your knees.'

He leaned forward obediently and she held her hand on his shoulder for a minute or so until he sat up again.

'How ridiculous!' he smiled at her, weakly. 'We seem fated to do nothing but ask each other if we're all right.'

Anne said, 'You remind me of Paul. My son. He cut his foot once on the beach – I was remembering it just now – on some broken glass or something and wouldn't look at it for hours because he was sure his toes had come off. He was six or seven. Have you always been like that about blood? Hold it over the sink now. Don't look.'

'Just about always. Not a good failing for a schoolmaster. Have you any idea how much bloodshed a medium-sized boys' school averages per week?'

'Pints, I should imagine. Sorry, I'm getting your sleeve a bit wet.' His hand, under hers, felt cold. Fishing, of course, gives you cold hands. Her father, coming in on summer evenings, would lay his on her cheeks, either side, teasing, to warm them.

'As for National Service . . . I spent my time quaking at the sight of those sabres on the wall in the officers' mess.'

'How awful. But what do you do about fish? Bashing them on the head?'

'Oddly enough, that I can do. Fish blood seems different.'

'I find that inconsistent. There, it's nearly stopped bleeding now. Can you press it together for a few minutes?'

'No, I'm much too infirm.'

'Oh, dear,' she said, 'Then I shall have to.'

The single chromium spout of a pair of mixer taps, stared at with intensity, becomes the arched neck of some misconceived prehistoric creature, presenting a bright, elongated reflection of anyone who faces it. Two people, side by side, flow one into another; formlessly pink, brown and green. Fortunately, perhaps, the reflection is too distorted to return anything so precise as an expression, as eyes, or mouth, or nose.

Anne said, 'I really think that's all right now.'

'If you say so.'

'I'll just put a bit of plaster on and then we might have a cup of tea.'

'That would be nice.'

They sat facing each other across the kitchen table, silent now, and then both speaking at once.

'Have you been teaching in Lichfield long?'

'Berkshire, you said you lived in, wasn't it?'

Anne said, 'Yes, a village near Reading.'

'Ah. Commuter country. That's a kind of landscape I'm not too familiar with, being a provincial lad by birth and upbringing. I'm used to places people live in rather than work from, though I don't know you could say that of these parts, nowadays. Brum spreads its tentacles a long way. I grew up in Nottingham.'

'I've never been there, I'm afraid.'

'I don't recognize it, nowadays. New shopping centres as far as the eye can see. Ring-roads and flyovers and what have you. Now there's a town that's been progressively raped over the last fifty years. It used to have a seventeenth century town hall, did you know? That was pulled down in the nineteen twenties.'

'I thought it was notorious for its slums, once.'

'Oh, yes, them too. We lived in lower middle-class Nottingham, respectable little streets, most of them are getting bulldozed now. My father was a grocer. After Cambridge I came back and taught in the local schools for ten years or so, then a stint in Manchester, then here.'

Anne said diffidently, 'I teach too.'

'Your father never mentioned that. But then I must admit he didn't often talk about you.'

'Only in a very small way – some O-level history at our comprehensive. I'd like to do more, though, eventually.'

'Another historian,' said David Fielding, 'We're an unfashionable lot.'

'What do you mean?'

'The tide's against us, hadn't you noticed? People haven't got that much time for the past nowadays. They want vocational instruction.'

'Oh, come,' she said. 'I can't entirely agree with that. I should have thought it had never been more popular, literally popular. Cheap Book Club editions of history books all over the back of the *Radio Times*; millions of people tramping round stately homes every weekend; the last hundred years in some aspect or other being re-hashed on the telly every time you turn it on.'

'The past as entertainment.'

'Well,' she said, 'if you put it like that, I suppose that's one way of looking at it. But all the same I . . .'

'But when it comes to the past as instruction, that's another matter.'

'Is it instruction?' she said. 'Should it be? I've never been sure about that. The lessons of the past and that sort of thing . . . Why should you learn from history? Why not just learn about it?'

'When you start arguing you look like your father.'

'Do I?'

'And you have his way of picking a subject up and chewing it like a bone.'

'I'm sorry,' she said, offended. 'I didn't mean to be boring. I thought it was quite interesting.'

'You aren't a bit boring. I don't know when I've been less bored.'

'Oh,' she said. 'Good.'

'Go on.'

'I've finished that now. I can't remember what I was going to say. Would you like some more tea?'

'Yes, please. And what else do you do, down in Berkshire, apart from making sure history isn't too instructive? You've got children?'

'Two. Boy and girl. Fifteen and thirteen. What about you?'

'Two boys. Same sort of age. But, dear me, don't let's start talking about our children, I have enough of that professionally. Trading parental experiences is seldom a rewarding pastime. Best left to educationalists or psychologists. Your father had the measure of that. He seldom spoke of you or your brother – which I don't for one moment imagine meant lack of affection.'

'No, I don't think so. Though he was always a bit detached from family life. It's odd, but I keep getting this feeling now, going through his papers as I have to do, of only partly knowing him.'

'Presumably one only does know – see – a parent in one dimension?'

Yes. Yes, I suppose so.' She went on to speak of her thoughts that morning, of the deceptive picture of a life as presented by bits of paper.

David said, 'More selective than a museum archive, presumably. He must have chosen what to keep.'

'But the same emphasis on economic life.'

'To the exclusion of the passions?'

'Well, yes,' she said.

'Are your children going to find a drawer of love-letters?'

'I don't suppose they are.'

'You see . . .' he said. 'But there'll be expired passports and old insurance documents by the dozen.' He was silent for a moment, contemplating his own plastered thumb, resting on the yellow formica table. He went on, abruptly, 'Why are you doing all this now? You could leave it for a bit.'

'Until he dies?'

David nodded.

'I'm not sure, really. To start with because I had to – to sort out money things, you see. Partly because in some peculiar way I want to. It's not like me,' she added. 'I hate tidying. I'm very disorderly. My husband complains.'

He ignored this. 'The death of parents – of a parent – is a climacteric business, in all sorts of ways. You feel older, and younger, both at once.' He lifted the tea-pot and topped up both cups, spooning sugar into his own. 'May I? My father died about fifteen years ago. He was the kind of grocer that doesn't exist any more – the old-fashioned corner shop – I'm glad he didn't live to be capsized by the age of the supermarket. When he died I had to clear out all the shop accounts. Pathetically small sums of money – going back into the twenties, you see, people owing three and six till Friday, that kind of thing. And all those scraps of paper to do with what a person is, that you've been talking about. Every certificate of mine. He didn't have your father's reticence, I'm afraid, about his offspring. He was the Ancient Mariner where his son was concerned – the neighbours must have shrivelled at the sound of my name.' He laughed.

'Presumably he was proud of you. That's not a crime.'

'Yes and no. He thought it was a fine thing to have a boy at university – that was unheard of in our street. But he was a midland business man, in however small a way – he thought a schoolteacher's income a very poor return on all that educational investment.'

'It is.'

'If you look at it like that.' He sounded suddenly sharp.

Anne said in embarrassment, 'I don't. But I see what he meant. If you've spent . . .'

'I'm sure you don't. I didn't mean to slap you down – sorry. What does your husband do?'

'He's a solicitor.' Down in Berkshire, she thought, in somebody's sitting-room, on somebody's lawn, they say at this point, 'Oh, really?' in a bright, approving voice that means: ah, now I know where I am, who you are, how rich, where your children go to school, what you are likely to feel about things.

David Fielding said, 'Sensible fellow, I daresay.'

Outside, it was dusk. In the field, a shroud of mist now hid the line of willows. The garden fork stood stark as a gibbet where Anne had left it upright in the rose-bed. A motor-bike crashed down the lane through the silence and David said, 'I'd better go.'

At the door he said, 'I'll go in to see your father, of course. When will you be up again?'

'In about a fortnight, I expect. Unless they think I should come before.'

'Perhaps I'll see you.'

She said, 'I hope so.' After he had gone she sat in the kitchen, doing nothing, staring at the dirty tea-cups. The telephone ringing made her jump.

It was Graham. 'Anne? Look, I've fixed things to come up on Friday.'

'Good.'

'Everything O.K.?'

'More or less. Graham – one thing . . . Did father ever have anyone he gave some kind of allowance to? A pension or something? That nurse person we had in the war, when mother was working – what was her name?'

'Search me.'

'Not Barron?'

A fractional pause. Graham said, 'Don't think so. What's the problem?'

'Nothing, really, it's just there's this Mrs Barron he has a standing order for at the bank. Fifteen pounds a month.'

A longer pause. On another line, voices faintly chattered. 'Look,' said Graham, 'I shouldn't bother about it. Just leave it.'

'But we've got to know who she is, this person, for goodness' sake!'

'Not necessarily.' Was that what he had said? There was a windy sound in her ear now, as though he was yawning, or sighing, down there in London. 'Not to worry anyway.'

'I'm not worrying,' she said crossly.

'Jolly good, then. Well, I'll keep in touch.'

'Right you are. 'Bye.'

''Bye.'

She slept badly, falling from long wakeful stretches into a fitful sleep, tumultuous with dreams and images. She got up early with a headache, projecting forwards into the day so that in her mind she was already back at home and about the things that would await her there. It was as though the lengths of road in between did not exist, as though you cut from one place to the other as in a film. She bustled round the house, closing windows, pushing her things into a bag, thinking of a meal for tonight, of what she had to do tomorrow. But sitting at the kitchen table over a cup of coffee she saw again David Fielding's hand with plastered thumb laid against the speckled grey and yellow formica.

With the sharpened observation of hindsight she saw too his hair fringed with grey above the ears, the unravelled stitches at the cuff of his sweater, the cracked bowl of his pipe. She wrote 'mince, onions, carrots, pickle' on the back of an envelope – the evening meal could be bought on the way home – and thought: he must keep father's rod, I should like that, it's much the most sensible thing, I'll talk to him about it again, sometime.

Three

'Fill her up' said Graham, and the garage attendant, laying a lascivious hand on the car's expensive rump, thought: what a waste, an old bloke like him having a job like this, it's not bloody fair. He slammed the cap back on the tank, not properly screwed up so like as not it would drop off within five miles, and came round to the window. 'Four fifty, sir.'

And Graham said, 'Well, that's how it goes,' so the boy thought for a minute he was taking the mickey and was going to come back at him, hard, till he realized it was the money he was talking about. 'Daylight robbery,' he said with a grin. 'Goodnight, sir.' From the office he watched the tail-lights of the car link up with the rush-hour traffic.

Graham, two and a half hours of the M1 ahead of him, flicked the switches of the radio and settled for the news. He sailed through darkening counties, informed of this and that, sliding from one lane to another, reasonably comfortable, reasonably content, moderately tired. At the ends of weeks, nowadays, he tended to feel a bit done in, which of course meant nothing at all, nothing a bit of a holiday, come the summer, wouldn't put right. Around Luton he thought, for a while, of the divorced lady with whom, other things being equal, he usually spent Friday nights. He thought that somehow there might not be a lot more of those nights, but it wouldn't be much skin off his nose, one way or the other, all things considered. I could do with a rest, a bit of time off all that. I'll go down and see Annie and the kids next weekend, ought to keep up more than I do, months since I saw her. Northampton coming up, not bad time, there before eight, anyway.

* * *

Not even houses are inert: everything moves on. Anne, stepping into her home, felt herself reclaimed by the place, her attention at once arrested by all those minute and instantly discernible changes produced by time. Tuesday had given way to Thursday; on the hall table, two letters, a circular and a bill; in the kitchen, crockery in the sink, clothes flung down in one corner, something decaying in a saucer on the fridge. Her children, banging into the house in the tailend of the afternoon, seemed to swamp her with demands.

'What thing on Saturday? Oh, I suppose so, if I've got time.' To Judy, hunched at the kitchen table, wolfing bread and jam, she said, 'Aren't you going to ask how grandfather was?'

'Sorry. How was grandfather?'

'He isn't very well, I'm afraid.' Pity eclipsed her irritation as she saw the girl with momentary detachment, suspended in that eternity between childhood and womanhood. 'Don't eat so much bread, darling, it's so fattening.'

'I'm fat already. So what's the point?'

'You could get thinner. I've put on weight, too. We'll go on a diet together.'

'I'd still have spots.'

'We'll try a different kind of stuff from the chemist.'

The girl said nothing, tranced in gloom. Anne thought: poor things, they don't know what they are, what's expected of them, it's a rotten time – what nonsense is talked of childhood, of that bit of childhood.

She said, 'I was looking at all sorts of old photos at grandfather's, of you and Paul when you were little – I meant to bring them back, they might have amused you.'

'Mmn . . .'

'At Poppet Sands. Do you remember that holiday at Poppet Sands?'

'Not really. Mum?'

'Yes?'

'Can I have 25p to get Susie a birthday present?'

'All right,' Anne said. Not even, yet, sustained by memory – they haven't that crutch, so far. She went to the kitchen window and stood looking into the garden, at the raw green leaves of the lupins that had climbed a perceptible inch or so since she had left, at the blazing polyanthus and the crocuses now spurting untidy greenery above the tattered flowers. The roses were in full leaf, the chestnuts offered embryonic candles, the grass of the lawn was long enough to cut: next week the school holidays would begin.

Paul put his head round the door and said, 'Sandra Butterfield's here. You have been warned.' Anne, drawn up defensively against the sink, abandoning the garden, thought: no, I will not offer her tea, or she'll be here an hour or so and I've a hundred things to do. She watched Sandra bustle past the window, head down over a fistful of papers that she shuffled through as she walked. What is it this time? Liberals; Oxfam; Christian Aid Week? She went to open the door.

'My dear, I mustn't stop – I've got all the C.P.R.E. stuff to push round – but I did just want a word with you or Don about the Traffic Action Group. You see the thing is . . .'

Anne said, 'Come into the kitchen.'

Sandra Butterfield sought causes with the fervour of a medieval churchman in pursuit of a heresy. Her small, tubby person exuded energy and indignation. Propelled by her and her followers, over the years, this spruce Berkshire village had embraced liberalism, cherished the environment, fought the threat of a motorway, restored the church spire. Denied the need to work by her husband's income, she pursued occupation. Hers was the stocky, tireless physique of a peasant woman bowed over a cornfield in some nineteenth century painting; transposed into her large modern house in this tranquil commuterland, she seemed to dart hither and thither with the undirected pent-up energy of a clockwork toy. A prettier woman would have taken up adultery. Sandra, bundled into woollies and tweeds, sat now at Anne's kitchen table, spread out her papers and envelopes and put a large red biro tick against an item on a list which, Anne could see, said 'Recruit Lintons for Traffic Group.'

'The thing is,' Sandra was saying, 'that the traffic density's gone up by a hundred and twenty percent over the last year. What? Well, of course it's not *absolutely* exact but we've done this spot check outside the school now three times and it's definitely up. Those gravel lorries are simply pounding through – well over forty, time and again – I mean, the young mums with prams just have to leap for the pavement if they're to preserve life and limb. So we feel the first thing is a Protest Meeting – to get some attention, whip up feeling and everything, you know – and a bit in the local rag and all that, and then . . .'

She's got older, Anne thought. It's funny, you see people year in and year out, sometimes missing a month or two but seldom more, and you don't notice. When we first came here Sandra was a young mum. So was I. She was even a bit sexy, then. Graham got her tipsy once after some children's party, for the hell of it – she kept asking after him for years, he must have patted her bottom or something. He wouldn't now – Graham's girls get younger, not older.

'. . . And the other thing I wanted to talk about is, what are we going to do about Splatt's Cottage?'

'Splatt's Cottage?'

'My dear, it's going to be pulled down, hadn't you heard. Some wretched spec builder.'

Anne said, 'Oh, but that's awful.'

Ten years ago, coming to this place, she had hunted for its origins. She had looked its name up in the *Dictionary of English Place Names* ('Cuxing Brk [*Cucingam* 872 ASC, *Cucingas* DB, *Cucing* 1170] *Cuc* or *Cuca*'s people. *Cuc* or *Cucu* is a short form of names in *Cwic* –. . .'), wandered forth from her own Edwardian brick house in search of something that would tether the village more nearly to time and to region, that had more conviction than the housing estates that cartwheeled out from the church and the High Street. The church ('Norman in origin, Perp W tower, the rest 1880 by W. Young . . .') named and recorded. The War Memorial intruded large events into a small place. Here and there, the names of streets or fields preserved archaic functions – Pound Way, the Brickfield. But of the visible past there was little. A terrace of Georgian brick cottages had been done over by young couples commuting to Reading or London; primrose front doors alternated with rust and eau-de-nil, wrought iron lanterns glowing discreetly above them. In the High Street, some half-timbered façades canted out above the plate-glass windows of Boots and Mac Fisheries. The market cross, pock-marked stone with outline blurred almost beyond recognition, was clamped behind an iron railing beside the public lavatories. And at the far end of Swan Lane, squatting morosely beyond an airy development of Span semis, Splatt's Cottage clung to a precarious half-life, its windows smashed in and boarded up, the thatch slipping from its roof, its walls daubed with football slogans. It was a cruck-frame farmhouse, reputedly dating from the fifteenth century.

'Surely they can't do that?'

'They can and will,' said Sandra. 'That's just it. It's not scheduled, apparently, and now Pym's – you know, the builders – have bought it off old Mr Taylor *and* the adjoining land and they've got planning permission for five bungalows. It's taken everyone by surprise. Of course we should have spotted what was going on but one can't keep tabs on everything.' She sighed theatrically.

'It's surprising no one's bought it to do up, long ago.'

'Well, of course it would cost the earth to make anything of it. But the point is that we can't stand by and see it pulled down. I mean, the Pickerings had someone staying at the weekend who knows about that sort of thing and he says it's about eight hundred years old.'

'I don't think it can be quite that,' Anne said. 'I've always understood it was fifteenth century.'

'Well, anyway, it's tremendously old, that's the thing, and it absolutely must be preserved. So we'll have to have another Action Group and I was wondering – I'm up to the eyes at the moment with the traffic stuff – I was wondering if you could take that on.' She stared across the table, almost accusingly. 'I thought you'd be just the right person, teaching history and everything. I mean, you do actually care about the past, don't you, and then you've got a car so it's easy for you to buzz round getting people interested.'

'I suppose I could.'

'You're only working part-time, aren't you?'

'Yes.'

'I do envy you. I'd have adored a career but I never coped with all those exams and things. You're awfully lucky to have had time for all that. Well, I'll leave Splatt's Cottage to you then.' She took up her fistful of envelopes. 'You'd better check with the builders what they're up to.'

Anne thought: now what have I let myself in for? She went upstairs to have a bath and from her bedroom window saw Sandra's bulky figure further down the street, talking to someone, the late afternoon foot-traffic of school children and shoppers dividing around her. The greengrocer's daffodils and tulips stood on the pavement in shocks of colour; Marinas and Cortinas were bringing husbands home from work. Anne undressed, thinking of Splatt's Cottage and remembering a ritual, when Judy was small, wherein she must always lift the child to peer through the dusky windows in search of heaven-knows-what private fantasy in those empty rooms, abused by vandals and stray cats. Sandra's right, she thought, I suppose she's right and I suppose I'll have to do something – but I wish she hadn't nailed me like that, just now, this spring, with father ill and everything. I shall be up and down there all summer, I shouldn't take on much else.

Lichfield created itself in her head; her father in the white embrace of those hospital pillows, the empty house, the patch of sunlight shifting around his study, that stubborn rose root, its years of growth driving it deep down into the ground. And, accompanying these images, there came what seemed the most unaccountable, the most perverse sense of well-being, of undefined expectation, as in childhood there lay offstage the promise of Christmas, of birthdays, of a treat.

* * *

'How was Harlow?'

'It was there.'

Once a month Don visited the company at Harlow for whom he acted as legal adviser.

'Just that?'

'Just that, to all intents and purposes.' Meaning, mostly, I can't be bothered to talk about it; partly, it wouldn't interest you. He smiled, placatingly, over the top of the paper.

Anne said, 'I went through Oxford on Tuesday.'

'You needn't have done. I told you. The bypass takes you round.'

'I know. I just felt like it, suddenly. I went down Leckford Road, past your room there.'

'Those were awful digs.'

'I suppose,' she said, 'you think that's sentimental, going there.'

'It would have been simpler to stick to the bypass, that's all. Oxford traffic's a shambles, nowadays.'

'I'm not talking about the traffic. Don't you want to know what Leckford Road looks like now?'

'What does Leckford Road look like now?'

'It looks much the same. It was fairly unresponsive.'

'Isn't that,' said Don, 'what places are supposed to be?'

'I daresay.'

In the next room, the children's room, the television quacked, erupted into applause, quacked again. The hall clock whirred its overture to striking the hour. Don said, 'I'll just have a look at the news.'

'It's going to mean going up and down to Lichfield a good bit, for the next few months.'

'Yes, I imagine so.'

'There's a lot of sorting out to do, at the house, apart from seeing father.'

'Sure,' said Don. He went through to the other room.

Later, in bed, he laid his hand on her thigh. 'Annie?'

'Yes,' she said. 'Yes, that would be nice.'

* * *

She visited Splatt's Cottage. The adjoining Span estate had won an architectural award. Its houses were cleverly stepped to take advantage of the site's contours and the existing trees (a chestnut, a clutch of silver birches) had been incorporated into the plan and now looked more groomed and gracious than ordinary trees, presiding over the shaven lawns and paved approaches. Children's chopper bikes and tricycles leaned against walls and doors, a baby fretted in a sleek black pram; this was an estate of young marrieds, Sandra's mums who must be protected from the rogue lorries. Outside one of the houses, the old village pump had been preserved, tastefully displayed on a little island of turf, quite detached from any function and more like some piece of sculpture in an open-air exhibition.

Just beyond the houses, Splatt's Cottage, lurking behind the hawthorn hedge of its garden, seemed seedy by comparison, not charmingly old but inappropriately so, perhaps even a little obscene, its crouched and sagging form reminiscent of some early Flemish or German woodcut suggesting faintly evil goings-on, undefined medieval perversities. And, as though to confirm this, the ditch outside its garden gate offered scrumpled handfuls of lavatory paper and the pale extended tube of a condom. Anne pushed open the gate (which lurched from its one hinge) and went down the brick path to the front door.

It was locked, though she could see through the broken window beside it that people had been into the cottage. There was a beer can on the floor and some old newspapers. She walked round the outside, examining the structure as revealed externally in the curve of the crucks, the horizontal timbers, the infilling of herring-bone brick work plastered over but showing here and there where the plaster had cracked off in chunks. I'll have to do some homework, she thought, get a book on timber-frame buildings, try to find out about this place, how old it really is and all that. You can't defend something efficiently unless you know what it is you are defending.

The back door was wide open. There was evidence in the kitchen of recent, and transitory, occupation. A nest of newspapers and broken-down cardboard cartons in one corner; an empty cigarette packet, more beer cans; a scrawl across one wall – Leeds Rule OK?; lengths of light flex spewing from the walls where fittings had been torn away.

How long since anyone had lived here? She moved through the small rooms, trying to extract information from objects. There was a square stone sink and grooved wooden draining board in the kitchen, and an iron range. No bathroom and only an outside wash-house and lavatory. Small decorative Victorian grates in the bedrooms. In one upstairs room a twenties fluted glass lampshade had escaped the vandals. If the past had been cherished here, it was because of poverty, not good taste.

And further back? I don't know about this sort of thing, Anne thought, these beams might be any age. She tapped the wall above the brick fireplace in the sitting-room and thought she detected a hollow noise. An open fireplace? Inglenooks? The bulge beside the back door must surely be a bread oven, entombed now in the wall. And had the ground floor been always this warren of tiny rooms? Surely, once, one big open place – wasn't that how these houses were laid out originally? Extraordinary, really – you take a tree and chop it in half and build a house out of it, and people come along, hundreds of years later, and stick iron ranges into it made in Birmingham and glass lampshades from Woolworth's. And somewhere along the line there is some curious adjustment to the way people feel about the past and it becomes immoral to knock the place down.

The interior walls were blistered with damp. There was a smell of cat. Closing the back door behind her, engaging its feeble latch (as though that would keep anyone out) she tried to re-animate the affection she had once felt for this place, and failed. Ten years ago, when they came to Cuxing, she used to bring the children down here on afternoon walks, when they were three and five. To walk this lane now was to feel again their small hands cling to hers as they darted back from private sorties to the ditch, the five-barred gate to the field, the arthritic branches of the willow at the corner. Passing the Span houses, she had caught herself in an automatic glance to see if the ditch was flooded, a possible child-hazard. But the Span houses had not been built then: there had been a field of cows where they stood and the ditch was drained and tamed now, nothing but a sulky lair for nettles and docks. Splatt's Cottage had seemed, then, entirely different, a faintly mysterious place, the beckoning climax of a walk (summer walks, in recollection, but surely there must have been winter days, too, cold and wet, and why, remembering, were the children never demanding or recalcitrant?), a Hansel and Gretel house in the woods. Yes, that of course must have been its allure for small Judy, held up to project her infant imagination into those murky rooms; a gingerbread house, a fantasy place.

But I liked it too, Anne thought, it had some special meaning for me, then, though it was just as run down, just as seedy. I can't quite see why, now, though I can see that Sandra's perfectly right, one can't stand by and let it be pulled down, it must be the oldest building in the village.

And, walking back past the Span houses (the young mums, trousered and smocked, herding their children back now from the primary school) she decided that it was they, the new arrivals of brick and pre-cast concrete, that made the cottage seem a profane intrusion where once it had stood so appropriately in its landscape of field and cow, water and willow. And of course, she thought, that is what does happen – the present does alter the past, quite true. But that's not an argument for knocking down Splatt's Cottage. She found an envelope in her pocket and scribbled on the back of it the names of those whose finer feelings might be appealed to on its behalf: old Miss Standish, the Pickerings, that retired Professor.

She told Don of her visit and, stung by the mild derision of his response, found herself repeating Sandra's phrase – caring about the past. It sounded absurdly pretentious and made her more irritated still. But look, she said, one can't just sit back and do nothing, can one? And imagined that behind Don's shrug and his indifference (his laziness, she said to herself) lay the thought that she was becoming one of those women herself. And, thrashing about in this mire, she made it worse.

'You never commit yourself to anything. I mean, not to anything that's going to cost.'

'Cost?'

'Cost emotionally. Oh, I don't mean that everyone should rush round having causes, like Sandra. But just sometimes you have to identify with *something*.'

'And you feel identified with Splatt's Cottage?'

'No, of course not. Well, yes, in a stupid kind of way. All right, caring about the past is a silly expression, but that is what it's about, I suppose. I mean, the place isn't especially beautiful – in fact yesterday there was something a bit repulsive about it – but in the last resort it is a very early building and there aren't many of them in Cuxing. It stands for something.'

Don said, 'You certainly expect a lot of the inanimate world.' And smiled, that cat-like, placating smile. End of argument. Except, of course, that the argument had never been. We have never, she thought, never ever had a stand-up row, because Don cannot be bothered with that kind of thing. Once, in her extreme youth, in the days before Don, she had had a lover with whom she fought devotedly. Aged eighteen and nineteen, they had blazed their way in and out of bed, through partings and reconciliations. Married to Don, she had thought how childish all that seemed. This, she had said to herself complacently, is how grown-up people behave, with restraint and consideration.

'That,' she said now, 'sounds just too clever by half, frankly. All I'm doing is give up a bit of my time to something that might be worth doing.'

* * *

Graham telephoned to say that he had been up to Lichfield and that if it was all right with them he'd pop down to Cuxing for the weekend. 'Time I gave your kids the once over. Don't put out any red carpets.'

'I wasn't proposing to,' Anne said, 'And furthermore you'll have to come with us to an extremely dull local party on Saturday night.' With a sudden spurt of warmth she added, 'I don't mean that – it'll be good to see you.'

* * *

Paul said 'I mean what exactly *is* Uncle Graham? Like Dad solicits or people are engineers?'

'You may well ask,' said Don.

'He always seems to have pots of money.'

'Your uncle,' said Don, 'is a media man.'

'I know he does things for the telly. But what, exactly? I mean, you see his name on something but it's come and gone before you've had time to find out what he did.'

Anne said, 'He's a producer. He arranges and organizes programmes. Works them out in the first place and then hires actors and people and oversees everything.'

'Do you think he knows the Goodies?'

'I've no idea. Anyway, he doesn't do that kind of thing. He does drama series, or serious plays.'

'Your cultural stuff?'

'Vaguely cultural,' said Anne, 'I suppose.'

'Pity. Now if one had an uncle who knew the Goodies, that would really be something.'

* * *

He was late, of course, for lunch on Saturday, arriving in a sports car that she thought ludicrous; she felt again the sting of exasperation with which, years ago, she had watched him arrive at home, always inconvenient, always in possession of something new (clothing, car, girl) that patently could not be afforded.

'My god, you're getting a paunch!'

'If your husband weren't around I'd pass a comment on your grey hairs. How are you, Don?'

But he was at his best, out to please, chatting up the children, telling jokes that thawed even Don's immemorial distaste for his brother-in-law. He was a person who could induce emotional schizophrenia, always had been; in childhood, she had swung between bitter hatred and passionate support. Now, in a muted form of this, she watched him wash the dishes after lunch, clowning unfamiliarity with a perplexing ritual, encouraging Paul in schoolboy horse-play, and glared beyond him at the car, toad-like in her drive.

'What a ghastly car!'

'All right, all right. Tart-traps, they were called, in our youth.' He winked at Paul.

'Well, we aren't any more, are we?' she said 'Young.'

'Oh, come off it, Annie, What's up with her?' he said to the children. 'Does she always put on this premature senility act?' They were fascinated by him, Judy blushing scarlet every time he came near her, exuding sexual awareness.

After lunch he walked with Anne to the shops.

'Did father know you?' she said.

'Hard to say. On and off, I think.'

'I've started sorting things out at the house, papers and that. I'm putting all your stuff in one box.'

'I know. I saw. You could leave it for the time being, surely?'

'I had to see to some bills and letters and then – oh, I don't know, I just felt I ought to, and I kept coming across things I'd forgotten about, stuff from years ago. I don't know what to do with it all.'

'Chuck it away,' said Graham. 'Anyway, the nursing-home seems not too bad a place, bar the po-faced nurses, but I'm afraid Dad's rather beyond noticing them, poor old chap. Is it pricey?'

'Fairly, but I went through things with the bank manager – it should be all right. That reminds me – who on earth do you think this Mrs Barron can be? You know – that I told you about on the phone.'

They were at the corner of the High Street. She turned to him and he said, 'Where are we going now – over there? Right.' And took her arm, shepherding her over the road, piloting her between lorries. How odd, she thought, Don never does that, never did, it must be one of those basic differences between men, those that do and those that don't. Achieving the pavement, almost giggling, she said, 'Here – what's all this? Anyone would think I was one of your girls.'

'Critical as ever. Seriously, though, Annie – it's good to see you.'

'Come down more often, then.'

'You know how things are. One gets so tied up.'

'Hmmn . . . This Mrs Barron, Graham . . .?'

'Ah, yes. Look, Annie, don't fash yourself about that. I'll have a check myself, next time I go up.'

'There's no point in us both doing all this.'

'Maybe. What's this party tonight, then? Good do?'

'Nothing for you, I should imagine, unless you fancy Berkshire housewives.'

'If sufficiently deprived in that direction I can fancy almost anything.'

'Thanks very much. And just you behave yourself.'

'Yes, auntie.'

Later, pressed into a corner of someone's sitting-room (Speed and Morden maps of the county on the walls; collection of Victorian souvenir mugs in a cabinet), she watched him across the room, his back to her. His back, she saw, had a slight, as yet very slight, stoop, and there was a hint of pink scalp through his thinning, just perceptibly thinning hair: she felt a lurch of compassion. Him too. Even Graham. 'Yes,' she said to the man who was talking to her (a man, she seemed vaguely to remember to be in some way connected with local government). 'Yes, we're thinking of going to Scotland this year.'

When Graham was twenty-four and I two years younger there was that business, that ghastly business, with the pregnant girl. I never, in fact, knew her name. That, he said, was neither here nor there, not really the point. What was very much to the point was the lolly, the cash, the wherewithal. He does not, in fact, still owe me twenty-five pounds (my Post Office savings, all but five quid) because he did, in fact and rather to my surprise, pay it back. Where he got the other seventy-five I'll never know, or if he paid that back.

'. . . get my wife to let you have the name of this place in the Trossachs.'

And we have never mentioned the subject again to this day, though, of course, it is lodged there for both of us like sediment in a pond. Neither have I ever mentioned it to Don, for one reason or another. What reason? Don wouldn't actually disapprove of abortion, he doesn't really disapprove of anything except fuss, bother, demands. Suppose, she thought, suppose *I'd* got pregnant, that weekend in Broadway, before we got engaged? That would have been a bother all right, even Don couldn't have quietly slid away from that one. But of course I didn't; we were luckier.

'I'm sorry,' she said, 'there's such a racket. . . . Glenelg, did you say?'

Or more careful. Don was always dead careful; he knew more about my periods than I did. He'd never have got into that kind of trouble. Graham, of course, didn't see it as trouble; just a passing difficulty. I felt sorry for the girl, the girl whose name I never knew. I wondered if she loved him. I thought a great deal about love then.

'. . .warn you against the west coast route.'

'Excuse me,' she said, 'I can see my brother making signals.'

Only very subdued ones, in fact; a catching of the eye, a lift of the eyebrow. He's got stuck with the retired general, he won't like that. And here's Sandra, doing the rounds. Has she spotted Graham, I wonder?

'Anne dear just a quick word . . . I'm told the chap to get onto on the R.D.C. about Splatt's Cottage is a Mr Jewkes. He's apparently really quite enlightened and prepared to listen, so long as we can make out a good case we can get him on our side.'

'Yes, I see. I went down there yesterday – to the cottage It is in a mess, isn't it?'

'I'd see him myself, of course, only just now I haven't a moment. Is that your brother over there?'

'Yes. Sandra, do you think one should preserve *any* old building?'

'Well, for goodness sake one has some responsibility to future generations.'

'Yes, of course. But carried to extremes you could get a situation where . . .'

'I thought,' said Sandra, 'you were a preservationist.'

'Up to a point. Well, yes, naturally I am. But if you take age as a virtue in itself – if you sanctify the past just for its own sake . . .'

'Your sister,' said Sandra, 'is using the most frightfully long words. It comes of all that education, I suppose – very confusing for homely girls like me.'

'Homely?' said Graham. 'What absolute nonsense. Let me get you another drink? Annie?'

'We met once at some ghastly children's beano. You won't remember.'

'But of course I remember. Are you drinking red or white?'

Liar. And that expression could almost – most certainly will in ten years' time – be called a leer. Sandra's, I suppose, is a simper.

'Share the joke, Anne?'

She worked her way to the window and stood looking over the lawn that ran down to the trim banks of the Thames. It must be an expensive house, this, all that river-frontage. Boats, as spruce and painty as toys, were moored at intervals; small craft with outboard motors and here and there a canal narrow-boat meticulously restored in traditional colours and patterns. They had roses and pictures of castles painted on their sides. Anne remembered visiting once, with the children, a waterways museum where this vanished life-style was lovingly enshrined, pots and pans and plates and faded sepia photographs of coal-blackened bargees. Now, down there on a leisure-time river, a girl emerged from the cabin of her boat and stood in the spring evening sunshine, wearing jeans and sweater, a can swagged with painted roses in one hand and a transistor radio in the other.

'Thinking of a boating holiday?' said Don, appearing at Anne's side. She slipped her arm through his, feeling slightly tipsy. 'Not on your life. Shall we go? Where's Graham?'

'Somewhere around. Nice house, though.'

'I s'pose so.' She couldn't remember who their host was. Someone she'd barely met, someone Don knew through work.

'We might think of moving somewhere like this when I take over from Thwaites.'

'Why?' She stared at him in amazement.

'More garden. Quieter. Good investment.'

'Oh,' she said. 'But I like our house, we've been there so long now, what's the point of moving? Such a bother,' she added, with craft, 'all that fuss.'

'O.K.,' he said. 'Just a thought.' But if she had not been just a little drunk (and looking round now for Graham) she would have seen the insincerity of this, not giving in but postponing.

'Good,' she said, her arm still through his, Graham contacted now, by eye, the host located, there by the door. 'Good, now we can go.'

They drove home on a tide of good spirits induced by drink and a united front against people they had talked to at the party.

'What a bunch! Sorry we wished that on you, Graham.'

'Don't mention it – a laugh a minute, I assure you. I particularly relished the military bloke.'

'Ah,' said Don, 'the general. He's one of my favourite characters, too. Strictly after the event, mind.'

'Pull in here a minute, Anne, will you.'

They watched him vanish into the White Hart. Anne said, 'For goodness sake, couldn't he wait till we get home for a pee?' She felt restless, edgy, for two pins she would go trotting in there after him, like a wife chasing up a roaming husband: she put her hand suddenly on Don's thigh. 'Here,' he said, 'what's up with you? Here's Graham, anyway.'

'Oh,' she said. 'Look, he's got a bottle, bless him. Champagne, at that, if you please!'

She glanced at Don, to see how he took that. Time was, that would have got his hackles up, so far as anything did. When they were young, he'd resented Graham's affluence – Graham's illusory affluence, as it in fact was, his conspicuous expenditure of money he did not in fact have.

'He's a spiritual Scot, your bloke,' Graham had said, when Anne and Don were engaged. 'You'll never catch him buying a drink out of turn. Better watch it, Annie – don't you know what they say?' And gullibly she'd said no, she didn't, and Graham had produced these saloon bar analogies between tightfistedness and sexual restraint. She'd flown at him (and quite right too, she thought now, indignantly), and she'd flown at him again when he laughed at Don's building society savings account – his pre-marital building society savings account. It's very sensible, she said, and anyway it's none of your business. Oh yes, said Graham, it's sensible all right, all too bloody sensible. Christ! And went on laughing. And of course they never got on, he and Don, or at least they never overtly quarrelled (because, she thought with surprise, come to that you can't have a row with Graham any more than you can with Don, he backs away too, slips out of the room, changes the subject, only he's usually laughing at you while he does it) but they avoided one another, or exchanged platitudes. How many brothers-in-law, though, could do better, she wondered. It's an impossible relationship in any case – unsought by either party, without the rival love for the person in between that makes some kind of getting-on-together effort unavoidable between children and parents-in-law. You aren't exactly loved by a brother. Attached to, though, yes.

Graham insisted on the children being given champagne also. They were both a little frenzied by it; Paul apeing sophistication, showing off, Judy incandescent and eventually somnolent, pecking at her glass like a wary bird. Graham entertained (the professional guest, Anne thought, the bachelor singing for his supper, he must do this a lot). He told stories that became more and more indiscreet; in sudden alarm she packed the children off upstairs, and came back into the room to find a tension between the men. Graham said, 'Don reckons I've been corrupting your young.'

'I wouldn't put it that strongly,' said Don.

'Judy's only thirteen, remember – it's bewildering, that kind of grown-up talk.' She plumped a cushion, sat on the floor by the fire, looking for a diversion, thinking, I don't want an argument, it's been a nice evening. And Graham as though in agreement began to talk to Don about inflation. A good safe subject, she thought, like the weather, the rain it rains upon us all, and no two ways about it. Thank God for the course of history. How many fragile family occasions, back in Starbridge, had been saved by recourse to such matters? We all of us deplore – deplored – the Cold War, the H-bomb, the housing shortage, air pollution, sliced bread, muzak. But for God's sake keep off all those things whereby people define themselves. She remembered a friend of hers who claimed that disagreement with her parents had extended to so many areas that they had been obliged to spend the whole of one Christmas talking about new species of rose. But why, when between friends discussion is the very stuff of life, should it have such potential danger within families? Harmony between relations, she thought, has to be built up of evasions – the deft avoidance of all those rogue subjects that can shatter the smooth passage of a meal, an outing, the three days of Christmas. By the collusion of all parties, they have to be smothered for the sake of appearances (or, when no one can stand it any longer, invoked so that everyone can hang onto their self-respect). At Starbridge, they might as well have been inscribed upon the kitchen wall: Modern Art (except Lowry and Augustus John), artificial fertilizers, birth control (except in mother's absence), phonetic spelling, Aneurin Bevan, D. H. Lawrence, the Trent River Board, Coventry Cathedral.

'Do you remember,' she said suddenly, 'going to Coventry that time? Soon after it was built – some Christmas.'

'You and Dad having an argument about stained glass and stuff? I couldn't see what all the fuss was about.'

'Tastes.'

'Never worth a barney,' said Graham with a yawn. Don said he'd better see about the boiler and went out of the room.

'I don't agree. But that's not worth an argument now.' They grinned at each other. Outside in the kitchen Don clattered with coal hods.

Anne said, 'You ought to get married.'

'Why, for heaven's sake?'

'Oh, I don't know. One thing and another.'

'Someone to look after me in my old age.'

'That, even.'

'Christ,' said Graham, 'I haven't come to that yet.' He slumped in the chair, a glass in his hand, watching Don go past the window to the coal shed. 'How's it worked out for you, then, Annie?'

'How's what worked out?'

'Twenty years with old Don.'

'Seventeen as it happens. Fine. Just fine.'

'All right, then, don't say. I'll tell you one thing, though, I thought he was doing pretty well for himself at the time.'

'Don't be an idiot. I wasn't your type of girl at all.'

'Oh, that's true enough – you'd been ruined by education. I like my women pure and uncorrupted. I still thought Don was onto a good thing, though.'

'Hmmn. Well, I don't know how you find these uncorrupted women now, after twenty years of university expansion. Even in your murky world.'

'I must admit, it's getting harder. They do tend to mellow, of course. Like you, if I may say so – you've mellowed. Not quite so many principles around. Less inclined to leap into the breach.'

'Thanks very much,' said Anne crossly. What about Splatt's Cottage? she was going to say, and then thought: no, dammit, I'm not embarking on that, it's too late and I can't be bothered. But that, of course, is precisely what Graham means.

'And so,' he went on, 'have I. I'll save you the trouble of saying it. Truth to tell, I get a bit whacked these days. O.K. if I help myself?' He waved towards the whisky bottle.

'Go ahead.'

'It's a bit disconcerting when you look round a table, at a script conference or something, and realize you're about the oldest person there. Or you find yourself working with some director young enough to be your son.' He kicked a log back onto the fire. 'Not of course that it matters. You just feel a bit – crept up on, I suppose. And I get these bloody stomach aches.'

'You should see someone about that.'

'Will do. Sometime.'

'Well,' she said, 'I like you better a bit mellowed, myself. Except for that ludicrous car. Good thing father was spared that. That reminds me, Graham – this Mrs Barron. I really do have to sort this bank account out, you know.'

Graham put his glass down. He swirled its base in the circle of damp it had left on the table. Outside in the kitchen, coke cascaded into the boiler. Graham took a handkerchief from his pocket and wiped the wet patch and the base of the glass. He put the handkerchief away and the glass down and said, 'Yes. The fact is. . . . Look, Anne, I always imagined you had some idea.'

'Some idea of what?' More coke pouring. Diffused spatter of an overspill.

'Well, clearly you didn't. Look, Annie, you aren't going to like this, but the fact is Dad had a lady off-stage for a long time. In Gloucester or some such place.'

The lid of the boiler clunked shut. The hod was dumped down on the floor. Now Don was washing his hands.

Anne said, 'You cannot, you simply cannot be telling me he had a mistress.'

'Oh, Annie, be your age. It does happen, you know.'

Don put his head round the door and said, 'I'll just put the car away. Did you leave the keys in it?'

'What?'

'Keys. Car keys.'

'Oh – yes, they're in it.'

After a moment she said, 'You *knew*. Since when?'

'Only kind of vaguely. I rather stumbled across it once – years ago, I really can't remember now – and just filed it away as one of those things. A fact of life.'

'Did father know you knew?'

'I imagine not.'

'And this Mrs Barron. . . ?'

'Oh, good lord, no,' said Graham, 'she's not her. She died sometime ago. Before Mum in fact. This is her daughter.'

'What!'

'Oh, not *their* daughter. Christ, no. Nothing to do with us. This is a daughter she had already.'

Outside, headlights swept the drive, washed across the window, went away. 'Well,' said Anne, 'that's something to be grateful for. At least one thing stays the same. There's only the two of us.'

'I know it's a bit of a shock. Truth to tell, I'd almost forgotten about it myself. I was surprised when I first realized about it, way back – it just didn't seem Dad's line of country at all – but there you are. It wasn't any of my business, our business, I thought, best to leave well alone. Mum never knew, I can tell you that.'

'Good.'

'You won't – you're not going to say anything to Dad about it?'

'Oh, Graham, what do you take me for?'

'After all, it doesn't make him a different person. He's still exactly the same bloke you always knew.'

For forty years, if you can count the first three or four as knowing. A person who, once, taught one to swim in a grey, foam-marbled sea off Suffolk; who hummed when content but out of tune; who ate boiled eggs narrow end first; who voted Conservative or occasionally Liberal; was usually in bed by eleven, could recite great chunks of Wordsworth, tied his own trout flies, served on many committees, and, it now appeared, had been able to love two women at once. Can you? she thought. Do people?

'Not quite,' she said. 'No, Graham, not quite.'

'Bugger it,' said Graham. 'It's a pity you had to know this. Simpler if you never had.'

'Much simpler.' Outside, Don's footsteps crunched past the window.

'Forget about it.'

'Oh, *Graham*. . . .' She took his glass from him and re-filled it. Then her own. 'You know a person, up to a point, how they react to things, what they're likely to feel about something, to some extent even what to expect of them – you know all that partly from observation, partly from what you know *about* them, about what they have been as well as what they are. Where they've come from. What's happened to them. But if you find suddenly that some large chunk of information has got left out – you'd never realized they had cancer, or had murdered their mother, or spent half their lives in a mental home – then you revise things a bit in the light of it. No, you don't revise, not quite that. Everything just shifts slightly, nothing can be quite the same.'

'You're leaving me behind, Annie. I daresay you're right.'

Don came in. 'What's she right about?'

'I said Graham should get married.'

'And I said I know what's good for me better than she does.'

How easy to fall into a conspiracy of exclusion. Oh, she thought, I shall talk to Don about this at some point, of course I shall, it's just that I need to sort it out for myself first before I can talk about it to anyone. I don't even know what I think about it yet. She got up, gathering glasses.

'Well, bed as far as I'm concerned. Get up when you like in the morning, Graham.'

She lay awake, listening to the house settle itself around her; final closings of doors, flush of a cistern, sluggish creaks of contracting wood and metal. She clasped her hands behind her head and stared into the darkness of the room, beginning the slow re-adjustment of the past, roaming to and fro across the years, without regard to chronology, sifting through a jumble of events and occasions. What I thought was thus, was otherwise. Things that appeared so, were not.

Four

Don got up to buy his brother-in-law a beer and thought that he was the only person he'd ever come near to hitting and even so that wasn't very near, and a long time ago. He couldn't remember, now, the occasion, only the emotion, and that because it was such a rare one. As a national serviceman he had to do bayonet practice under a sergeant of astonishing ferocity: with a relish that was quite undisguised the man hurled himself at sacks and twisted the blade in their guts. One by one the platoon had to emulate him, eighteen and nineteen year olds summoning up astonishing histrionic powers to avoid being singled out for criticism. Don's performance had been the most totally unconvincing. 'All right,' the sergeant said wearily. 'Look, think of some bastard you hate. Right? And get stuck into it again.' And Don had thought: but I don't hate anybody, what does he mean, what help is that? But he had, once, thought it would be nice to hit Graham, and looking at him now, sitting there beside Anne in his combat jacket and denims (why the hell did people in his line of business have to dress as though for a bout of guerrilla warfare?) the spectre of the emotion hovered for a moment.

'Pint?' he said.

'Thanks.'

It was partly that he brought out the worst in Anne. Either they were spatting at each other, or involved in some kind of undefined conspiracy. At least, that was how it seemed to be, back when he and Anne were first married. Nowadays, of course, they hardly saw him from one year's end to the next, just large cheques blasted off to the children at Christmas (too large) and some peculiar present for Anne. A nightdress, once. An absurd diaphanous nightdress. She never wore it, on the grounds that it was too cold. Surely, he thought, people don't give their sisters nightdresses? He had no sister himself and felt on uncertain territory. Wives one knew about, children, colleagues, secretaries, people one dealt with in one way or another. Sisters, no. He bought a lager and a couple of pints of bitter and noticed they'd been tarting up this pub, putting in strip lighting and wrought iron and a thicket of potted plants in the fireplace. He carried the drinks over to Anne and Graham, and sat down to hear Anne say '. . . and it used to be so nice, stone-flagged floors and benches with high backs like church pews. A real pub.' Here we go, he thought, all change is for the worse. . . . And switched off, as it were, so that he could sit there with his foxy smile, to all intents and purposes one of the company, in fact hearing nothing and doing a bit of work on some stuff he was involved in at the office. It was a most convenient knack, this; without it, he often thought, paternity would be quite intolerable, and marriage, too, from time to time. He had no idea if other people did it, and didn't care. He sat and thought about Sadler v. Baines, and watched Anne and Graham open and shut their mouths like goldfish.

*   *   *

Judy said 'Why were you ringing up the Pickerings? I thought you weren't all that keen on Mrs Pickering.'

'Oh, just about Splatt's Cottage. I'm not, really, but . . .' Anne shrugged, but, she thought, we all have to suffer in a good cause, or some such nonsense.

'What about Splatt's Cottage? Do you mean that place down past the Span houses?'

'That's right – where we used to walk when you were little. It may be going to be pulled down – we're trying to save it. Do you remember how you always had to be held up to see inside the windows? What did you think there was there?'

'Eels.'

'Eels! Why, for heaven's sake?'

'Because once we saw an eel in the ditch there, Paul and I, and I thought it came out of the house. I thought it was full of them and they came out into the ditches. I hated going there.'

'But you never said a word.'

'I s'pose it was too horrible to talk about even. And anyway you mightn't have taken any notice.'

'I wasn't that heartless, surely?'

'Jolly good that it's going to be pulled down,' said Judy. 'Why do you want to stop it?'

'It isn't good at all,' said Anne crossly. 'You shouldn't just destroy old buildings, that's vandalism. . . .' She lectured, and saw the child's eyes glaze over with inattention, her fingers prodding a pattern of dents into the rolled pastry on the table. 'Judy, do leave that alone – your hands are filthy.'

'What's it for?'

'Bacon tart. When I'm away tomorrow.'

'Where are you going?'

'Lichfield. Did you listen to a word I was saying – about Splatt's Cottage and places like that?'

'What Mum means,' said Paul, turning suddenly from some private communion with the transistor radio, 'is it's posh to like old things.'

'I don't mean anything of the kind.'

'Antique furniture and houses with beams everywhere, and vintage cars. And old maps. Dead posh. It shows you've got nice taste.'

He sat at the table, disembowelling the transistor, for some reason, hair flopping over his face, flopping, mercifully, over the spot that blazed like a beacon above his right eye. He didn't look like her, nor much like his father, a lank dark boy, but staring at him now she saw for a moment that uncanny reflection of herself that most people see, if only once or twice, in a child, as though for a moment one glimpsed oneself in a state of fission. There am I, but not I.

'Personally,' he said, 'I like things up to date. Your modern, today world, see?' He peered at the innards of the radio and said, 'Aha! All is revealed.'

'Well, of course,' Anne said 'we all do, up to a point. But the thing is you have to be selective, you have to look at buildings, and objects or whatever, and ask yourself whether. . . .'

'Mum,' said Paul, 'you were being teased. You don't want these bits of pastry, do you? Thanks a lot. See you later. . . .'

First tedious, then absurd. Once upon a time, she thought, sweeping flour from the table, rinsing her fingers under the tap, once upon a time parents are just a great omnipotent presence; immutable, heroic personalities beyond analysis or criticism. They simply are, and could not be otherwise. Only later comes the reduction to universal proportions; they are strict, unreasonable, unpredictable (or too predictable), they are stupid or sarcastic and should not wear the clothes they do or have the occupations they have, their friends are dull or mad and their tastes perverse. Everybody is diminished, she thought, as their children grow. She wiped her hands, looking out of the window at the translucent leaves of the chestnut tree (unfurling visibly, it seemed, in the sunshine) and remembered the day she had discovered that her best friend's father did not object, apparently, ever, to people jumping downstairs. And you could walk on his flowerbeds. And the mother of the family next door, she had presently observed, was pretty. Thereafter her parents had been flawed, as are all parents.

'I'm sorry,' she said to Judy, 'about the eels. I had no idea you were frightened.'

'It doesn't matter now,' said Judy graciously. 'Why are you going to Lichfield again?'

'To see grandfather.'

'Will you be back for the school fête?'

'Probably.'

Too late, she thought, much too late, thinking not of the school fête but all those mistakes and misunderstandings, eels and harsh words or no words or offences against the awful vulnerability of children. One of her friends, haunted by the warnings and admonitions of books on child psychology, had spent most of her time explaining and apologizing for her actions to her children. 'So long as they know why one is doing what one is doing, and why one behaved as one did, then it must be all right,' she would say, desperately. 'Mustn't it, Anne?' The children, bored, seethed around their feet. And presumably, in the end, digested their mother's behaviour as her particular flaw, as such flaws are digested and become, in the end, familiar things one could not do without. Like, she thought, mother's flights from decision; father's array of dislikes. It would have been entirely disconcerting, in the end, to find mother make up her mind lightly whether to shop in the morning or the afternoon, to have father announce an admiration for Picasso. In the end it is consistency you want in people, not perfection. Betrayal is to find them do what you would not have expected. Just that.

* * *

She drove north again, the next day, through kaleidoscopic weather. The landscape blazed in sunlight, or sulked beneath leaden clouds. When it was not raining, the wet road shone as a mirror image of the sky. She was distracted by the beauty of it, removed from the purpose of the journey so that sometimes she seemed to be travelling simply for the sake of moving like this along gleaming roads, between towns and villages that existed only as names on signs. Again, places that she had never visited – Tamworth, Stafford, Warwick – offered themselves as legendary and significant, detached from the real world of housing estates and supermarkets. The spires and towers of churches flamed where the sun caught them. Time and again her attention was arrested by the antiquity of buildings; timber-frame and mellowed brick seemed to dominate the landscape. And it had assumed an extra dimension, expanding with the spring, the flatness of fields turned into exuberant relief by greenery: she found herself driving slowly to examine the shape of a tree, the sparkle of flowers on the verge. With regret she reached the outskirts of Lichfield, threading through the streets that led to the nursing-home.

Her father was out of bed again, sitting up in the armchair, wedged in with pillows, a rug across his knees. The carpet was rolled up and a woman on hands and knees swabbed the floor energetically around him, pausing only for a moment to say good morning to Anne and remove her dusters and polish from the other chair. When she gathered her things and departed the room was very still and empty without her brisk presence. Beyond the closed door, in the passages, the comings and goings of the place, footsteps and voices, seemed also to abandon the neat room and the hunched figure in the chair. Anne wondered how far her father was conscious of all this. She said, 'Are they looking after you well, father?' But had to repeat it many times before he took in the question, and then he only mumbled something she could not follow. They sat together in silence, Anne read the newspaper and made out a shopping list. From time to time she looked across at the old man, staring at him intently and with a kind of guilt. It seemed wrong to watch him in this way, when he barely knew one was there, his head nodding, moisture creeping from his eyes, as though one were spying on his senility. Once, she got up and adjusted the rug that was slipping from his knees, and held his hand for a moment. The fingers clutched hers.

It was mid-afternoon before she got out to the house, and flung herself into more clearing and sorting, glad of the activity. Graham, she found, had done nothing. His brief presence showed only in a couple of empty beer cans on the kitchen dresser and an ashtray of cigarette stubs; they felt oddly companionable. He seemed not to have touched the study; the papers on the desk were exactly as she had left them. The cardboard carton in which she had put stuff relevant to him personally was almost as she had left it. A school report on top had been picked up and dropped again beside the box; the pile beneath was unpenetrated. She could not understand such incuriosity. For the next couple of hours, she went through files of her father's letters and papers, copies of official correspondence about schools and educational projects. The vigour and fluency of the language seemed to come from someone quite other than the man she had just left. She realized that he had been very good at his job and thought also that this was something she had hardly ever considered before.

At last, at seven or so, with the sun slanting low through the windows, she put the files away, tidily sorted into those examined and those not, and labelled according to whether she felt they could, eventually, be destroyed. She went upstairs, changed into a pair of old trousers and a warm sweater, and tied a scarf round her head. Standing before the mirror for a moment, staring at herself, she picked up a lipstick, and then changed her mind. She combed her hair and wondered if the fringe she wore (had worn, heavens! since she was sixteen or seventeen) was too young a style. The rest of her hair rose and fell by a few inches every year or two, according to whim. The fringe, dark brown, showing now the neat furrowings of the comb, was exactly the same as it had been twenty years ago. The grey hairs to which Graham had referred did not in fact exist. Oh well, she thought, next year, sometime, we'll have a re-assessment, consider the matter of the fringe. All in good time.

In the cloakroom, she found a pair of her mother's old gumboots and put them on. Then she set off briskly through the garden, stopping once only to inspect the bed she had weeded two weeks before. It was peppered with weed seedlings again, and the roses were in full leaf. There must have been rain, up here. She ducked under the fence at the end of the lawn and struck out across the field.

Lapwings lifted from the grass ahead of her, retreating waves of black and white against the green. The evening sky was a deep and vibrant blue, orange-rimmed at the horizon, bare except for the crescent moon poised like a feather above the telegraph pole by the roadside. Her father's house was at the edge of the village, the last in a row of unappealing pre-war buildings; now, more stringent planning laws curbed its further expansion. Even so, the surrounding countryside was faintly scruffy, scarred by the corrugated iron of sheds and barns, dumped down in the corner of a field or the apex of a lane. Lines of telegraph or electricity poles severed the brown sweep of plough or the green furrows of winter wheat. The skyline of the village was a jumble of television aerials and wires tethering roof to roof, pole to pole. Only the church spire showed a clean, neat outline. The flatness of the landscape eliminated much sense of distance. It was hard to realize that the Derbyshire hills lay not far away.

By the river there was a sense of something more natural, less man-made. Here, it was possible to understand the appeal this place had held for her father, over thirty or forty years. It was a trout stream, winding between banks that rose high in some places, crowned by willow and alder, and sloped to shingly beaches in others. For long stretches the water ran shallow and clear, river crowfoot pouring just below its surface, already spattered with the first white flowers. In others it slowed suddenly to the dark stillness of pools. Anne, standing beside one of these, where the river turned and wound away out of sight, masked by the bank, saw the exploding circles of a rise, gilded by the setting sun. She peered into the water, searching for fish, and saw only her own face, split and refracted by the ripples.

She began to walk along the bank. Here, often, she had walked with Don during weekend visits to her parents. The children had fished, ineffectually, with bent pins, or paddled in the icy water, teetering from one shore to the other on weed-covered stones. Out of sight, round a corner, on some undisturbed stretch, her father would be about the serious business of the river, his stocky figure bisected by the stream, up to the waist in his waders, the line hissing in the air as he cast, slung about with the paraphernalia of the fisherman.

It could have been him she saw now, standing on a spur of shingle there. There was merely the possibility, she told herself, and of course I did not know he would be here and would have walked down to the river, in all probability, anyway – it is chance, just mere chance, and nothing else.

David Fielding called, 'Hello.' He began to wind in his line, the familiar noise again reconstructing other times, another person.

She came up to him and said, 'Hello. Don't let me disturb you.'

'You're not. I was just going to pack it in anyway. It's too early in the year to expect much. I hadn't realized you were up here again. How's your father? I'm afraid I haven't managed to get in to see him this week.'

'Much the same. No, that's not quite true. A bit worse. I can see a difference from last time I was up. It's as though – as though he were getting a little more indistinct all the time. Fading.'

David nodded. She saw the red line of a scar on his thumb as he fiddled with the reel and said, 'How's your cut?'

'Fine. Thanks to your ministrations.' He delved in a canvas bag. 'My thermos will stretch to two cups, I think. Only tea – I'm afraid. Your father would have had a flask of brandy, I seem to remember.'

'Thanks.'

They stood on the river bank, watching the water. David said, 'A dipper – look.'

'Where?'

'There – on that stone.' His hand rested for an instant on her back, between the shoulder blades, turning her in the right direction; she could feel it as a phantom pressure after he had taken it away.

'Oh, yes – on the island.'

The river divided around a hummock of turf, creating a scenery of miniature rapids, the water whitening over pebbles and catching at a projecting stone. The dipper bobbed, and flew away upstream. They drank the tea, hot and sweet (man-made tea, Anne thought, women never make tea as strong as this, he made it himself). She said, arbitrarily, 'What *is* the fascination of rivers?'

'Speculation about what might be in them, as far as I'm concerned. There – something rising again. They always do just as you've packed up.'

'Oh, I was thinking much more confused things,' she said, 'about the continuity of places and all that.' She turned to look at him and was dazzled by the setting sun, seeing only his hair fringed with a halo of light, his face in shadow. He said abruptly, 'Would you like to have something to eat in the local pub?'

'Thank you, that would be nice.' Walking across the field, she thought: isn't his supper waiting for him at home? His wife?

They reached the road and passed, on the outskirts of the village, an ancient and desolate house that reminded Anne of Splatt's Cottage. She told David about her involvement with it, and the ambiguity of her feelings towards its preservation. He said, 'We're not so squeamish in these parts. Someone would have taken a bulldozer to it, one fine day, and no more said.'

'Well, I don't approve of that, but I do wonder if . . . oh, well. It used to have some awful fascination for Judy, when she was small. Apparently she thought there were eels in it.'

'Freudian, I suppose.'

'What on earth do you mean?'

'Well, eels are a sexual fantasy, aren't they, in dreams, anyway? How old was she?'

'Oh, very small – three or so. Actually I think they were perfectly straightforward eels. There was one in a ditch there, once, she said.'

'I thought these things never could be straightforward. Here we are

– it's fairly basic, I'm afraid, as pubs go.

'It's nice. Father used to come here.'

Anne went to a settle by the fireplace while he stood at the bar. She picked shreds of dead grass from her trousers and threw them into the fire, watching them curl and spark, and was suffused with a sense of the most extraordinary pleasure. I am extremely happy, she thought, for really no reason at all. And when David stood before her, holding beer and plates of food, she found herself smiling with a radiance that must, she thought, seem affected or ridiculous. They ate, perching plates on the too-low table.

'Still sorting out the past?'

'I suppose so. It'll be a long job. Father seems never to have thrown anything away.'

He drank his beer, looking at her over the mug. 'Why do you feel so driven to impose order? Is all your life so tidy? No mysterious corners?'

'I'm afraid not.' Really not, she thought. Hardly any concealments, except a parking fine I never mentioned to anyone, least of all Don, because it made me so cross. I have only been unfaithful to him in thought, which presumably he has done too so it doesn't count. 'Oh, I've done things I'm ashamed of,' she said. 'Things I'd rather not talk to anyone about.'

'I worry more about the things I haven't done. Ambitions unfulfilled. Compromises. All one's craven moments.'

'I wouldn't have thought you were all that craven.'

He said, almost sharply, 'Well, I am.' And began to talk about something else. The impression he gave of stillness, of wariness, she realized, concealed some kind of restlessness, suppressed energies channelled into many directions – work, involvement with local activities, chairmanships of this and that. Like Sandra? she thought. And then, no, not like Sandra at all.

'Well,' he said. 'How does it strike you, provincial life?'

'I live it myself.'

'Rubbish. The home counties are entirely different.'

'Oh, come,' she said, and saw that she was being teased. They laughed, and David went to buy more drinks.

When he came back he said, 'And how long will all this re-arranging of the past take you?'

'Ages.' She drank some more beer. 'As a matter of fact, I wish I'd left well alone.'

'Why?'

'I've come across something I knew nothing about. My father had a mistress, for many years, it seems. My brother knew. I had no idea.'

David Fielding said, 'How extraordinary. I'm very surprised.'

Why did I tell him that? she thought, have I had too much to drink? But she felt quite clear-headed, had spoken with deliberation.

He said, 'Would you prefer not to have known?'

'I'm not at all sure. In some ways I feel cheated at not having known for so long.'

'Cheated by your father?'

She was silent for a moment. 'No, I don't think it's quite that.'

'He presumably wanted to spare you embarrassment. Or distress.'

'Graham – my brother – says it doesn't alter the person he was. The person one knew. The whole person, I suppose he means.'

'That's a somewhat naive view, possibly.'

'I thought so too.'

'It's upset you?'

'In a way. Confused, perhaps, more than upset.'

'I can understand that.'

'The odd thing is,' she said, 'that I find I want to go to see this woman.'

'It could be disconcerting.'

'I know.'

'Where does she live?'

'Gloucester.'

'I'll take you if you like,' he said casually, looking away.

'That's very kind. Thank you.'

Yes, she thought, it is kind and I would like that so much. She wanted to say so, with more enthusiasm, but in the slight pause an awkwardness had already grown between them: David Fielding was fiddling with his plate, and then caught the eye of someone he knew at the bar, with something that seemed like relief. The man joined them for a few minutes, a local man, talking pleasantly of local things, small, safe, humdrum things. He had known Anne's father ('Not well, mind, just to pass the time of day') and asked after him. When he left them Anne said, 'I should get back.'

They walked through the darkened village. David said, 'I met your brother once, briefly, I think, last year. Cheerful kind of chap.'

'Yes. We're not much alike.'

'I haven't found you particularly sombre.'

She smiled. 'Good.'

'Truth to tell, I found him a bit out of my world. Television, is that right?'

'Yes. He's a producer.' He didn't like him, she thought, and David said, 'I think I might find him a bit difficult to get on with.'

She could feel him looking at her, prepared to have offended, suffering the compunction of those driven always to say what they think, or feel. 'He's not so bad really. A bit selfish, I suppose. But then he's not married so it doesn't matter all that much. He's got no one to be selfish at.' She laughed, trying to put him at his ease again, but he said nothing and they walked on in silence.

Outside the house they stopped and stood for a moment, both speaking then at once. 'Do come in for a minute, I think I can find some coffee. . . .' 'Well, I mustn't keep you up, let me know if. . . .'

Inside the darkened hall, the telephone began to ring. Anne broke off, fumbling in her pocket for the keys.

David said rapidly, 'Thanks – thanks for the evening. Bear Gloucester in mind, won't you?'

'Yes, I will. And thank you.' Turning at the door, dragged by the noise of the telephone, she saw him walking away. She picked up the receiver and said 'Yes?' again, the front door still open, framing the crescent moon now high and bright above the rooftops.

'Anne? Where on earth have you been?'

'Just having a meal. Sorry, darling. I had a meal at the pub. Is everything all right?' The street was empty now. She pushed the door shut with her foot.

'There's some fuss about a shirt. Here's Judy.'

Judy's voice, petulant, distant, said, 'Mum, I can't find my clean school shirt *anywhere*. . . .'

'Oh God, really, Judy – I told you, in your top drawer . . .' The moon was a line of splintered light now, in the frosted glass of the door panel; down there, in Cuxing, it would appear, at this time of night, just a little to the left of the house opposite and immediately above the yew tree in its garden. '. . . Give the phone to Dad now. And get up to bed. Don?'

Going to bed herself, presently, she opened the window of her room and fancied she could hear the river rustling in the distance at the bottom of the field. Or was it too far, and the noise repeating itself merely in her head, an echo from earlier in the evening? She lay awake for a long time, in what seemed a state of acute consciousness, haunted by images and snatches of talk.

* * *

Thursday, thought David Fielding . . . Thursday, which is the Staff Meeting, and the Oxbridge Entrance lot, in the afternoon, and after school the parents of Kevin Grant, to whom I do not know what to say. Thursday, he thought, will be a varied day. And after Thursday there is Friday, which is the interviews with the candidates for the chemistry post, and in the evening the Music Society AGM, which just about accounts for Friday. And then there is Saturday, and then there is Sunday. And then Monday, which is Oxbridge Entrance again, and the Lower Fourth, amongst whom there are one or two problems, and the History Club in the dinner hour. He went to the bottom of the stairs and called up, 'I'll be in for a meal tonight.' A voice came back acknowledging this information, and he went out to the garage and got into the car. I measure out my life, he thought in Thursdays and Fridays and Mondays and Tuesdays, which I suppose is not so very pitiable, all things considered. As mother would have said, it's nice to know where you are. I know where I am all right.

The Midlands, he thought in the Staff Meeting, is a funny place. Are funny places. Now here am I, and there is George Barnes over there, and we were born not many miles apart in, I should guess, around the same year, and I daresay to the unpractised eye we might seem pretty much of the same ilk. We both speak with what is called an educated accent, behind which, nonetheless and I suspect rather to

George's annoyance, our origins are detectable. I say 'poonch' for 'punch', as Doctor Johnson is alleged to have done. I don't know about George, never having heard him say the word that I can recall, but I, and most people in these parts, could nail him after three or four sentences as a Leicestershire man. It is not merely a question of pronunciation, either, this subtle difference so unapparent to the uninitiated. George would prefer to be somewhere else; he is here because he is not, frankly, all that good and has never landed one of those jobs in minor public schools or the big direct grant schools that he would like. I am here because I want to be, for reasons I find difficult to define, especially to myself. And now, if we are not going to run on into the next hour, I am going to have to shut George up. He knows, and I know, and we all know, that there is very little if anything to be done about the delays to the new science block. He cleared his throat and set about shutting up George Barnes.

Would you like, he said, two hours later, to the Oxbridge people, would you like an essay on 'What is meant by historical method?' Something along those lines?

The third year sixth (History) thought the matter over and were unenthusiastic. Paul Craxton said he thought that was a bit general. He said he felt he needed to get down to things more.

'Why do you want to read History at university, Paul?'

Paul Craxton said, smartly, that he felt we could all understand our own society better if we knew more about the past. I mean, he said, you can sort of evaluate social problems and interpret things better if you know what has happened before. And the past can warn us about the future, can't it? You know where you are better, he said, don't you, if you know some history. But I suppose you don't say that in an interview, do you, at least not about knowing where you are? The others laughed. If I get an interview, he said, which I shan't.

David said, 'Ah . . .' He looked at Paul Craxton and thought of Paul Craxton's father, with whom he had spent nearly half an hour two weeks ago. Paul Craxton's father was a Sales Manager in an engineering company and was worried about what Paul was going to do in the end, ultimately, after university. He'd seen the way the wind was blowing, nowadays, in industry, and frankly you could be out of work just as easily with a degree to your name as without. It just doesn't, Mr Fielding, he said, have the pull it used to, fifteen, twenty years ago. It was only a thought, mind, but he'd been wondering if Paul mightn't maybe do just as well to pack it in now and go into the works right away. There was an opening he'd been told about, and he'd talked it over with Paul's mother, and they couldn't help wondering.

David, listening to him, had thought of his own father and said, 'What does Paul think about it?' And what Paul thought was made manifest now, by the fact that he was still here, on a Thursday afternoon, saying that what he'd really rather do for this week would be to go over some old Entrance papers again. He didn't know a thing, he said, about the rise of the gentry. And none of them, said Tim Langdale, had done much on Tudor economic stuff.

David said, 'I think, all the same, you can do an essay on the kind of thing I suggested.' Read Butterfield, he said, and Marc Bloch. And you could look at E. H. Carr. And Marx, come to that. Think about it, he said; if you're really set on spending three years studying the past you might as well be sure why you're doing it. You might as well know where you are. The third year sixth laughed, writing down names and titles.

'Ah . . .' he said, to the parents of Kevin Grant. 'Do sit down.' He couldn't remember having met them before. They drew their chairs together as though, David thought, closing ranks. The woman was smartly dressed, carefully made-up, her head straight from the hairdresser, but her glance slid past him, avoiding his eye. He wanted to put them at their ease.

'I'm so glad you've come to see me,' he said, 'I've been wanting . . .'

The man interrupted, leaning forward a little, his hands planted on his knees. 'One thing,' he said, 'we'd better get clear from the start. We're not taking him away from the school. That's definite.' His wife nodded. 'And it seems you can't ask us to, seeing as he only got probation. I've checked on that – had my lawyer check on that.' He looked defiantly at David and David thought in bewilderment: what the hell has been going on here, what have these people got into their heads?

He said, 'But there's no question of that, Mr Grant. We don't want

Kevin to leave the school. All we want – and presumably you too – is to try to see that he keeps out of this kind of trouble in future.'

The man said, 'Most youngsters get in a bit of trouble, one time or another.'

'Mr Grant,' said David, 'not many appear before a juvenile court three times in one year. You realize that if it happened again he would be unlikely to get probation? He and his friends did several hundred pounds' worth of damage, I gather.'

'Asking for trouble,' said the woman suddenly. 'Leaving that place empty at night. What do they expect? Boys of that age, they're bound to be a bit high-spirited. You must know that, Mr Fielding.'

David said tersely, 'I know that. And what they expect, Mrs Grant, is that people treat public property with the same respect as their own. Do you allow Kevin to tear your house apart?'

'That's different.'

'I don't think so.'

They sat staring at each other in hostility. Well I'm damned, David thought, I didn't think it would be like this at all.

'Personally,' the man said, 'I believe in giving kids a bit of a free rein. Letting them do their own thing. I'm not saying I approve of what Kevin did, I don't, but the fact is he's old enough and that it's not altogether our business, my wife's and mine.'

'It's only up to a point you can interfere, nowadays, isn't it?' said Mrs Grant. 'I mean, it's the way things are, with young people.' She smoothed her skirt over her knees with rosily manicured fingers. 'You can't fight the times, can you, Mr Fielding?'

David said, 'You amaze me.' He got up and went over to the window. There was a solitary car in the Visitors' Car Park. He said, 'Is that your car?'

'Is it in the way? I'll move it.'

'No,' said David. 'It's not in the way.' He looked across the car park to the playing fields, where boys eddied to and fro, including probably Kevin Grant, aged fourteen, whose parents owned an expensive new car and were complacent in their respect for the times. Beyond the playing fields the cathedral squatted against the skyline. Nearby, invisible behind rooftops, stood Samuel Johnson's birthplace. Lichfield schools had been catering, in one way or another, for the sons of Lichfield tradesmen since before the days of Samuel Johnson. He turned back to Mr Grant (whose occupation was given, in Kevin's file, as company director) to hear Mr Grant saying that he did not think they need take up any more of Mr Fielding's time, now that they all knew where they stood. He watched Mr and Mrs Grant leave the room and sat alone for several minutes, thinking not of them, but of the sound of the river running over stones, out at Starbridge.

Five

Sandra said, 'Your brother was looking awfully well, I thought. I didn't think he'd remember me, but we had quite a chat, really very interesting, about a play on Northern Ireland he's producing. He's a very committed sort of person, isn't he, I mean, he really does take things seriously.'

'I wouldn't entirely say so.'

'Well, he's your brother, you should know. But I must say he's the sort of person we could do with more of here. I'll come into the library with you, I want them to put up the notice about the Traffic Action Group. Does he come down often?'

'Not all that often.'

'Pity. I say, Anne, do you really get through all those books in a week? I envy you, I'm always wishing I had more time to read. Oh, that reminds me, I've still got that book of yours on old farmhouses and things.'

'M. W. Barley. Did you think it was interesting?'

'Well, truth to tell I never got around to reading it from cover to cover. I did dip into it a bit.'

'It has a long section on cruck-framed buildings like Splatt's Cottage. How the internal arrangement changes – starting off with just one room, and then a kitchen being added at one end, and upstairs rooms and so on. And external chimneys.'

'Yes,' said Sandra vaguely, 'I did have a look at that, I think.

Anyway, I must let you have it back.' She moved away, and through the book-cases Anne could see her manœuvring her notice into a favourable position on the library's pin-board. Returning, she peered at the books in Anne's shopping basket.

'Of course, I suppose you have heaps of time in the holidays. Why Gloucestershire?'

'Oh, just I was thinking of going to Gloucester cathedral sometime.'

'Lincoln's the one I adore. That is the one with all those figures on the front, isn't it?'

'That's Wells, actually.'

'Oh, of course. Anne, I've been meaning to ask you about your father. How *is* he?'

'So so.'

They walked together down the High Street. Sandra, it seemed, had had a perfectly ghastly time with James's father, the year before last, endless visiting at that hospital somewhere on the absolute outer rim of north London, and then of course she'd had her own mother in the house for ages, really hardly able to do a thing for herself. 'So you have all my sympathy, I know what it's like.'

'I think it's father who needs sympathy, really' said Anne.

'Surely they're doing everything they can.'

'Oh yes, they're doing everything they can.'

'Well,' said Sandra. 'This is where I must love you and leave you.' She passed on the brink of the zebra crossing. 'By the way, have you got the Pickerings lined up yet, over Splatt's Cottage? And the R.D.C. man?'

'No, I'm seeing him tomorrow.'

Anne went into Dewhurst's and bought two pork chops for supper. Paul had gone away on a school camp. Judy was spending a few days with a friend. Later, eating in the kitchen, she said to Don, 'We could go off for the weekend. Why don't we? First time we've been on our own for God knows how long.'

'Go where?'

'Oh, I don't know. Anywhere. The Cotswolds. Remember Broadway? Walk, and look at things. Stay in a nice hotel. Why shouldn't we? Please let's.'

'Why, particularly?'

'No reason. Just it would be nice. I'll ring somewhere up, shall I – book us in?'

'If you like,' he said. 'If you want to.'

* * *

They drove west beside the green flanks of the Berkshire Downs. We walked, said Anne, up there, do you remember, years ago, after a dance or something, when we hadn't known each other very long. We got a bus out from Oxford and had lunch in a pub that had tables outside and a dog that fetched stones if you threw them for it. Remember? And Don said, not the dog, frankly, no. And a bit after that, she said, in the vacation, that weekend we met in London, we went to bed together for the first time. Yes, said Don, that sleazy hotel in Kensington. Not sleazy, she said, I can see it now, not sleazy at all, marvellous, special. Well, he said, that's as may be, and it's just as well you can see it now because it's not there any more. Knocked down for a new block of flats, I was noticing the other day. Isn't it? she said, isn't it? I didn't know that. You never told me.

* * *

'You're very restless,' he said. 'What's the rush? I'd have had another beer.'

'But we want to see Hailes Abbey. And Belas Knap.'

'Do we?' he said. 'If you say so. You drive, I'm having a snooze.'

The hills presided over Gloucestershire and the Vale of Evesham, the Malverns whale-blue in the distance, limestone villages burning in shafts of sunlight. Counties met and interlocked; the Welsh mountains lay like clouds on the horizon. They climbed away from the valley up a field whose pitch silenced them, walking through cowslips. At the top, on the level, Don said, 'What is it, anyway?'

'Darling, I told you. A burial mound. Neolithic.'

'Fine view, I'll say that.'

The barrow crouched among fields of kale, its age and function explained on the Ministry of Works notice. Don stood in front of it, reading, his hair lifting in the wind. Anne climbed the turf mound and stood on top, cushioned by the same wind, looking up the valley. There is Winchcombe down there, where we shall sleep tonight; Cuxing is over to the right somewhere, miles and miles away, quite out of sight; the Lake District where Paul is in some tent is due north, straight up the valley, on and on. And Lichfield, she thought, Lichfield is that way too, more to the right, the road to Lichfield is not so far off, north-east, over there.

'Come up here,' she said. 'You can see for miles.'

He came and stood beside her. She put her arm through his. 'Aren't you glad we came?'

'Mmn. Good idea. We should bring the children sometime.'

'No, we shouldn't, it's our turn now.'

'I daresay. What's that place down there?'

'Winchcombe, where we're staying. Do you realize we're standing on top of a family mausoleum?'

'So it seems.'

'You can't begin to imagine what they were feeling, those people, trailing up here burying each other with pots and brooches and goodness knows what.'

'Oh,' said Don. 'Reassurance of some kind. Investment in the future. Sensible enough.'

'What nonsense! Mumbo-jumbo, that's all. Superstition. Just like any religion. Leaving money to have masses said for your soul, burying provisions with the dead – it's all equally mad. You can't plan the afterlife, even if you suppose there is one.'

'But you don't believe in planning life, either.'

'No, I don't,' she said crossly.

'That's a kind of superstition, too.'

'I don't see why.'

'Well,' said Don. 'It's a way of refusing to anticipate things. If I don't arrange for it, it won't happen.'

'Now you're talking like an insurance agent.'

'Maybe.'

'I just don't think,' she said, 'you ought to rule anything out. Did you know Sandra and James have already bought the house they're going to retire to? Twenty-five years ahead. Fancy deciding where you're going to be in twenty-five years' time.'

'I'd rather like to know,' said Don, 'where I'm going to be for the rest of the afternoon. What else have you in mind for us? You seem to be the planner today.'

* * *

Did I tell you, she said, driving down the hill to Hailes Abbey, did I tell you about this man I saw yesterday? About Splatt's Cottage. It didn't work out quite how I'd expected. I'm in a bit of a muddle about all that.

* * *

She had been passed from voice to voice, on the telephone, from office to office in which typewriters clacked and heels tapped echoingly across floors. You want our Planning Department; Mr Hanson deals with that area; do you know the application number? 'I believe there's a Mr Jewkes I should speak to,' Anne said. And at last there came Mr Jewkes on the line, saying perhaps the best thing would be if she could pop along and talk it over. Yes, he said, he knew about Splatt's Cottage.

They sat facing each other in an office whose walls were lined with maps of the county. Maps showing density of population; maps showing distribution of industry; maps of town and country and road and rail networks. Berkshire was analysed and dissected, arrangements made for its future, schools planned for children as yet unborn, expansion areas designated for the housing of couples still unknown to one another. Amid these predictions, Mr Jewkes sat behind his desk, a man of amiable concern, more like an old-fashioned doctor, Anne thought, than a planning officer. He said, 'It's not scheduled, of course.'

'No, we realize that. But we feel that all the same this application should never have been granted – that it's a building of historic importance and ought to be preserved at all costs.'

Mr Jewkes said mildly, 'I did of course go into it myself, when the application was made.'

She had expected someone more ruthless than this, a more clinical figure, disposing in this godlike way, changing landscapes at the stroke of a pen. He had gone over to a map cabinet now and came back with a sheet. 'It's marked on the 1875 Ordnance Survey, of course,' he said. 'The twenty-five inch. Rather interesting – you'll see if you look, Mrs Linton, the ground plan shows some outbuildings that seem to have disappeared, or at least I could see no trace of them when I went there.'

'Splatt's Cottage', it was spelt, in copperplate print, quite isolated among fields. The ditch curled around it. Like an eel, Anne thought.

And he had done his stuff, Mr Jewkes, more deliberately, she realized with annoyance, than they had themselves, she and Sandra and Mary Pickering, in their desultory attempt to establish some facts about the place. Structurally, Mr Jewkes said, it was in a very dickey state, very dickey indeed. Dry rot, woodworm, the lot. You name it, he said, and it's got it, poor old place. I had one of our public works chaps go over it pretty thoroughly and his report was rather daunting. He reckoned the costs of restoration would be fairly astronomic – always assuming the present owner could find a buyer for it at all. I can show you his report, if you like, Mrs Linton, said Mr Jewkes.

Anne said, 'No, I'll take your word for it. But even so – even so buildings like this *have* been rescued. I mean,' she said sternly, 'cruck-frame farmhouses of the early fifteenth century don't exactly abound.'

'Quite,' said Mr Jewkes. He looked at her over gold-rimmed spectacles. 'That thought did occur to me,' and Anne, feeling herself rebuked, looked away in discomfort. 'Curiously,' Mr Jewkes went on, 'it's not mentioned in Pevsner, whereas the Old Mill, which I've always thought rather dull, is. But that's neither here nor there. We did, I assure you, Mrs Linton, think long and hard about this. And then, of course, there was the question of the amenity value of the proposed bungalows. The acute need for this kind of housing for old people.'

'But you can't be sure they'll go to old people.'

'Ah,' said Mr Jewkes, 'I think perhaps you're not quite aware. . . . Have you seen the terms of the application?'

Anne said, 'No.' She felt doubt take hold, insidious, like the early symptoms of a cold.

'Let me just explain, then. What the builders have in mind is a group of purpose-built bungalows for the elderly. They are intending to keep the price low and are giving an undertaking that first options should be given to local people – to people born in Cuxing. Mr Pym is himself a Cuxing man, of course.'

Sandra would say, Anne thought, this is a fix. 'It sounds very altruistic,' she said.

'And builders,' said Mr Jewkes, 'are not always remarkable for their altriusm. I can imagine you may be thinking that, Mrs Linton. Quite. But sentiment apart, Mr Pym had also to reckon with the possibility that we would not grant planning permission. I think you could call this a scheme whereby the vendors benefit – though by no means on the scale they might – and the village gains some much-needed accommodation for its elderly. So you see, it was a question of expediency. Which do we need most – a building of admitted historic interest, but very uncertain future, or housing for old people?'

Game, Anne thought, and I think probably set and match. She said, stiffly, 'I see your point. I shall have to talk this over with the rest of the committee.'

'Naturally,' said Mr Jewkes. He rose, and held out his hand. 'And of course if you'd like to look in again, I'm always available. It wasn't an easy decision, I do assure you, Mrs Linton, but decisions have to be made. Nothing stands still.'

* * *

And I haven't yet, she said to Don, had time to talk to the others about it, but I must say as far as I'm concerned I feel a bit uncertain about the whole thing now. I feel, she said, a bit foolish. I wish I'd never got pushed into it.

Hailes Abbey, too, burned in the sunshine. They toured its nave, its aisles, the conjectural site of its altar, the skeleton of its cloisters, refectory, undercroft, all mounted on grass neatly banded by the mower, any insecurities of structure attended to with fresh mortar or discreet splintings of iron. Hailes Abbey, what there was of it, was all set for the next hundred years. Don said he'd had enough sight-seeing for now, if she didn't mind, and sat in the sun on the cropped wall of what was once the monks' frater, doing the *Times* crossword. Anne moved from glass case to glass case in the museum, poring over chunks of limestone that flowered into all the riotous creatures of medieval fantasy, and innumerable fragments of tile, their colours snuffed out by five centuries. Emerging, she saw Don sitting in exactly the same place, but the sun had gone in and the stone was drained of colour, grey not gold. She felt suddenly dispirited and remembered how her mother's moods would fluctuate with the weather, and how this had always annoyed her when she was young. Oh dear, her mother would say, look at the day, pouring, doesn't it make you feel low? and she would argue that how you feel comes from inside, not outside. And I still, she thought, am not much uplifted by weather, or otherwise, so there is no need for today to be spoiled by a few black clouds. 'Coming?' she said. 'There's the church as well.'

They studied the wall-paintings. 'I can't make it out,' said Don. 'What's it supposed to be?'

'St Christopher. Look, there's his staff, and his legs, and the wiggly lines are the water he's walking through. He's a charm against death, you know, like touching wood. That's why he's in so many churches – if you saw him you were all right for the rest of the day.'

'In that case,' said Don, 'let's tackle the hazards of the A46.'

* * *

Leave the wretched crossword, she said, in the hotel bar, talk to me. Have you enjoyed today? We should do this more often. And Don, folding the newspaper (but right side out, she saw, ready for later) said, yes, very nice, I daresay we should, what about the summer, then? Scotland, isn't it, we fixed on?

Oh, Scotland, she said, I didn't mean that, that's different. Scotland's the statutory two weeks holiday, so we've got something to talk to people about in the autumn. I meant days like this, she said, just for us, just for you and me.

What's up, Annie? he said, you're very sharp, all of a sudden. What's got into you? Nothing, she said. Nothing at all. Everything and nothing. Not to worry, as Graham would say. Come on, let's have a look at their menu, I want my money's worth, four courses and no nonsense. Prawn cocktails, duck with slices of orange glued on, the lot.

* * *

They returned home to the phone ringing in the empty, dark house. Fumbling for her keys on the doorstep she thought, in dithering sequence: Oh God, Paul, there's been some accident. . . . And then: Judy, Mrs Shapton ringing about Judy. And finally: father, the nursing-home, that Matron.

But it was none of those things, merely Farrer, from the comprehensive, the headmaster, saying if it was not too inconvenient could she look in one day this week, just to have a talk.

'Yes' she said, bored. 'Yes, of course. Wednesday. Right you are.' And put the receiver down thinking, Thursday I'll go up to Lichfield. Thursday or Friday.

'Who was it?'

'Farrer. He wants to see me. Syllabuses for next term, I suppose. D'you mind if I go straight to bed? I'm flaked out – all that fresh air.'

They had walked for miles, through a day of crystalline clarity in which, from the hill-tops, each detail of the landscape stood out minutely: the shape of trees, the swirling plough-marks on fields, smoke from chimneys, flash of light from car or window-glass. And then, in late afternoon, the day had mellowed to a dusty haze and the sunshine had streamed down through golden clouds in great shafts and pillars, so that it seemed as though a William Blake God, or angels at least, should descend upon Gloucestershire. They had walked apart, coming together only to consult about time, or direction. Anne, plodding over fields, climbing hillsides, crossing lanes, had felt alone. Don's footsteps, a dozen paces behind, made no demands. She thought of nothing, except that she would like to get very tired, physically, and when, at some point, Don suggested they go back, said, you go, if you want, I'll meet you later, it won't be dark for ages yet. And had not for several minutes thought to look back for him, nor had been surprised to see him still there, hands in his pockets, following. Sorry, she said, arriving back at the car, you needn't have come, I just felt like a good walk, and he'd shrugged, meaning, she supposed: why not? One might as well as not.

* * *

The Splatt's Cottage Preservation Committee ('It's awfully cumbersome,' said Sandra, 'as a name. We need something snappier than that. Anyone got any ideas?') met at the Pickerings. It would be so nice, Mary Pickering had said, now that we've at last got rid of the builders, we thought perhaps after dinner, if that suits everyone, and we can talk about it over a drink, nice and informal, I hate committees, actually, don't you?

'She paints, you know,' said Sandra, turning the Renault in at the Pickerings' gates. 'And he lectures in something at the Poly. Design, or graphics or whatever. Is that right? You know about that kind of thing, Anne.'

'Do I?'

'Actually,' said Sandra, 'he's a bit hard to pin down, if you see what I mean.' The car slowed, awash in newly-laid gravel. They got out, and waded across to the front door. Sandra went on, 'They've done wonders with this place, apparently.'

The committee sat on low long sofas and immense patchwork cushions and drank a wine cup thick with borage and lemon balm from the garden. Old Miss Standish, having arrived, it seemed, inconveniently early, sipped gingerly and eyed Mary Pickering's long, patterned dress and sandalled feet.

'Gorgeous batik,' said Sandra. 'I suppose you did it yourself, Mary? I do envy you – how lovely to have time for that sort of thing. So restful.'

The forge, bellows and anvil which had once been the house's *raison d'être* were cunningly incorporated into the design of the living-room. The bellows, renovated and softly lit from some concealed source behind, looked like a piece of controversial sculpture. The anvil, polished to a sharp glitter, stood against a background of copious indoor plants. The forge itself made up one wall of the room, its awkward angles smoothed out by built-in shelves and cupboards housing bright paperback books, pieces of pottery and displays of dried leaves and flowers. An open-tread staircase rose to the floor above. The ceiling beams, recovered and exposed, carried spotlights angled towards the bare white wall on which old agricultural implements were displayed – sheep-shears and sickles and flails and a scythe.

'I say,' said Sandra, 'what an awfully good idea.'

'They're such super shapes, aren't they?' said Mary Pickering. 'Lovely clean lines.' She pointed out the old bread-oven, restored and with a glassed-in front, making a display cabinet for some choice pieces of china.

Sandra, still intent on the agricultural implements, said. 'Now what would that have been for?' They all looked at a piece of iron neatly pinned beside the door.

'As a matter of fact,' said Brian Pickering, 'I couldn't exactly tell you. It's a thing we picked up in Wales once. But it's rather nice, isn't it?'

'That's a dibble,' said Miss Standish suddenly, 'for planting seeds. Making the holes, you see. You had a man or a boy go along the rows sticking it in ahead of the man who was sowing.'

'Really?' murmured Mary Pickering. 'I had no idea.'

Miss Standish, encouraged, went on, 'I know because of course I remember it as a child. They still did it like that then, you see, and there were horses in the fields, not tractors. I can see it now,' she said, 'as though one were still there. Silly, isn't it, the way that kind of thing stays with you . . .' her voice trailed away.

'Yes,' said Sandra. 'Fascinating. Now had we better get on, I wonder?' She shuffled the papers on her knee. Brian Pickering went round filling up glasses. He had a beard, and wore denim trousers and checked shirt. 'Top you up?' he said to Anne, leaning across her, and she nodded, reminded somehow of Graham. A muted, more settled Graham, she thought, what Graham might have been if he'd done one thing rather than another, fancied girls like Mary Pickering instead of the kind of girl he does fancy. Brian Pickering, sitting down cross-legged on one of the patchwork cushions, smiled at her, a wet, pink smile from the recesses of his beard. Like a sea-anemone, she thought, in seaweed, not nice really, and jumped to find Sandra looking sternly at her.

'The Planning Officer's attitude,' said Sandra. 'I think you're going to tell us about that, Anne, aren't you?'

'Yes' she said, and paused, thinking: I've got to be careful about this, this is awkward, I don't know how to put this, really. She saw Mr

Jewkes again, framed by his maps and predictions, charting the future of Berkshire, with official backing.

'It's not,' she said, 'quite as simple as we thought. It isn't just a straightforward application by a spec builder. Apparently what this man has applied for is planning permission for a group of bungalows for old people, and the idea is to keep the price low and give first option to Cuxing people.'

Sandra said, 'Huh! We've all heard that before.'

'Bungalows,' said Mary Pickering. 'But that's horrible. I mean, at least the Span houses *look* nice.' Her husband nodded.

'Actually,' said Anne, 'I did feel he'd gone into it all pretty thoroughly, this Mr Jewkes. He wasn't somehow the villain of the piece I'd been expecting.' She smiled, but no one else did. 'The truth is, I felt a bit silly. In the first place for not having looked at the application properly – so that he was one jump ahead as it were – and then . . .' she wavered, 'and then because I must admit when he put the case it did seem to make sense. I mean, there *is* a desperate need for housing for old people in the village. For housing at all. And apparently the cottage is in the most appalling condition – he's had the council people look at it and apparently it would be almost impossible to put right, to restore.'

There was a pause. Then Sandra said, 'I wish I'd gone to see this chap myself.' She did not look at Anne. 'I've been snowed under just recently, that's the trouble.'

The retired professor, silent hitherto, said 'There are several points that are murky, to say the least of it. In the first place, what guarantee is there that these bungalows go to the deserving elderly of Cuxing?'

'Quite,' said Sandra.

'What is meant by an intention to keep the price low? How low? And what if there are no takers at that price? And in the second, as Mrs Pickering pointed out, there are important aesthetic and environmental considerations. Any development down there goes beyond the present boundaries of the village – is this the thin end of the wedge, as it were? The next step is ribbon development all the way to Barton.'

Anne said, 'Oh, I don't think . . . I did feel this was an isolated case. That they'd looked at it all very carefully, and weighed up the pros and cons, not been irresponsible, in the way that I suppose we imagined . . .' She hesitated.

'Well,' said the professor drily, 'he must be a very persuasive fellow, this Planning Officer. He seems quite to have won you over, Mrs Linton.'

'Not at all,' said Anne, irritated. 'I still think there's a case for preserving the cottage, but I did feel perhaps we'd rushed in a bit fast without looking at it from every side, as it were.'

Brian Pickering got up and went round with the jug again. Back on his cushion, hands clasped behind his head, he said, 'I must say I think a rash of bungalows down there would be quite disastrous. Actually these old people would be far better off in flats in Reading, nearer to the shops and hospital and all that, anyway.'

Mary Pickering said 'Yes, it's all quite unrealistic.'

'Frankly,' said Sandra, 'I smell a rat. I don't blame you, Anne, being taken in – I know these people can be most awfully convincing, but one simply does have to take a stand. I'm prepared to bet this builder's just putting one over – no doubt he's in cahoots with your Mr Whatsit. This kind of thing crops up time and again and one simply must not let oneself be sidetracked from the main point which is to save a fine old building. I mean, do we or do we not, want to see Splatt's Cottage bulldozed out of existence?'

A murmur ran round the room. 'That's what we're here to stop,' said the professor. He held out his glass. 'Thanks very much – er, Brian – yes, I will.'

Anne thought: Oh God, I wish I hadn't come. She sat staring at the Pickerings' array of rusting tools, some of them, she now saw, sandpapered and polished up, like the anvil. The scythe had a chaste gleam, picked out by the spotlights, that reminded her of a vast Victorian oil-painting of Old Father Time wielding just such an implement in a field of, she thought, fleeing people. Where on earth had that been? At school – yes, she remembered with satisfaction, at school, that's it, in the dining-hall. One sat looking at it every day, over the spuds and watery cabbage.

'Look, Anne' said Sandra. 'If you feel like this would you rather step down as secretary? I mean, it's a bit awkward if you're not one hundred percent convinced.'

'Perhaps I'd better,' she said.

'Possibly Mrs Linton would feel happier off the committee altogether,' said the professor.

Good lord, she thought, amused, they're ganging up on me now. And, examining her feelings, found none, even that earlier flare of irritation snuffed out now, quiescent in the comforting, comfortable atmosphere of the Pickerings' living-room. The old railway clock on the wall said nine. Monday evening, she thought, Tuesday. Wednesday. Then Thursday.

'Oh, nonsense,' said Sandra. 'Sorry, I don't mean to be rude. But of course Anne's on our side, aren't you, Anne? Naturally she wants to help but if we're going to have a tough campaign then we're going to have to be a bit aggressive. Now what I think we'll have to do is . . .'

Anne sat silent and acquiescent as the professor, with token reluctance, emerged as her successor. Tactics were discussed, letters drafted, a time-table of events drawn up. Mary Pickering, leaving the room, unobtrusively, returned with a plate of pizza. She handed it round, smiling that warm, unaltering smile, the same for everyone, a helping each, like the pizza.

They broke up. Getting into the car, shouting at the Pickerings' closing front door, 'Thanks for an awfully nice evening,' Sandra humped herself behind the driving wheel and shot a sideways glance at Anne.

'I hope you don't feel miffed about that, or anything. He seems an efficient sort of chap, this professor person.'

'Absolutely,' said Anne, 'and absolutely not. Not miffed, I mean.'

'Good. Actually I daresay you've got quite a bit on your plate, with your pa and all that.' Struck by a sudden thought, she crashed the gear-change, turning out onto the main road. 'I say, do you think your brother could pull strings and get us a bit of telly time? You know, one of those interviews about how awful it is. That sort of thing?'

Anne said, 'I doubt it. That isn't really what he does.'

'Oh, pity.' Sandra was silent for a minute, taken up with a forward move in the chain of red lights that winked ahead of them. Then she said, 'They're awfully interesting, the Pickerings, aren't they?'

'Are they? I don't feel I know them all that well.'

'He's – well, he kind of gets you a bit, doesn't he? I rather like these artistic types. By the way, did you have a nice weekend?'

'Mmn. Very nice.'

'Marvellous to be able to just take off like that. I can never get James out of the garden at weekends. Well, I'll put you off here if that's all right.'

* * *

The comprehensive school had been built, fifteen years before, as a secondary modern. Now, its function redefined, it was in the throes of extension and addition. Contractors' vehicles had ploughed the dirt of the car park into mud. Anne, picking her way through it, thought again of Mr Jewkes, and wondered what strokes of his pen had allowed the new language laboratory, pushed the frontiers of the games field across the lane and up to the edge of the housing estate. And did those projections on his wall, those maps for 1990, know already, to the nearest round number, how many children would be spilling out of its plate-glass doors in ten years' time? Presumably they did, or claimed to. What an odd job, she thought, providing statistics for what has not yet happened.

She walked down the empty corridors to the headmaster's room and knocked at the door. Going in, she was surprised to find him alone.

'I'm sorry . . . Have I got this right, I thought it was a staff meeting?'

Farrer said 'No, Anne – just you. Sorry – I didn't make myself clear.'

It was all christian names now – even with impermanent people like herself, teaching just a few periods a week. Farrer was new. He had come three months before, from some big London comprehensive, to succeed the retiring Head. Anne had seen little of him; he was said to be a big wheel in the educational world, full of new ideas, very radical.

'Do sit,' he said. 'Look, I'd better come straight to the point, I think. As you've no doubt heard, we're making quite a few changes in the school. To be frank, I've had to take a new broom to the curriculum. It just didn't stand up to inspection in this day and age. Far too much dead wood.'

He sat on the edge of his desk, looking past her and out of the window. Taking a packet of cigarettes out of his pocket, he offered her one and lit one for himself. 'I don't blame my predecessor, of course,' he went on, 'not entirely. It's all too easy to get out of the mainstream of educational thinking – not have much idea of what the innovations are. But there's a lot to be done – this curriculum's cluttered up with outdated concepts and the kids need a chance to get their teeth into some of the new projects. The fact is,' he said, 'that History's one of the things I've had to rethink. We're not going to do a History O-level any more, which means, I'm afraid, that unless you'd like to switch to something else we can't offer you those five periods in future.'

Anne said, 'History's an outdated concept?'

'Quite. Or at least history the way it's been taught hitherto. Narrative history. The fact is, Anne, there's been the most extraordinary amount of ignorance about the effect of this kind of teaching on kids. Have you looked at the Halliday Report?'

'No.'

'Well, you really should. That's a most interesting piece of research which proves fairly conclusively that children under fifteen just aren't ready for a chronological approach to history. And yet here we are teaching them history as narrative, one thing after another.'

'That's what it is. One thing does happen after another.'

'Yes, but that's a very sophisticated concept, Anne. They simply aren't ready for it at the O-level stage.'

Anne said, 'I entirely disagree.'

He dropped one foot on the desk, hooking his arms round his knee and looking at her over the top of it, seeing her, apparently, for the first time.

'Really?'

'I certainly do. As far as I'm concerned children of ten or eleven can grasp quite clearly that the Saxons come before the Vikings who come before the Normans. And I wouldn't know how otherwise to teach history.'

Farrer said, 'Oh, dear me.' He unhooked his arms, got off the desk, went round and sat behind it. He flicked open a file on the blotter and stared into it for a moment.

'You're a graduate, I see.'

Anne said nothing.

'No Dip.Ed., though. Have you ever thought of something in that line now? An in-service Degree Course or something of that kind?'

Anne said, 'What are you going to teach instead of History?'

'Sociology. And there's this new Social Science subject some of us have had a hand in planning. It's going to make a very nice option.'

'Not an option.'

'Sorry?'

'Not an option if there's no alternative. No History.'

Farrer closed the file and tapped its blue surface with his finger nails for a moment. It said, she saw: Linton, Ms A.

'Look, I'm really very sorry about this, Anne. I know how you must feel. But that's how it is. Times change. You're a historian, you'd be the first to appreciate that' – he smiled persuasively – 'and the educational system of all things must bow to change. Move with the times. We have to keep re-thinking what kids need. What's relevant.' He got up, and came round the desk, holding out his hand. 'And of course I don't even need to say there's nothing personal. Your work here has been much appreciated. And I don't have the slightest doubt you'll pick up something else in Berkshire easily enough. The Training College. One of the private schools.'

'Somewhere more relevant?'

'Quite so.'

She left him, and walked out into the sunshine, where yellow bulldozers were busy rearranging a few more acres of Berkshire for a useful and productive future.

* * *

She said to Don, 'History's an outdated concept.'

'Is that so?'

'Apparently.'

'What are you going to do about it? The chap's right, this headmaster, you could easily enough find something else.'

'I don't think I'll bother,' she said. 'Quite frankly. I just don't think I'll bother. Maybe I need to do some re-thinking. About history. And by the way I'm going up to Lichfield tomorrow, did I tell you?'

Six

James Stanway dreamed he was playing football. His bare knees ached with the cold; he charged up and down a pitch. He slipped, and felt silken mud and grass under his hands. He got up, wiping his hands on his shorts, and the other players had all gone. He stood now in the classroom of a school, looking at a board on which were chalked the declensions of a French verb; he studied the back of his hand and listened to the headmaster explain his staffing problems. 'Quite,' he said, 'quite. I think you've a case for an extra part-timer, at least – I'll certainly support you there'; outside the window children clamoured. He was seized with restlessness; work, he thought, I must work, there is no end to what can be done.

He woke, and knew that this was reality, however improbable it might seem, this bed and this room seen indistinctly through unspectacled eyes and these hands, these veined and knotted hands held in front of him in a basin of water. Old hands.

Other hands, thin, dexterous hands, came down and soaped his, took them from the basin and dried them, laid them on the sheet, one at either side. He said, 'I need my glasses,' and a voice, a kindly, young, female voice, said, 'You're very spry today, Mr Stanway, that's nice. Going to sit out in the chair later on?' The glasses arrived on his nose and the room cleared itself a little, but not much. He lay and thought about a friend he had had at college, whose name he no longer remembered but who lived, he knew, in Dorset and had ginger hair. I am ill, he thought, and tried to say as much to the girl who came and went on the cloudy fringes of his vision. He shouted, I am ill, but she smiled and straightened his pillow and talked of cups of tea. Where am I? he said, but she fed him with a spoon and then went to the door to stand talking with someone else. James Stanway watched something shadowy form and re-form at the foot of the bed. It annoyed him that he could not tell what it was. A tree? Clouds? 'My glasses,' he said, 'I need my glasses.'

* * *

'He was very *compos mentis* earlier,' said the nurse. 'But he's wandering again now, I'm afraid. You can't get much response. Did you have a good drive up?'

Beyond her, Anne looked at the old man propped up on the pillows, blinking and muttering. 'Yes, fine, thanks. There's no change, then?'

The girl said, 'Not really, not to speak of.' She glanced back to the bed and said, 'I'll just draw that curtain, the light worries him, I think. There's been something bothering him this morning, but he can't say what, bless him.' She twitched the curtain and came back to the bed. 'That better, then, Mr Stanway? O.K. for a bit, Mrs Linton? I'll pop in later and toilet him.'

Anne sat watching her father, letting the tension of the journey slip away from her. She had set out early and had gone to the house before coming to the nursing-home. There is a change, she thought, he is different, just, from the week before last. It could not be defined. It was as though he had become more indistinct. All the euphemisms about death as departure came into her head. Her father seemed to be in retreat, not propelled by anything or anyone but of his own volition. She stood over him and took his hand and presently he turned his head and said quite clearly, 'Anne?' Pleased, she pulled the chair closer to the bed and talked to him, about the children, about his rose-beds that she would weed again this evening, about her weekend in the Cotswolds. She brought the sheaf of photographs out of the envelope, and the two albums put together by her mother, the second one ending in 1965, the year of her death, with a dozen blank pages after the last entry.

'I thought you might like to look at some photos, father.' She propped the album in front of him and turned the pages over. 'Can you see all right?'

He said something about his glasses that she could not catch and she adjusted them for him. 'Goodness, these go way back, I hadn't realized. This must be you and mother on your honeymoon, I think. Cornwall, is that right?'

And from the sepia views of Mevagissey and St Ives there grew, a page or two later on, Graham sitting owl-faced in a high black pram and presently herself shawled in her mother's arms; digging a sandcastle on a beach in the year of Munich; parading with gas-mask in 1941. 'Look,' she said, turning pages, 'I remember her; how that house comes back, the one we had that summer; what was that dog called, father, can you think, the one that got run over?' Her father peered at the pages, mumbling something every now and then. Once or twice he groped with his hand as though to stay hers, to keep her from turning a page.

They grew and shed their skins, Graham and herself, mutating from one page to another, from infant to child to adolescent to young adult. Don arrived, standing on the lawn of the house in Putney, screwing up his eyes against the autumn sun of 1956; off-stage, unmentioned, lay Suez and Hungary. Marriage. More swaddled bundles. On the last page, two months before her death, her mother stood against a gatepost in the Lake District, taking second place to the landscape, like the figure posted before mountain scenery in a romantic painting. 'Saddleback, father?' she said. 'Is that Saddleback? Or Skiddaw?' And her father blinked at the photograph and coughed. She wiped a trail of spit from the corner of his mouth.

The trouble with all this, she said to him, is that it leaves so much out. Almost everything. Such, for instance, as this lady of yours whose name, yet, I do not know and who must have loomed large behind all these snaps, but of whom there is no sign at all. Like Suez and Hungary she can only be filled in once you know about her. I begin to see how slippery the past is. It is not, as Farrer would have it, that chronology is a difficult idea to grasp. The problem is the shadows it throws. This happened, and then this, and then this. But if you keep your eyes only on that, you miss another dimension and end up with something that is not the truth at all, or only part of it.

For instance, she said, you didn't know, in that photograph where we're all grinning away outside the church at Starbridge, that I almost called the whole thing off, the week before. And then panicked, and couldn't. I walked down a street with Don, a street in London with lime trees just in flower – I can smell them now – and thought: I'm not sure I want to marry him, not absolutely, totally sure. I like him and probably I love him but sometimes ever so faintly he irritates me. And I pushed the feeling away and we did get married and we've been perfectly happy, I think, on the whole, by and large, ever since. We don't nowadays, talk to each other a great deal.

Did you talk to mother?

The nurse, coming in, said 'Family photos, now that's a nice idea.' She hung for a moment over an open page, 'Don't they look funny, those clothes? And it's not so long ago, is it, 1961? Could you give me a hand, dear, lifting him?'

The old man, in their sturdy grasp, dabbed feebly for the album as it slithered from his lap.

* * *

'The open window,' said the note on the mat, 'suggested that you were up here again. I spent a few minutes with your father last week; he did not know me, I'm afraid. I'll look in later this evening to see if you'd care for a drink.'

It was a sheet from an exercise book, folded into four and then in half, like, she thought, the notes passed from hand to hand along a line of desks at school. She read it and re-read it, made a cup of coffee and read it again. Outside the window a robin sang with piercing sweetness; the spring grass blazed from end to end of the garden; the sun on her back was as warm as the touch of a hand.

She went upstairs to have a bath, and lay smiling at the yellow plaster of her father's bathroom ceiling.

* * *

David said, 'I thought we might go a bit further afield. There's the Plough at Yoxley which isn't at all bad. Do you fancy that?'

A filmy golden moon, plumped out by two weeks, rose above the house opposite. 'I haven't,' he went on, 'had any fishing since I last saw you, what with one thing and another, but now it's the holidays, there's a bit more chance . . .' Getting into the car, he talked without looking at her, fiddling with keys, starting the engine, swinging out onto the road too fast and braking as the headlights of another car swept round the corner. 'Sorry.'

You cannot say calm down to a man you hardly know. Neither, much as you would like to, can you reach out and put a soothing (or otherwise) hand on his thigh. Anne said, 'Have you had a good week?'

'Two weeks. Two weeks and two days, in fact . . .'

I know that, too.

'. . . So so. Fairly run of the mill. No, not entirely. I met some parents of one of our boys who startled me rather – I'll tell you about that. And Mary had an accident with our car. This belongs to a friend of mine.'

Mary. Mary, she is. 'I hope she wasn't hurt?'

'No. And what about you – you'll have finished your term, too.'

'Very much so. I've got the sack. Did you know that chronology was a very difficult concept? Too difficult for people of fifteen?'

'I did not. Tell me.'

Sitting in the Plough at Yoxley, while David, his back to her, waited his turn at the bar, she studied the row of prints on the wall opposite: they presented a series of scenes that seemed as though they should be connected, like episodes in a strip-cartoon – a stage-coach drawing up at a Dickensian hostelry, early Victorian squires in the hunting-field, similar people carousing round a laden table. She turned from them to find him watching her across the room.

He brought drinks and said, 'I've come across that type myself. Usually at conferences. He'll go far, I fear.'

'Oh dear, do you think so?'

'Probably. People who generate theories tend to, in the educational world. Even if they're thoroughly bad theories. I'll give you a job. Come and live in Staffordshire.'

'How I wish,' she said, 'I could.' And then, quickly, to break a threatened silence, 'You were going to tell me about some parents . . '

Going into the Ladies, towards the end of the evening, she caught her own face unawares in the mirror, sideways, the reflection thrown back by another mirror in the opposite wall, and saw a woman who did not (she thought) look forty, smiling to herself, reaching in her bag for a comb, momentarily a stranger, or a friend long unseen and half forgotten. She looks nice, Anne thought – I look nice. Quite pretty too. The reaction surprised her; she had never been vain. Her own looks had never much interested her; it was with relief that she had shed the intense physical self-consciousness of a young girl. It seemed an odd bonus, at the end of all those years of neglect, to have emerged really quite nice-looking, no worse, certainly, than many women whose time and energies must have been devoted to self-preservation. She combed her hair and washed her hands, looking again at her own face in the mirror and thinking of how her mother used to insist on the connection between good looks and a state of mind. 'You can't be thinking nice things and look an ugly person – it's written on a face, how a person feels.' It's not true, of course, not true at all. Except just in this one thing. Which is why I must not go on looking like this. I could, she said to her face in the mirror, I could be entirely wrong. Completely and utterly wrong. I could have made the most awful and embarrassing mistake, which is why, among many, many reasons, I must not look like this. She went back into the pub, trying to restore anonymity to her expression.

* * *

David thought: money I've never regretted, I'm not equipped to be a rich man, possessions don't mean much to me. I have had a good deal of satisfaction from my work and great pleasure from my sons. I have adapted to other circumstances. Until now, I believe, I did not think I had been too badly done by. I would not have thought of myself as a dissatisfied man.

He got up abruptly, as Anne returned, and said, 'Shall we go?' Walking to the car, he kept apart from her. As they got in, she said, 'Was your car badly damaged?'

'It's mendable.' He started the engine, and said, as they drove out of the car park, 'My wife will probably lose her licence. She had had too much to drink.'

There was a long pause. Anne said, 'I am sorry.'

'I wasn't with her. She hadn't been to a party or anything gay like that. She doesn't often go to parties. She simply, from time to time, has too much to drink. She has done that for a long while now.'

They drove, in silence, through a half mile or so of Staffordshire. David went on, 'She isn't an alcoholic. The problem, if that is the right word for it, is contained. And now let's talk about something more cheerful. How is your campaign to cherish the past? This derelict farmhouse of yours?'

'Oh, that,' she said, 'I'm in a dreadful muddle about that.'

He listened to the story, chuckling once or twice in the darkness. 'What an extraordinary place Berkshire sounds. I daresay there are people like that up here, though. I just don't move in those circles. So you're going to abandon Splatt's Cottage to its fate?'

'I don't know,' she said, 'I really don't know.' They were back at the house. Her hand on the door, she said, 'Thank you so much, David, I did enjoy . . .'

'Could we meet for lunch in Lichfield tomorrow?'

'Yes. Yes, I'd like that.'

'After you've seen your father.'

'Yes,' she said. 'That would be lovely.'

'Yes,' he said. 'Well, then. Well, I'll see you tomorrow.'

'Where?'

'Oh – yes, where? Somewhere central. The cathedral? No, make it the square.'

'Johnson's house?'

'Yes. Johnson's house would do fine.'

'About half past twelve?'

'About half past twelve' he said.

He drove home, put his friend's car into the garage, picked up his son's bike which had been left flung down in the drive and leaned it against the wall. He went into the house and listened to the sound of bathwater running. 'I'm in,' he called up the stairs, and above the noise of the water a voice called back, 'Yes, I heard.' He opened the door of his younger son's bedroom and looked for a moment at the hunched shape under the bedclothes. His elder son, coming out of the lavatory, said 'Hi, Dad.' He said 'Hi there,' and went into his own room. He undressed, got into bed and lay staring at the window. The bathroom door opened and closed, and another door. He turned out the light.

* * *

After Paul's birth, Anne had wept. She had howled at the ceiling of the hospital labour ward and Paul, in the crib beside her, had howled also. Don, arriving late from the office after some confusion about messages, had been disconcerted by them both. He said, 'What's the matter?' to Anne, and stared with doubt at Paul. 'Nothing. It's just such an anti-climax, that's all. And I'm so relieved.' He patted the baby, gingerly, and said, 'Relieved about what?' 'Relieved it hasn't got two heads or anything.' Don said, 'It was never really on the cards that it would.' He sat uncomfortably on the chair beside the bed and took her hand. 'This really isn't any time to be in tears,' he said, 'do stop it, Annie.'

A baby, a small, flesh-and-blood baby, seemed such an anti-climax to all that time thinking about getting married, and then getting married, and being married. Out of that, came forth this. Paul lay raw and angry in his cot, a chrysalis whose future yawned unpredictably ahead. He might grow up or he might not; he might die in infancy or the world might come to an end while he was a child. She was alarmed not by him, but for him. Don said, 'For goodness' sake, Anne, it'll all work out all right, you see.' And, fifteen years later, she had to admit that it had. Paul was alive, well, and showed no sign of being the cataclysmic force for good or bad that she had imagined. He was simply there, and a world without him was unimaginable.

She thought of this as she dressed, looking out of the window at the garden where the thinner sprinkling of weeds on one of the rose-beds marked her efforts of a few weeks before. Elsewhere, groundsel and couch grass were taking over. She thought of David Fielding's son, born at around the same time, and of the woman who had given birth to him. Who, from time to time, drank too much. She went down into the kitchen and made coffee: beyond the window the spring day shone. She was seized with amazement at the progression of seasons, at the ceaseless passage of one condition to another, at the state of change in which we live, at the beauty of it. The willows in the field were explosions of colour; the whole landscape promised. Is it always like this? she wondered, is there always this feeling of what is to come? She sat looking into the garden and remembered wanting passionately, as a child, to hold onto a moment of happiness, to freeze it, to remain within it for ever. She thought: I will do something that on the face of it is ridiculous. I will plant things in the garden, for summer. She took a purse and walked down into the village, to see what she could find.

She had done the same in that first house of theirs, in the London suburb in which Paul was born. It was she who had been proud of the house, not Don. For him, it had been a stop-gap, a makeshift, the best they could do for now. But I don't want, she said, a posh Georgian thing in Kensington. I like this, it's lovely, it's just right. And she had polished its ugly thirties bow windows and planted tiny plants in its long thin garden. Paul and the plants grew together. Don had been working in a big London firm of solicitors, in a junior capacity. That, too, was a stop-gap. Out of sight, she knew, round the corner, lay that partnership in some well-established provincial firm, and in due course (after that summer at Poppet Sands, when Paul was six or seven) it had come. And, a little sadly, she had abandoned the plants – waist-high now, or overflowing walls and paths, according to their patterns of growth – and the cherished house and moved, or been moved, to Cuxing. What's the matter? said Don, this is a much better house, for goodness' sake, Annie, it's cost half as much again, and you've always said you wanted to live in the country. She had planted things once more, though not, she realized, for some time now. Nowadays she watched things grow – saw with surprise that the rambling rose put in when they first came had reached the gutters, that the buddleias were old and woody and should be cut right back, that the rock garden was matted with growth and the rocks submerged.

The Post Office sold seeds. She tried to remember, from the London suburb days, what you grew in the open ground, and chose love-in-a-mist, marigolds and something that looked gaudy on the packet called lavatera. She walked past the churchyard; an old man was pushing a hand-mower between the gravestones and rooks called among their nests in the trees behind. She stood listening and the old man, stopping, straightened up and saw her. He said, ''Morning. Nice one.'

And she said, 'Yes, it's lovely, isn't it.' He looked at the packets in her hand. 'Nice to look ahead. Ground's a bit cold yet, though.' 'Is it?' she said, anxiously, 'is it too early, do you think?' 'No,' he said, 'no – bit more sun, that's all we need. You get them planted, they'll be fine.'

Back at the house, she found a fork and rake and went out to clear a bed. Down at the bottom, beyond the lawn, near the top of the field, there was a place where her father had grown vegetables – a few lettuces and carrots, some rows of spinach. She forked out last year's spent plants, dug and weeded the bed. Beyond her in the field the lapwings kept up a continual plaintive wailing; sometimes, looking up from her work, she saw them tumble from the sky in mating rituals, spiralling downwards to the grass like stalling aircraft. Out of sight, the river poured over stones in a shallow place.

She cleared the bed and scattered the seeds in random groupings, raking soil over them. It occurred to her that they were an odd mixture, inappropriately chosen: her garden would be gay and tasteless, like a child's garden. She snapped some sticks from the hedge and threaded them through the seed packets like flagstaffs, and stuck them into the earth. As she knelt to do so, there came again a memory of that holiday as a child in Southwold, crouching on damp sand to build a castle, and her father making a flag for the battlements from a piece of driftwood and the green paper of an unfolded Woodbine packet. She saw her father's face, his pipe tucked sideways in his mouth, the smoke streaming away in the sharp East Anglian wind. Further back on the beach, her mother sat on a rug and knitted. Graham stood at the water's edge with bare bony torso and shorts that reached to his knees. It was the summer of Munich. Ahead, off-stage, lay the war, her father's move to the Ministry, evacuation to Wales for the rest of them. And off-stage too, not far ahead, she supposed, was Mrs X, with whom her father had stood on a windy day, in Dorset in 1940 or thereabouts, the hair blown across her face confusing her identity until you knew, and looked more closely, and saw that this was not mother's shape or stance, but that of a stranger.

She stood for a moment admiring the tilled brown surface of her seed-bed. It seemed amazing that its anonymity should be charged with the latent energy of all those seeds. 'Flowering period July–August,' the packets had said. The seeds affirmed the inevitability of July, of the summer, of other times.

* * *

She walked from the car park and he was standing outside Samuel Johnson's birthplace, looking away from her. (Thus, time out of mind ago, Don waiting under the clock at Paddington. No, no – not like that at all.) She walked past Boswell, dapper in bronze on a stone plinth, and past Johnson's brooding back. Separated from David by a shunting lorry, she tried to scour from her face the look that really would not do, and, the lorry moving off, found him confronting her across the road, seeing her now at last, his face reflecting hers.

Not a ghastly mistake. True, quite true.

He said, 'I can't think at all where to take you.'

'Anywhere will do.'

Sitting on the shiny red vinyl of some Lichfield Lounge Bar, flanked by sales reps, choice of Ploughman's Lunch or Sandwiches (Ham, Cheese, Beef), a jukebox Out of Order in the corner, he said. 'I suppose you're going back.'

'Yes. Now. Soon. I said I'd be home for supper.'

'I was afraid of that,' he said.

'I'll be back.'

'Yes. Then that will have to do.'

They walked round the cathedral and Anne said, 'It's not all that nice, as cathedrals go.'

'I suppose not. Better inside than out.'

'I like Norwich best. Then Canterbury. Then Durham I think. No, York Minster perhaps.'

'Gloucester's well spoken of.'

'I've never seen it.'

'We're going there together.'

'Yes. Yes, so we are.'

Squadrons of ducks patrolled the water beside the car park, their wakes fracturing the surface into diamond patterns. David said, 'I don't want you to go. How long does it take you?'

'Three hours, usually. Five minutes more, and then I must.'

They sat on a bench and were contemplated by the ducks. He reached out and took her hand and Anne, looking at ducks, water and red sandstone thought: I am quite wrong about this cathedral, in fact it is marvellous and eliminates Norwich absolutely, once and for all.

'I do really have to go now,' she said. 'Look, it's nearly four.'

She drove out of Lichfield into rain. Huge apocalyptic rainbows straddled the landscape. Storms battered the windscreen and then swept away to right or left. She drove faster than usual, from the A446 to the A452 to the A41 to the A423. The road unreeled behind her, taking with it Lichfield, Coleshill, Kenilworth, Banbury. She stayed in Lichfield, sitting on a bench with ducks quacking in front of her on choppy water that reflected trees and red sandstone while someone else, some efficient automaton, good with indicator and accelerator, drove the car to Cuxing, put it away in the garage, got out coat and handgrip, and went into the house.

* * *

'Of course none of us imagined they'd move so fast,' said Sandra. 'I mean, we knew perfectly well time wasn't on our side but nobody thought they'd be getting the bulldozers in quite so soon. The field's practically a building-site already. Are you feeling all right, Anne?'

'Yes, fine, thanks.'

'I just thought you looked a bit washed out. But anyway Professor Sidey's been most awfully efficient and done some detective work and he reckons they're going to pull the cottage down after Whit – he's been chatting up the contractors' men and that kind of thing. So that's where we move in.'

'Move in?'

'Do something. In fact, we think, demonstrate. Always assuming more passive methods have failed and we haven't managed to get the planning permission revoked.'

'Yes, I see.

'I assumed you'd want to know, that's all. You seem a bit detached, I must say.'

'Sorry, Sandra. Actually I haven't been sleeping too well.'

'Oh, bad luck. So we're warning everyone they may have to turn out at the drop of a hat – I mean, we shan't get much notice. We're putting leaflets round now and Brian Pickering's getting some banners and things done, ready.'

'Are you going to sit down in front of the bulldozers?'

Sandra said suspiciously 'It's not a laughing matter, you know. Anyway, I take it you'll be there yourself. You're still on the committee, aren't you?'

Anne thought: I've no idea when Whit is. I don't really know when anything is, except next week. I'm sorry, I'm sorry – I'm in love, you see, it takes up all my time.

'I must say the Pickerings are the greatest asset,' Sandra was saying, 'and Professor Sidey. Of course poor old Miss Standish is a bit of a dead weight, but one doesn't want to hurt her feelings.'

* * *

She said to Don, 'Did you ring on Thursday night?'

'No. Why?'

'Just I went out for a bit – I thought I might have missed you.'

'It's fifteen pence now for three minutes, you know, to Lichfield,' Don said. 'No point unless there's something particular to say.'

Quite.

'That's all right then,' she said. 'So long as I didn't miss you, that's all.'

* * *

The children, when young, she remembered, used to challenge you to an impossible feat whereby you put one hand above your head and rotated it in one direction and the other in front of your stomach and rotated it in the other. It couldn't be done: the brain rebelled. But the brain – or whatever controls these things – does nothing to hinder the co-existence of emotions. How is it possible to experience, in quick succession or even both at once, joy and guilt? With an intensity hardly felt since childhood.

Or since, at any rate, about 1956, for the first, and for the second, further back yet.

Once, knowing quite well that it was forbidden, one went into father's study and fiddled the papers on his desk (ah! there, then, is the taboo ancestral to the uneasy feeling that accompanies the sorting-out, now). And in so doing one knocked the jar of ink (Quink, blue-black) and in one appalling, stomach-shrinking moment it had fallen and blue-black Quink coursed over blotter, papers, desk, floor . . . And one fled, shrivelled, and lurked at the furthest end of the garden, waiting.

Waiting for what? Retribution? Or peace of mind?

Since then, guilt has been experienced in only a very desultory way. The occasional lapse from maternal or housewifely duty; the class at school scamped because of a headache or boredom; inadequacies (minor) of friendship or relationship. The emotion, in its full, hot-blooded state, was almost forgotten.

As for the other.

The loose spoke of a bicycle wheel; Leckford Road; a hotel in Kensington (now, apparently, pulled down). Shadows, merely. Echoes. Documentary evidence of what was. As are also Paul and Judy evidence, of a kind. 'Bacon?' she said to Paul. 'Mushrooms? Fried bread? The lot?'

'Yes, please. What's all this? I thought it was only cooked breakfast on Sundays?'

'I'm feeling generous.'

'Suits me. I thought I'd been told off or something.'

'Told off?'

'It's what, Mum' he said, 'you used to do when we were young and you'd belted us or bawled us out. Be specially nice for hours and hours afterwards. To make up, I suppose. Can I have an egg too?'

'Did I?'

And outside the kitchen window the spring is more exultantly green by a week, and the kitchen garden path leads to the road which leads in turn to the village street from which you reach the A423 and from thence the A41 and the A452 and the A446.

* * *

David Fielding sat beside old Mr Stanway's bed and said: I love your daughter, that's the problem. I really don't know how this has happened, he said, it is not a condition with which I am familiar. Not for longer than I can remember, and perhaps never.

I am emotionally disturbed, like some of the children with whom I have had to deal.

James Stanway saw the shadow at the foot of his bed quiver and spread and disgorge a second shadow which hovered above him and then settled at his side. He turned his head to examine it and a man's voice asked him how he was.

'I am not well,' he said. 'I am not well at all.' But the shadow was silent now and presently he forgot it. He floated from this indistinct place to another, where his wife stood by a gate before a mountain, and to others, where small children heaped sand upon his feet.

Seven

In a school hall in south London, hired by the television company for rehearsals, Graham sat on the edge of the stage and watched the floor manager chalk out the set dimensions. At the far end of the room, actors arrived, eyed one another, and took coffee from the machine. The new girl, he observed, was small, bright and blonde. He dropped from the stage to the floor and walked down the hall, stopping to check a camera angle, and said to the girl, 'Hello there – I don't think we've met. I'm Graham Stanway.' And she turned to smile (the eager, actressy smile already and only nineteen) but for not quite long enough nor hard enough. 'Everything O.K.?' he said. 'Just give me a shout if it's not,' and at that moment Jenny his assistant came up to say over her clip-board that there was someone on the phone, passed on from the studio. He padded through cloakrooms forested with empty coat-hooks and found a phone with receiver displaced out of which his sister's voice said, 'What on earth are you doing in some boys' school?' 'We work in these places,' he said. 'I'm lumbered with a new series, eight episodes of steaming history. Is anything wrong, Annie? Dad?' 'No, he's still the same. I just thought I'd let you know I'm going up to Lichfield tomorrow, that's all.' 'Right you are,' he said. 'You're a good girl, Annie. Is it on, all this commuting up there, with the kids and everything?' 'It's all right,' she said, 'I can manage.' 'Don's accommodating, is he?' 'Don's accommodating, yes. Try to get down to us again soon.' 'Sure,' he said. 'Right you are. Will do. I'll have to go now, love. Let me know how he goes on, the old man. 'Bye then.'

He went back through the coat-hooks and saw the new girl sharing her coffee now with the leading man. 'Right,' he said. 'Let's make a start, shall we? Ready, everyone? The castle scene, Jenny, O.K.?' His stomach ached already, and an eight-hour day to go.

* * *

I have never before, Anne thought, realized that cooling towers are beautiful. Or that the front gardens of houses are infinite in their variety. Or that clouds piled on the skyline take on the shape of castles and cathedrals. If fields are always that colour in late April, then it seems to have escaped me hitherto. And never have I sat in a traffic jam, sandwiched between two shuddering lorries, and hummed or tried to all I can remember of *The Marriage of Figaro*. I have never particularly enjoyed driving. I have certainly never realized that roads one has known for years could be sanctified in the course of three weeks.

She drew up outside her father's house, got out of the car, opened the front door, and the envelope on the mat was a brown one from the Post Office, addressed to her father, acknowledging no doubt her payment of the phone bill. She went into the kitchen and as she stood looking at the shrivelled daffodils picked the week before the telephone rang in the hall.

'Hello,' he said. 'You've come. When did you get there? I didn't know – I tried earlier. I thought perhaps . . .'

'Where are you?'

'I'm in Lichfield. I could come straight out to Starbridge,' he said. 'Should I do that?'

* * *

She said, 'You can hear the lapwings in the field. I've been using this bed for twenty odd years and never noticed that before.' She picked up his hand, lying across her breast, and ran her finger over the puckered scar along the thumb. 'It's quite healed, hasn't it, that cut? I never thought, when it happened, I never for one moment imagined this. Did you?'

'Yes, frankly. I've thought of little else.'

'I'm lying, I suppose – I couldn't believe it, that's all. I thought it was just me – being a bit unhinged. Back in Cuxing I feel as though I'd imagined you. I've thought I'd come back here and find you'd never been real at all.'

'I'm real all right,' he said. 'Look. Feel.'

'I've felt. It was lovely.'

And extraordinary. To do something in itself so utterly familiar, to lie under, and upon, and beside, another naked body and do things one has done a thousand times and find them new and strange. To lie with thighs clamped round unfamiliar thighs (not hearing, at that point, the lapwings) and be at one and the same time joyously involved and a detached and amazed observer of what is happening.

David said, 'Not was. It isn't finished.'

'It's two o'clock, and we haven't had any lunch. Shall I go down and make an omelette?'

'Later, possibly. Not now.'

'I've never done this before,' she said. 'I just wanted you to know that.'

'Then you're very competent, for one so inexperienced.'

'Don't tease me. You know quite well what I mean.'

'You mean that you don't make a habit of getting into bed with people. Neither do I, Anne.'

In Cuxing around this time one would be clearing up in the kitchen and about to sit down for a while with the paper and a cigarette. But one is a thousand miles from there, in every sense, and indeed unsure now that it exists.

'More?,' she said. 'Again? Oh, David . . .'

'Turn round, I can't see you. I told you, I've been thinking of nothing else. What do you expect?'

* * *

Drugs are said to intensify experience of the physical world. I wouldn't know about that, she thought, but I know what does all right. I knew that this morning, driving up here, and I know it now, walking across this very ordinary field, across which I've walked innumerable times before.

Standing on the river bank she looked down into the water and saw trees and bushes reflected with total clarity, perfect in every detail, as was her reflection and David's, fore-shortened and faintly quivering. She could see the glint of his watch, catching the sunlight, with ribbons of weed trailing underneath it, and his face transparent over the bark of a submerged branch, and his eyes, looking at her.

'What I hate,' he said, 'is that there's so much of you I've never known. Years and years of it.'

'Come now – I'm not that old.'

'I mean as you quite well know that I have to put up with being ignorant about practically everything that's ever happened to you. What did you look like when you were eighteen?'

'Like now, only more so.'

'And the other thing is that when you go away I haven't the faintest idea where you go to. What kind of house you live in. You go into a kind of limbo. You disappear.'

'I go to a somewhat dull bit of Berkshire, into a rather ugly Edwardian house.'

'With people in it who have always known you.'

She said, 'Let's not talk about that. Not just now.' And lobbed a stone into the water; the reflections dissolved into concentric rings.

'Have some respect for the fish,' said David. 'Your father would be appalled.'

'Could we go back to the house soon.'

* * *

They went together to the nursing-home but David waited outside in the car while she sat with the old man for half an hour or so. Coming back across the car park she could see the shape of him in the driving seat, his head bent over a book; she walked slowly, spinning out the fifty yards of tarmac.

Driving away he said, 'How is he?'

'Worse, a bit, I think. I saw the Matron. Apparently the doctor says there's no change to speak of, but he seemed to me different. They still say it could be months, even.'

'I've rung up home and said I shan't be back till late – very late.'

'We've got all evening, then?'

'Yes.'

They sat in the middle of Lichfield, trapped by rush-hour traffic. The cathedral, picked out by a shaft of sunlight, blazed gaudily above the buildings. David said, 'It was Tom who answered the phone, which was a pity. I've never deceived him in my life.'

'Would it have been better if . . .?'

'If it had been Mary? Yes, it would have been better if. Do you want me to explain why, or not?'

'I don't think, really, I do.'

'Then I won't. Or not now, if at all. Because I don't want to hear or even think – though I do – about your husband.'

'There wouldn't be anything to tell. And if there were I shouldn't because I feel awful enough as it is. Except that I feel awful and terribly happy both at once if such a thing is possible, which it seems to be.'

'We both,' said David, 'appear to have led rather sheltered lives.'

* * *

'I shall have to go home tomorrow afternoon – this afternoon – because I must take Judy to the dentist on Thursday, first thing.'

'I was afraid of that. And then?'

'And then I shall be back the week after.'

'Then that will have to do, I suppose. Though I don't at the moment see how. Don't put the sheet back. Stay like that. If you're cold then I'm afraid you'll have to put up with it.'

* * *

She lay alone and listened to the lapwings and said to David somewhere else – in his car, perhaps, still driving along empty night-time roads, or going into his alien, inconceivable home – I am amazed, when I have time to be anything. I am like someone with amnesia, untethered both from past and future. At least, the future reaches no further than twelve today when I shall see you in Lichfield, and the past to which I have paid so much attention has become simply Judy and her dentist appointment and the road back to Cuxing, which has to be taken, come what may.

* * *

'Judy did *what*?'

'Oh, Mum, for goodness sake, you don't have to go through the roof! She merely gashed her hand on this bit of barbed wire and Sandra Butterfield merely happened to call in with some guff for you about something and saw it and said she'd take her along to the surgery for an anti-tetanus jab because it might be shut by the time you got back. You don't have to carry on like that. She's not *dead* for heaven's sake. Here they are now, coming in through the gate. God, Mum, you're *shaking*. What on earth's the matter? You can see the stupid girl's perfectly all right.'

She stood in the hall for a minute, subsiding. Only, of course, from the religious is retribution exacted; the rest of us know that real life is not like that – the wicked go unpunished and the rich shall inherit the kingdom of heaven.

'Oh, Sandra,' she said, 'thanks so much – Paul's just been explaining to me – I should have been back earlier but I got a bit held up, I'm so grateful, Judy what on earth did you do, was it that old fence at the bottom. . . .'

'Of course I had no idea when she'd last had an anti-tet.' said Sandra, dumping herself down at the kitchen table. 'And she didn't seem to know herself but Dr G. looked it up on her card and she was due – overdue, actually, Anne – so it was just as well. I say, you do look done in – this dashing up and down to Lichfield's not doing you any good. Do you have to? I mean, does he realize, poor old fellow? I must say, if I were Don I'd be putting my foot down but of course Don's so frightfully easy-going, isn't he? If it were James he'd be creating, I can tell you – he doesn't like me larking off one little bit (not that you're larking, of course, Anne, I know that) which is a bit daft at our age and after twenty years of marriage, but there you are.' She chuckled complacently. 'I should be flattered. Do you know, I even had to trail with him to some business thing in Italy last year, right in the middle of the motorway campaign.'

'Where in Italy?'

'Oh, those lakes up in the north. I was bored stiff, I can tell you, I kept thinking of everything I ought to be getting on with here. Talking of which – that was what I dropped in about earlier, luckily as it turned out. D-day is the week after next.'

'D-day?'

'The Splatt's Cottage demonstration. Hugh Sidey's had his ear to the ground and it looks as though that's when the contractors' men will be moving in. You'll be there, I take it?'

'Well, it does depend a bit if . . .'

'I'm assuming you will,' said Sandra sternly. 'We have to turn out in force if it's to have any impact at all. I've brought you one of Mary's banners. She really has done them rather nicely.'

The banner, unfurled upon the kitchen table, was made of a coarse, expensive looking linen material, with lettering embroidered upon it in scarlet wool. It said SAVE SPLATT'S COTTAGE.

'Or there's this one,' said Sandra, 'if you'd rather. Pretty, isn't it? I must say when it's all over I'd rather like to hang onto them. They'd look rather good on a kitchen wall or somewhere.'

The second banner, in chocolate brown linen weave with white wool lettering, said WE CARE ABOUT THE PAST. DO YOU?

Anne said, 'I think I'll have the other one, Sandra.'

Paul, coming into the kitchen, stared at the banners and then at Sandra, and went out again, a hand over his mouth.

'We must rope in the children, of course,' said Sandra. 'I've already had a word with Judy.'

'What did she say?'

'Nothing much. Mine will all be there. I'm keeping them away from school.'

'What exactly do I do with the banner?'

'You put a bamboo through each end,' said Sandra tersely, 'where Mary's left those pocket things, and get someone to carry the other end. Paul, presumably, or Judy. Or Don, even. Well, I must fly now – here is Don, I'll go before he comes, I daresay you've got masses to talk about if you've been away since Thursday. 'Bye.'

Don, coming into the kitchen, looked at the banner and said 'That's Sandra, I take it.'

'That's Sandra. Hello, darling.'

'Hello. Just so long as you're not expecting me to carry it.'

'No, Don, nobody does. Where are you going?'

'Just to listen to the news. Where's the paper, do you know?'

'I don't, I'm afraid. You might give me a kiss.'

'Anne, anyone would think you'd been gone a month. . . . There!'

'That's better.'

'How's your father?'

'Much the same.'

'Well, I'd just like to catch the news.'

Through the open door, she saw him stop at the hall table and pick something up. 'This is from you.'

'Oh, yes. So it is.'

He stared at her, puzzled. 'You sent it yesterday?'

'Yes.'

'But you knew you'd be back today.'

'Yes, I just . . . I don't know – I just wanted to. I'm sorry,' she said stiffly. 'It just seemed an idea at the time.'

'Thanks,' said Don. He looked again at the card. 'Lichfield cathedral. I supose we must have been round that often enough. Not very exciting, if I remember rightly.'

'I suppose not.'

'Could we have dinner a bit early. I've brought a lot of work back I'd like to get on with.'

She peeled potatoes at the sink and thought: Don has never much cared for cathedrals or at least not cathedrals done yard by yard, guide book in hand, which is by no means unusual, lots of people don't.

The potato peelings unravelled and fell from her fingers and she stared out into the garden (the lupins a foot high now, the crocus leaves slumped against the grass, a yellow shock of forsythia by the gate) and thought of some occasion early in their marriage when she had toured a church, commenting on its features, she had thought, to Don at her side only to find herself turning to look into the perplexed face of a stranger, with Don nowhere to be seen (but found, later, tranquilly smoking in the cloister). He had not – or apparently had not – noticed her irritation and after a while she had forced herself not to feel irritated because it was a holiday and holidays must not be spoiled by things that are really not important.

And thus are habits formed, for better or for worse.

Father, she thought, now father was quite different. He was a great one for the minute and thorough examination and yes, now I come to think of it, there is Bodiam Castle or some such place with mother sitting patiently on a wall waiting for him to be done, and looking at her watch, but surreptitiously in case she be seen. And instinctively I think: poor mother. Why?

In Starbridge now, that same moon – chewed away, by a week, since last I noticed it – is seen, at this point in the evening, as you sit at the kitchen table, through the top right hand pane of the window, resting against the line of alders in the field.

* * *

David Fielding said to his son Tom, 'Look, I'm not absolutely sure I'm going to be able to manage this camping thing next week.'

'But you said you would. In the Easter holidays, you said. You promised.'

'I know,' he said wretchedly, 'I know I did. And we shall. But just not next week. Do you mind awfully?'

'I s'pose not. Why can't you?'

'Because – oh, because there's some committees and things I ought to be here for.'

'Can I come fishing with you instead?'

'You certainly can. By all means.'

'Ma said to tell you she's out tonight and there's a pie you can have in the fridge.'

'Right.'

I hate this, he thought, I hate this as much as anything I have ever done. Tom. Tom and Alan than whom, hitherto, nothing has been more important. He said to Tom, 'Come for a walk. I'm fed up with these scripts.'

'Sorry, Dad – I said I'd go round to John's.'

'O.K. I'll have to make do with my own company.'

Tom, he thought, who will in two years' time be eighteen and on the brink of all those choices that determine how things work out, and whom I can help only up to a point. Oh, we can pore over university prospectuses together, and weigh up the pros and cons of this place or that, this course or those options, and he will pay attention to me because he is a sensible lad and recognizes that I know a bit about such things. But of the rest I can say little, and he would probably listen less, for immemorial reasons. We all have to make our own mistakes, as my mother used to say; you make your bed and you lie on it. You drive a nail into your own coffin. But when you are eighteen – or twenty-three – it is inconceivable that the choices you make must be worn like albatrosses around your neck for the rest of your life. And when you are forty-two it seems the ultimate malevolence that one should have been faced with those choices at the point in life when most of us are least equipped to make them.

To make them not wisely but well.

To make them other than for craven reasons. Out of fear of hurting a person, or disappointing them, or just because it was expected. A man tripping up in the street is more worried about humiliation than death. I married Mary because it would have been too much bother not to, and one can always hope for the best.

And so, for good reason, because they are bright boys and not unperceptive, my sons will not come to me for advice about that kind of thing, nor shall I offer it.

I could pray, if I were a religious man.

I could tell them that perhaps they are lucky to be here, given that a few months – weeks? – after our marriage their mother said from under me, 'Look, I'd better tell you rather than go on pretending, I don't all that much care for sex.'

I could tell them that one adjusts to more than I would ever, once, have thought possible. And no doubt they – being bright – would say, but why, Dad, why go on? And I would have to say again, probably just for craven reasons, some more comprehensible than others.

We will never, of course, have such a conversation.

David walked into the Red Lion and said, 'Pint, George, please.' He sat by the fire and the landlord, putting on another log, said, 'Warmer today. Last time I'll light this, I reckon. We can make do with a potted plant next week. In the middle of your holidays, I suppose, Mr Fielding?'

'That's right.'

'Got any plans?'

'A bit of fishing, maybe.'

He sat in the pub, as he often did, until nine or so, and went home to eat the pie from the fridge and watch a television play with his sons, in companionable silence.

* * *

Graham telephoned Anne and said if it wasn't a nuisance he thought he'd turn up next weekend. 'I say,' she said, 'we are favoured these days. What's happened to all your ladies?' And Graham, indistinct in a call-box, besieged – as it sounded – by pneumatic drills, said or seemed to say that he didn't much care, just at the moment. 'Fine, then,' she said. 'We'll see you here. I'll have been up to Lichfield again by then, I daresay.'

* * *

James Stanway woke from what seemed to him to have been many days' sleep and said to the girl in a white apron beside his bed, 'How long have I been laid up like this?' He could not at first hear what she said in reply but then she leaned closer and he understood that she was pleased to see him feeling more himself today, and would he like a nice bit of fish for his dinner? 'Well,' he said, 'you know I think now I'm fit again I ought to be getting home, my wife doesn't care for being on her own for too long.' He waited for someone to do something about this, but when he looked around the room again the girl had gone and when next he was aware of a presence by the bed it was a very different one: Betty wearing the silk scarf he bought her once for Christmas, talking of opera, a taste of hers he had come to share. 'Well,' he said, 'I bow to your superior judgment, but I remain unconvinced that *Carmen* is a major work. What about Verdi, now? How do we feel about Verdi?'

Eight

'There's a quiche in the fridge,' she said to Paul, 'for tomorrow's lunch. And a hot pot for supper, that wants a good half hour in the oven, and there's some cheese-cake and a chocolate mousse and a bolognaise sauce for Friday night – you only have to do the spaghetti yourselves – and lots of cheese. Oh, and I've made some of that pizza you like – all you do with that is pop it in a hot oven for a few minutes. Do you think you'll be all right?'

'I should think we'll just about survive.'

'And remind Dad there's an onion tart for him because he doesn't care for spaghetti.'

'Right.'

'And there are some crumpets.'

'Mum?'

'Yes?'

'Whose birthday is it?'

'I just want to be sure I've left enough,' she said. 'And I'll ring tomorrow night, tell Dad.'

The road to Lichfield unfurls now in stages, each length known and experienced; it would be impossible any more to mistake the route though there is a temptation to turn off here or there and experiment with a side-road or diversion. One wants, now, to prolong the journey. One wants to savour it to the full, this anticipatory joy, slow down over favourite sections, stop even, once or twice, and postpone arrival for a little because the contemplation of it, the expectation, is almost as good as the thing itself. From the A423 to the A41 to the A452 . . . From that smooth sweep of fields to those lines of poplars funnelling the road away to a distant point to this factory chimney sending its spirals of smoke out into the clear blue spring sky.

In the nursing-home, she found her father lying with his eyes closed, breathing in lengthy rasps, as though his body existed for that purpose only. It seemed an absence of consciousness far beyond sleep, and the Matron, coming in as she stood over him in anxiety, said that yes, this was a coma, but he would probably come out of it and was in no immediate danger. 'We have to expect this kind of thing,' she said, 'especially as he'd been particularly spry and lucid lately. I wish I'd known you were coming up, Mrs Linton, and I'd have suggested you put it off for a few days. What a shame.' She laid her hand for a moment on Anne's arm. 'Rather a wasted journey for you – but let's hope you're more fortunate next time.' Anne walked out through the gardens to the car park and thought: I would, I think, if it had been possible, have told father about this, about what has happened to me.

In Starbridge, she set about going through his papers in the desk once more, since, the nursing-home visit having been cut short, there was an hour or so to spare. Less squeamish now, she emptied files onto the floor and sorted quickly through their contents, filling a grocery carton with discarded brochures, minutes of committees, reports on this and that. How little I know, she thought, about how he spent his life – that he was in Cologne in 1958 at some gathering of European educationalists, that he was a member of a committee studying the proposed changes in the O-level syllabus, that he once wrote a long letter to *The Times* about second language teaching in primary schools. So far as I am concerned – have been concerned – he existed to be my father, and now one finds that was not the case at all, or only a small part of it.

In one box she found a bundle of letters from her mother, hesitated, and then snapped the elastic band back around them and returned them to the box. There were letters from herself, also, which she read with interest ('I'm going to marry Don Linton – I've known him for ages now, two years on and off, and I know we'll . . .', 'Judy has a tooth now and howls day and night,' 'Paul is Gabriel in the school nativity play') and from Graham, which she read also. There were no others, except a few recent ones from friends or former colleagues. Anne thought: whatever he kept of her he kept inside his head, nowhere else, he had nothing, except that one photograph, which seems to be accidental. So many years, of what must have come in the end to a kind of domesticity, and not a scrap of paper to record it.

She heard David's car draw up outside and sat waiting where she was, on the worn Persian rug, calling out through the open front door, 'I'm in here.'

* * *

'I've never been to this place,' said David, 'but I'm told it's quite good, and we can't go on for ever eating omelettes off your father's kitchen table. It's run by some Russian called Joe.'

The restaurant was murkily lit and had a perfunctory décor of chianti bottles hung in clutches and swags of fishing net. Its walls were lined with photographs of wrestlers, scowling into the room in attitudes of menace. It seemed that they related to the past of Joe himself, shambling from table to table in striped butcher's apron, his huge paws engulfing the pencil with which he scribbled down orders. He spoke easy Staffordshire: only the slant of his eyes in his broad face was central European. The meal was surprisingly good. They sat over it as the restaurant emptied and were finally alone with Joe, who drank morosely in the cupboard-sized bar. When he came over with the bill Anne said, 'You do the cooking yourself?'

'Wasn't it all right?'

'Oh, it was fine. Very nice indeed.'

David said, 'Where are you from?'

'From?'

'Originally. I mean, in Europe.'

'Latvia. I am from Latvia.' And the man began to talk at random of his childhood, a jumbled account of incidents involving flights, journeys, arrivals, periods spent here and there, unnamed places in unnamed countries. 'My parents were farmers,' he said. 'Farming people. Rich people – quite well off. We had a big farmhouse, among fields – corn, some cattle. Very nice – a beautiful place, very good land.'

Anne said, 'Have you ever been back there?'

'No, no.'

'When did you leave, then?' said David. 'During the war? You must have been a child.'

'That's right, yes. Seven, eight . . . Nineteen forty-four.'

Getting into the car, Anne said, 'How strange to be someone like that. To have a childhood so removed in every sense – that you can't revisit in any way, or that anyone else you know remembers. To be quite cut off from your own past.'

'He certainly was. Because I think he was wrong about, it, anyway.'

'Wrong? How could he be?'

'Well – as far as I know Latvia was a part of Russia by nineteen forty-four so that it's very unlikely that if his parents had been prosperous farmers they would have remained so then. They would have been collectivized.'

'I see.'

After a few moments she said, 'Was he making it up then, I wonder?'

'Probably not. Just distorting in a muddled kind of way.'

'I suppose that's what we do. Not so much preserve things as distort them.'

A middle-aged Latvian long resident in Staffordshire remembers a farmhouse that possibly never was; I knew my father in one dimension only; in Cuxing people are prepared to go to surprising lengths to keep other people from knocking down a building that can never have been so valued before. She put her hand comfortably on David's knee and said, 'What a very nice evening.'

'Wasn't it . . .'

* * *

Down in Cuxing, divided from his wife by the road to Lichfield and much else besides, Donald Linton ate hot pot at the kitchen table, following it with fruit salad and a helping of cheese. He then watched, with desultory interest, a television documentary on northern Ireland (which seemed to him some way away and not greatly his concern). While watching it he considered, briefly, telephoning Anne and then, remembering the cost of a call to Lichfield, decided against it. When, half an hour later, she telephoned him, he was mildly irritated and cut short the conversation. He returned to the television and listened to the news, in which an item on a collapsing insurance company reminded him of an intention to take out some additional insurance, and sent him to check his policy. He read the small print with care, and filled in a form which efficiently summarized him as to occupation, marital status etc. He was surprised, just a little, to note that he had only twenty-three working years ahead – one had assumed, somehow, that there were more. But that, after all – this expansion of time had and reduction of time to come – was something common to all and not therefore a personal problem, particularly. He signed the insurance form and went to bed.

* * *

David said, 'He reminded me, that man in the restaurant, of a friend of mine, a Pole, in the sense of being someone with an impenetrable – or almost unimaginable – past. This man got caught up in the war when he was in his teens, lost all his family, fought Germans when I was still at school, drifted from one country to another after the war, finally fetched up here. He makes me feel in some odd way inadequate. Short on personal experience. Apologetic.'

'Oh, but that's almost masochistic. To feel guilty for not having suffered.'

'I daresay. But nevertheless I always find myself deferring to him, as though what he's been through made him know more than I do about everything.'

'I used to think that about my brother, just because he was two years older.'

'Do you still.'

'Oh, my God no!'

'I could stay tonight,' he said. 'I've kind of arranged things at home so it would be all right. If you'd like that.'

'Like?' she said. 'Like . . .'

* * *

'It won't be long,' she said. 'It really won't. Ten days. One does get through them. I know that now. There's some absurd business on Monday over this cottage I told you about – they're going to knock it down, or try to. I'll have a tale to tell, no doubt, next time I see you.'

'Go to sleep,' he said. 'What a disturbing person you are. You talk all night. Look at the time – after three.'

'It's a lovely time. I haven't enjoyed three o'clock in the morning for years.'

'Neither have I,' he said. 'If ever.'

* * *

'Nine-thirty,' said Sandra, on the phone. 'Not later. Oh, and I should bring a thermos or something.'

'A thermos?'

'It might be a longish business, if things get tricky. I'll see you in the morning, then.'

The field beyond Splatt's Cottage had been pegged out into rectangles, and trenches driven across it at intervals. In the far corner a bulldozer sat in the middle of a custard-coloured area of sludge and water. There was a cement-mixer parked by the edge of the lane and a mound of assorted pipes stacked in the ditch. From a green mobile hut by the gate of the field three men peaceably drinking tea from mugs eyed the Splatt's Cottage Preservation Committee and their supporters.

Anne said, 'Are they the ones who're going to do it?'

'That we're not absolutely sure about,' said Sandra. 'Ah, here's Hugh Sidey. Hello there!'

'No action as yet?' said the professor.

'Not so far.'

'Then I think we should take up a kind of waiting position and see what happens.'

One banner was stuck up in the hedge and the other draped across the front of the Pickerings' Fiat. The group, swollen now to about twenty-five or thirty, disposed themselves along the grass verges and in front of the entrance to the cottage, chatting.

Anne said to Professor Sidey, 'I gather you put in a formal protest to the planning people. I'm sorry I had to miss the last committee.'

'We did indeed. It might, of course, have been more effective if we'd been able to get it in before the application was granted. As it is we got a fairly dusty answer, as we expected – except of course for vague assurances about the external appearance of the bungalows and what they're to be used for. Which, of course, one has to regard with the utmost scepticism. Ah, now this, if I'm not mistaken, is our Mr Pym.'

'The builder?'

'The villain of the piece. Or one of them.' The professor bustled away to consult with Sandra. What had he professed, before retirement, Anne wondered? History? Probably not, on the whole.

The builder had left his car at the end of the lane, and walked briskly, now, towards the group. He seemed in no way perturbed. As he passed them he said, 'Good-morning,' and one or two people murmured 'Good-morning' back, and then looked away awkwardly. He picked his way across the field towards the workmen who had now finished drinking tea and were tinkering with the stationary bulldozer.

'Mmn . . .' said Sandra.

The bulldozer, starting up, began now to erode the bank at the far end of the field. Mr Pym, deep in talk with one of the men, walked to and fro among the tapes and trenches, referring periodically to some papers in his hand. Mary Pickering came over to Anne and said, 'Actually you would think wouldn't you that they'd need more than just one of those yellow things to knock a house down.' She wore jeans decorated with elaborate appliqué work and a thick hand-knitted sweater.

'Yes, I suppose you would.'

'I do hope we're not here for nothing.'

The small children accompanying some members of the group were playing happily now in a pile of building sand beside the cement-mixer. One of the mothers said anxiously, 'I hope that doesn't matter. Timmy, don't throw it about like that, it doesn't belong to us.'

Mr Pym had gone now into the mobile hut, and could be seen through the open door studying a large plan or map. The bulldozer was still busy at the bank, and the other two workmen were digging a trench in the distance. Sandra said, 'Anyone like a cup of coffee?'

It was now past ten. One woman had already drifted away, saying apologetically that she had to get into Reading before eleven. Sandra said to her departing back, 'No skin off our nose, frankly, the weak might as well fall by the wayside. Who's this now?'

'Oh,' said Brian Pickering, 'it's the photographer from the Reading paper. I rang them up and suggested they send someone along.'

The photographer got out of his car and came towards them.

'Look,' said Sandra, 'I should hang on for a bit. Nothing's actually happened yet, you see. You'll get a much better picture when they actually start doing something.'

The photographer said doubtfully, 'Yes.' He glanced at his watch. 'Trouble is, I've got an assignment in Wallingford at ten-thirty. Could you sort of gather round, with the cottage as a background. And with those banners – yes, that's nice. Just one more – thanks very much.'

'Pity,' said Sandra, as he drove away. 'Still, it's better than nothing.' She turned back to look at the field where Mr Pym was now leaving the hut, shouting something to the trench-diggers as he went. He came out of the field and up the lane towards the cottage.

'Off to get reinforcements, I imagine,' said the professor.

Brian Pickering said, 'Well, I rather hope so, because I've got to be at the college by twelve.'

Drawing level with them, Mr Pym now stopped and looked round at the group of people spread about the lane. He seemed curious rather than apprehensive. The professor said, 'Good-morning, Mr Pym.'

'Good-morning to you, sir. I don't think we've met, have we?'

'Sidey's the name,' said the professor tersely. 'No, I think not.'

'Newcomer to Cuxing, then?'

'You could say so.'

'Professor Sidey,' said Sandra, 'bought the Old Mill House last autumn.'

'And good-morning to you, Mrs Butterfield. Ah, now I remember the Old Mill when it was still in use. That sets the clock back a bit, doesn't it? You'll have had to do a lot to it, sir, I imagine? It wasn't ever meant for living in, not the way people like things now.'

'What we would like to say to you, Mr Pym . . .' began the professor, but Mr Pym was already speaking again.

'. . . Come to think of it, I daresay I remember more of Cuxing thirty, forty years ago than anyone else much in the village – more than anyone here, I'd reckon.' He glanced amiably round the group, 'You've been here, what? – nine, ten years? – Mrs Butterfield. And there's a lot of faces here I don't recognize at all. The village has seen some changes all right, but that's the way things go, isn't it?'

Sandra began, 'There's absolutely no need for them to go quite . . .'

'. . . And I think it would be fair enough to say that none of us old Cuxing people think anything but that newcomers are a good thing. Ladies like Mrs Butterfield here've done a lot to put us on our toes' – he grinned at Sandra – 'And, mind you, most change I've seen has been for the better. Take my grandfather now – I remember him living with neither hot nor cold running water and a privy out the back . . .'

'Possibly,' said the professor, 'But . . .'

'Mr Pym,' said Sandra loudly, 'I think it must be clear enough to you what we're here about. Are you intending to pull down this cottage today?'

Mr Pym's benevolent glance roamed beyond her to Splatt's Cottage. 'The old cottage? It's a shame it's been let go like that, isn't it? My grandparents had it lovely – to look at, that is – with roses round the door and a nice garden.'

Sandra said, 'I had no idea your grandparents lived in Splatt's Cottage, Mr Pym, and frankly I find that makes it even more extraordinary that . . .'

'Oh, I don't know,' said the builder thoughtfully, 'I don't know. . . . Of course, it's a pity it has to go – I remember playing in that ditch there when I was a boy, it was a lot cleaner in those days and you'd get tiddlers, sticklebacks and that.'

Brian Pickering said, 'We're here to see that it doesn't go, as a matter of fact.'

Mr Pym, ignoring this, went on, 'Of course my grandparents moved out before the war, soon as they could get one of the new council houses, and the place was bought up by Mr Taylor, up at the Hall. I think he had it in mind for one of his men but nothing ever came of that and it's not been lived in, oh, forty-odd years now. Funny, I suppose, it should come back into the family, as it were, at the end.'

'All this is a bit irrelevant,' said the professor. 'Now, we understand your intention is to go ahead with the demolition today?'

'Today?' said Mr Pym. 'Oh no, not today. I wonder what gave you that idea, sir? No, that's a job I'm handing over to a contractor, and I couldn't tell you right now what his schedule is. Would you like me to keep you informed?'

A murmur ran through the group, huddled attentively now around Mr Pym. Brian Pickering said, 'God, what a balls-up.'

'No, thank you' said the professor coldly. 'I must say I think your attitude . . .'

'You should be ashamed of yourself, Mr Pym,' said Sandra in strident tones. She stood foursquare at the gate of the cottage, the top of a thermos protruding from the pocket of her anorak. 'Here you are busy destroying the oldest building in the village – one of the oldest – without so much as a scruple as far as I can make out. Don't you feel you owe any respect to the past?'

'Hear, hear' said the professor.

'I'd mind that path if I were you, Mrs Butterfield,' said Mr Pym. 'There's a nasty old drain there that wants filling in. Been there donkey's years. Ah . . . I should have said sooner. Are you all right?'

Sandra, picking herself up, said 'Perfectly . . . As I was saying, one feels the village is being betrayed by its own . . .' Her voice trailed away.

'I say,' said the professor, 'sure you're all right? You came down rather hard, I'm afraid.'

Mary Pickering, taking Sandra's elbow said, 'I'll run you back to our place.'

'Really no need,' said Sandra.

'I'll have that drain seen to,' said Mr Pym. 'Hope there's no damage done, Mrs Butterfield. Well, I'll be on my way.' He turned to the professor. 'Nice to have met you. It's good to have a bit of new blood in Cuxing, these days – you don't want to have a place stand still, do you?' He glanced cordially round at the group. 'Good-morning to you' – and walked away towards his car.

There was a short silence.

'I was assured absolutely,' said the professor, 'by one of the men on the site, that the intention was to knock it down today. I assume of course that we have been deliberately misled.'

'Quite,' said Brian Pickering. 'He's an absolute rogue, that's obvious.'

The supporters were moving away up the lane. The children, well established now in the sand heap, were detached with difficulty.

Anne said, 'Are you O.K., Sandra?'

'Yes, thanks. Stupid thing to do. But actually I think I will get back now and put my feet up for a bit. Can I give anyone a lift? Anyway,' she went on determinedly, 'we've made our point, I feel, whatever happens now.'

'Oh, yes,' said Mary Pickering, 'it's been well worth it.'

Someone said, 'Aren't we going to turn up again, when the contractors' men come?'

'I suggest a committee on that,' said the professor. 'We may have to do a bit of re-thinking.' He moved away with Sandra towards her car, talking.

Anne walked up the lane in the wake of the group. The Span houses, their windows glittering in the sun, rose from their squares of green turf. Behind, the bulldozer could be heard rumbling to and fro in the field. Between them, Splatt's Cottage sat inscrutably behind its hedge. She looked into the ditch and thought: I should have asked that builder if there were eels as well as tiddlers and sticklebacks, now I'll never know. She walked towards Cuxing, past the house where Paul's one-time best friend lived, past the place where Judy in infancy feared a dog marauding behind a garden gate, past another house that Don had wanted, once, to buy. David accompanied her – his face, his way of walking, his voice, creating and re-creating themselves against this familiar background that he could not imagine.

* * *

Graham came down for the weekend and seemed, she thought, subdued. He talked dispiritedly of his work when he spoke of it at all, and was a more passive guest than usual. He spent a long time with Paul, helping him assemble some stereo equipment, and said afterwards, 'He must be quite nice to have around, that lad of yours.'

'You always used to say you thought people were mad, lumbering themselves with children.'

'Maybe I was wrong.'

He seemed content to slump in armchairs, glancing through newspapers or dozing by the fire. On the Sunday afternoon Anne took him out, protesting, to walk on the downs.

'I thought I was here for a rest, Annie. I notice Don gets let off.'

'Don's never been all that keen on walking.'

The huge downland fields, fawn or hesitant green, curved around them. They followed a chalky bridle-path between bushes from which flights of small birds erupted. Overhead, the sky was full of larks.

'I suppose it's not so bad,' said Graham. 'Do me good, no doubt. I saw a chap about these stomach aches.'

'Is there anything wrong, Graham?'

'He didn't think so. Said I should lose weight.'

She stopped herself from laughing at the sight of his face, sombre and unsmiling as he trudged along the ruts of dried mud.

'You should take some time off – get away somewhere.'

'I might do just that.'

She said, 'I've been thinking of going to see this Mrs Barron person.'

'Whatever for?'

'I don't really know. I just feel I want to make some kind of contact. I mean, we've been connected all our lives in an eerie sort of way, without ever having met.'

'It's a funny sort of connection.'

'It certainly is. It's this business of her having known a whole part of father that we didn't.'

'You want to talk to her about father?'

'I'm not even sure that it's that, exactly.'

They were following the track now along a ridge; Berkshire lay spread out below them in filmy sunlight; the chimneys of Didcot power station rose cathedral-like in the distance.

She said, 'Do you imagine they were unhappy together, mother and father?'

'Hard to tell, isn't it? It didn't exactly seem so, did it?'

'No.'

'I don't know . . .' said Graham. 'If it was some script for a play and you found this chap had had someone else on the side for years and years, well, you'd be in the thick of your marital strife stuff, repression and suppression and whatnot. But this is real life, which I've come to think is different. Sometimes I thank heaven for the conventions of drama. You know where you are with a properly set-up dramatic situation, and a good script-writer who knows his job when it comes to characterization, motivation and so on. But this foxes me somewhat, I must admit. No, I don't really think they were miserable together, or anything near it.'

'*Why* did you never tell me?'

'It honestly never really occurred to me to, Annie. Good thing I didn't, as far as I can see. It seems to have got you properly worked up.'

'Not really worked up. Just muddled.'

They stopped at a gateway into a field and leaned against it. 'He must always have known mother might find out,' Anne said. 'And yet father was never a person who took risks, or at least I didn't think he was. But he did. So it's all very confusing. I rang the nursing-home on Friday – he's still much the same. No more of these comas, so far. They'd been getting him out of bed again.'

In the distance a tractor crawled across the field and from the creamy spread of plough lapwings suddenly lifted, their cries loud in the stillness.

'Anne?'

'What? Sorry.'

'I said are you sure it isn't getting a bit much for you, all this popping up and down there?'

'No.'

'We could do it turn and turn about, a bit more. I'm not that pushed just at the moment.'

'It's all right, honestly.'

'Of course,' Graham said, 'you've got this fellow of yours to keep you amused up there, that schoolmaster.'

She turned on him. 'What the hell do you mean?'

'Nothing. Just a joke. Christ, Annie, you look just like when you were sixteen and I used to pull your leg.'

There was a silence. 'Cigarette?'

She shook her head.

'Just a joke, I swear. I don't know what made me think of him – just something about the way he asked after you when I was in with Dad one time he turned up at the nursing-home. Sorry, Anne – I've put my foot in it, haven't I?'

'It's all right.'

'Well,' he said, 'so what, then? The best of luck to you. Have a good time and don't look so screwed-up about it. It's a common enough occurrence, after all. Do you good. Damn – I'm almost out of matches. I don't suppose you've got any?' Turning to look at her, he stopped.

'I'm afraid not.'

'Annie – look, I'm sorry. I really did just mean a joke. It's a bit sour, I see now.'

'Never mind.'

They stood side by side, elbows on the gate; an aeroplane drew a thin white line across the sky, from west to east. 'Shall we go on?' she said. 'There's a track across here we can take.' They walked in silence for a while.

'You've surprised me somewhat, Annie.'

She said, suddenly irritable. 'Why? I'm younger than you are. It's a bit of a shock to me, too, though. It's a process I'd rather forgotten about. I daresay it happens to you all the time.'

'Actually, no.'

'What about all those ladies, then?'

'They're just ladies,' he said. 'If you're talking about what I think you are, then that's something I don't know much about these days. Haven't for a long time.'

'Oh, Graham . . .'

'So what now? What are you going to do?'

'I haven't,' she said, 'the faintest idea. Let's not talk about it any more. Forget about it, Graham – I mean that. Look – if we cut across that field there it comes out in the village and we can get you some matches.'

* * *

When I was fourteen, she thought, I hated you for a whole year on end, bar seasonal truces for Christmas and birthdays and those were pretty frail. You pulled my leg, as you put it, first because I had grown a bosom and then because according to you it was inadequate. You hung my bra out of the front window where it was seen, before I retrieved it, by the boy opposite at whom I could not look without risk of heart failure. You brought your friends to the house and with them made remarks of incomprehensible indelicacy at which I giggled, for fear of appearing innocent. You played elaborate practical jokes on me, borrowed my records and returned them scratched or not at all, caught me shaving my armpits with father's razor and told him, called me 'Fatso' and threw cold water on all my aspirations. Or so it seemed at the time. I daresay you would have a different tale to tell.

And now, for no reason that I can see except the passage of twenty-five years, I become increasingly fond of you and more tolerant of all those things about you that have from time to time exasperated me. You are getting a paunch and have gone thin on top and I think you are lonely, which causes me the most peculiar and confusing kind of pain. I am sorry for you. And to feel sorry for people is to feel guilty because things are not for you as they are for them. Not complacent, guilty.

Nine

'But if as you said yesterday he hardly knows what's going on now it can't make any difference whether you go up before the weekend or after.'

'I told them at the nursing-home I'd be up on Friday.'

'Then tell them you can't.'

'Oh, all right,' she said. 'All right if you insist. I must say there's nothing I want to do less than have dinner with the Thwaiteses. Why can't they make it a different day?'

'They've got other people coming.'

'He's a bore, Jim Thwaites. A complacent bore.'

'He's my partner, may I remind you.'

'You're welcome to him.'

Don picked up his brief-case and walked out of the room. At the door he turned and said 'I can tell Jim we'll be there, then?'

'I suppose so.'

We've had a quarrel, she thought. Goodness. When did that last happen? I'm sorry, she said to Don's departing back, I'm sorry about that because I was unreasonable and you are perfectly right, my father is far beyond knowing Friday from Monday or indeed one day from another.

She stood in the hall looking at the telephone and turned to find Paul leaned up against the kitchen door, watching her.

'For heavens' sake! You made me jump. What do you want?'

'Nothing. Why do you keep picking the phone up and putting it down again?'

'I'm not. I've forgotten someone's number, that's all. Hadn't you better get off to school?'

'I'm on my way. Keep your hair on, Mum.'

She got the number through directory enquiries, walked to and fro between kitchen and hall for ten minutes, and then dialled it. A secretarial voice said distantly, 'The Headmaster isn't here just now. What name is it, please?' 'Could you tell him that Mrs Linton rang to say that unfortunately she won't be able to be in Lichfield till next Monday.' 'Mrs Linden?' 'Linton.' 'Would you like him to ring you back, Mrs Linton?' 'No' Anne said, panic-stricken. 'No, there's no need.' Putting the receiver down she found herself trembling.

Five minutes later she went to the telephone again. 'Don?' 'Yes?' 'Sorry, is it a bad moment?' 'I've got a client coming any minute. What is it, Anne?' 'I'm sorry about just now. The Thwaiteses. It doesn't really matter if I don't go to Lichfield till Monday.'

Don's voice, muffled, talking to someone else said, 'Leave the file out, would you, Mandy – I'll be wanting it in a minute.' Clear again, and to her, he went on 'Right. Fine. Seven-thirty, Jim says. Anything else?' 'No, nothing. What time will you be back?' 'The usual time, why?' 'Well, I thought it might be nice if we went out for a drink or something – if it's a nice evening.' 'If you like,' he said. 'We'll see. I've got some papers I must go over.' 'Don . . .' 'Look, I am in the middle of something, actually. I'll see you later.'

'Yes,' she said. ''Bye then.'

It was May. The garden was encircled now by bolsters of green where, two months ago, the street and houses opposite had been visible through the twiggy screen of the hedges. Subtract two months, the inflation and deflation of two moons, the growth of much grass and leaf, and the clocking up of some nine hundred odd miles on the dashboard of the car, and you were back in March, with nothing more disturbing on the horizon than the odd decision to be made about Paul's schooling, and whether or not to apply for some O-level examining this summer. Father was, apparently, well and happy in Starbridge; you were reasonably clear of your position on a good many things, including the extent to which people are in every way sustained and supported by the past; there was nothing you particularly wanted, and nothing you particularly regretted.

She went up into the spare room, later in the day, and began to disembowel cupboards. Judy came and sprawled on the bed, watching her, her skimpy school tunic barely covering her thighs, her school tie unknotted and its ends crammed into her blouse. Anne said, 'Why don't you take off those awful things? Look, there's a shirt of mine here I never wear – it's pretty – would you like it?'

'No, thanks.'

'Why not? It would fit you – you're as tall as I am, almost. Try it on. Darling, don't put your feet on that bedcover.'

'Why are you chucking out all that stuff? You never tidy things up – I bet you've not opened that cupboard for years. Is someone coming to stay?'

'No. I just thought I'd have a clear out.' And I have to have something to do, rather than think, or remember, or face the fact that today Tuesday is removed from Monday of next week by five days. 'Come on,' she said. 'Help me take this lot down to the dustbin, and then I'm going to make a terribly complicated cake. Do you want to help? You used to like doing that. But put something else on – you don't need to wear school things at home.'

'It isn't worth it,' said Judy, 'What's the point?'

* * *

Don read through the Styles *v.* Jackson Construction Co. papers and thought (while noting that there were one or two tricky points in the case that would want watching) that Anne was being a bit trying these days. He didn't in fact find these trips up to Lichfield particularly inconvenient, and quite appreciated the need for her to go, which made this business tonight somewhat irritating. One would almost have thought that she *wanted* to be told to go more infrequently, or not at all – sitting there in that pub on the edge, it had seemed, of tears. Good heavens, Anne, he'd said reasonably, it's really neither here nor there to me, I'm awfully busy these days. Come on – I must get back now.

It hadn't seemed the moment to bring up that house he'd heard of in

Wallingford, with the garden going down to the river. It might take time, getting her round to the idea of a move, let alone enthusiastic. One should be thankful, presumably, and indeed one was, not to be married to someone extravagant, or demanding of expensive holidays or objects. Oh, he thought, I'll get her round to it, with a bit of time and tact.

* * *

In the Thwaites' drawing-room the shine of the parquet was interrupted here and there by oriental rugs, deep red and prussian blue, balding a little in the centres. Massive sofas and armchairs of the nineteen thirties were moored at the edges of the room, each with its attendant small antique table for glass, or cup, or ashtray. Anne put her sherry down carefully and listened to Joan Thwaites tell her about her granddaughter's equestrian triumphs and the fortnight they had had in Greece, and the forthcoming R.D.C. elections. Yes, she said, did she really? no, I hadn't heard that; I don't think actually I've met him. Released by Joan Thwaites (rising now to greet new arrivals, and dealing them around the room, planting out her guests by fireplace or window) she studied without seeing it the Leader above the mantelpiece and observed without noticing that the Lalique bowl on the table beside her had a minute flaw in its rim. She took another sip of sherry and travelled to Lichfield and back, turned with an attentive smile to the neighbour on her right and composed, as he spoke, a letter of grief and culmination, tore it up, and allowed herself to be conveyed from drawing-room to dining-room and installed on one of eight (reproduction) Chippendale chairs at a diagonal slant from Don, taking his turn now beside Joan Thwaites. She ate an admirable cold consommé and heard from Jim Thwaites about the weather in the Peloponnese in April and the rapacity of Greek hoteliers. The woman opposite (sixtyish, determinedly spry and vivacious) said 'How I do envy you, Jim, it's five years and more since I managed Greece.'

'Well, of course,' he said, 'as far as I'm concerned, as a classicist, it's a bit of an infatuation. I suppose I first went, as an undergraduate, back in – dear me, in around 1935. Do you know Greece at all well, Anne?'

'No.'

'Oh, my dear,' said the woman, 'what a treat to come.' She picked up a fork, tidied the salmon and salad on her plate, and smiled kindly at Anne.

'You'd get so much out of it,' said Jim Thwaites. 'We must see that Don takes you before too long. Anne teaches history, you know. At – at the comprehensive, is that it?'

'Now that must be so interesting.'

Anne said, 'I did. I've lost my job, as it happens.'

'That's too bad,' said Jim. 'Presumably you'll pick something else up easily enough? Now Sybil here writes.'

The woman dipped her head modestly towards her plate.

Anne said, 'What do you write?' On the wall opposite a selection of English cathedrals, reduced and framed in gilt, offered themselves unobtrusively above the sideboard (pudding plates laid out ready, and glass dish of wafer biscuits); the third from the left, almost certainly, was Gloucester. At the other end of the table Don was discussing, it seemed, local politics with Joan Thwaites.

'Sybil does the most charming travel pieces for *The Countryman*,' said Jim.

'Actually rather more for *Country Life* now,' she broke in. 'And *Vogue*. That kind of thing.'

'Is that so? I very much liked that article Joan showed me on these archaeological tours in the eastern Med. That really whetted one's appetite, I must say.'

'They are most awfully good value. Archaeology, of course,' she smiled again across at Anne, 'is rather a pet interest of mine. I've got a treat coming up next month – I'm getting to Ephesus for the first time, which has always been a bit of a lifetime's ambition.'

'Ah' said Jim Thwaites 'We shall want to hear all about that, Sybil. You're one up on me there, I must say.'

'But you've done Knossos, Jim, haven't you?'

'We have indeed. Marvellous experience.'

'Of course,' said Sybil, 'these places aren't what they were, in this day and age of the package tour. Before the war, one really had that sense of somewhere absolutely untouched for thousands of years, and the people were so unspoilt. I dug,' she offered to Anne, across Jim

Thwaites's approving attention, 'in Palestine as a girl. One of the Dead Sea sites.'

Anne said, 'That must have been interesting.'

'It was incredible. I can smell it now – the heat, you know, and that extraordinary middle-eastern feeling, there's nothing like it.'

The Thwaiteses' gilt wall clock, with palest of chimes, announced nine o'clock. Removed from eleven by two hours and from next week by uncountable hundreds. Anne said, 'Don and I were at Belas Knap last month.'

After a fractional pause Jim Thwaites said, 'Let me see now, I should know . . . Turkey, is that?'

'In the Cotswolds. Near Winchcombe. It's a neolithic long barrow.'

'I'm afraid I'm frightfully ignorant about English archaeology,' said Sybil. 'It never seems quite the same, does it?' She laughed. 'Dear me, we did go to Fishbourne a few years ago, I remember – all those poor souls trenching in the mud, one really had to take off one's hat to them.'

'And a few miles from here,' Anne said, 'on the Downs, there's an earthwork that goes for about four or five miles – you can follow it on the ground, apparently it's thought to be a celtic estate boundary. And then of course there's the Ridgeway itself, and Uffington. I don't care for the very done-up Roman places, myself, like Chedworth, but I think North Leigh has a lot to be said for it. And then there are the Rollright Stones.'

'One really must,' said Jim Thwaites, 'make an effort and take in what is on one's own doorstep. Mustn't we, Sybil?'

'If it wasn't for the wretched climate . . .'

'If only, as you say, there wasn't the wretched climate to take the edge off things.'

From the end of the table, handing out lemon mousses, Joan Thwaites said 'I saw your picture in the paper, Anne. Demonstrating about that cottage.'

Ah. Yes. Lined up with Sandra, the Pickerings, *et al*. Wearing trousers and warm jersey, scarf round head, expression made the more inscrutable by fuzzy grey newsprint; a concerned and responsible person, doing what she thought proper about something that mattered.

'I gather it's all a bit in the air still – whether it'll get pulled down or not?'

'Yes,' said Anne, 'I think it is.'

'It really would be a shame. Have I done everyone? Do please start.'

Spoons chinked on glass; a blackbird, behind Jim Thwaites' left ear and on the other side of the window, patrolled the bright May lawn; in Staffordshire now the lanes are fringed with cow parsley and the trees more lavishly green than one would ever have thought possible; the birdsong is amazing, the dawns a blaze of sound; on the river the crowfoot is like snowflakes.

Sybil, on the opposite side of the table, who wrote, was saying that one felt trapped these days, simply trapped, with the pound in its present state and travel quite prohibitive. 'Tell me,' Anne said, 'isn't the climate in the Dead Sea pretty unpleasant? I haven't, of course, ever been there but I somehow thought it was nasty.'

A fading, now, of the kindly, older-to-younger-woman smile; a glance shot leftwards at Jim Thwaites ('Attend, please, to this guest of yours'); folding of napkin with pink-painted nails. 'Oh, goodness, are we back on archaeology? Well, it was a bit sticky of course but one was so engrossed it didn't really matter.'

'I see.'

Simultaneously, a clearing of the throat and scrape of chair from Jim Thwaites. 'Now, I think Joan will want us in the other room for coffee. Shall I lead the way?'

A quarter to ten.

A disposal now of the company; Sybil safely on the far side of the room, Don two chairs away with Jim Thwaites, one's personal allocation a youngish accountant from Henley, diligently seeking common ground.

Ten o'clock.

The common ground for which the poor man has had to work so hard (forgive me, I am not really as unresponsive as this nor have I any reason at all for disliking you; it is just that I am not really here) is found at last. His wife's parents live in Lichfield.

And how, without my being aware of the process, or, so far as I know, having lifted a finger to help, have we arrived in Lichfield?

'Where, exactly, does your father live?'

And of course he knows Starbridge, too, has driven out there of a summer evening (escaping from the parents-in-law?), walked down to the river, had a pint in the Barley Mow.

Yes, I've been into the pub once or twice.

And, if one is looking for somewhere quite nice to have a meal, there's a new place in a village – oh, three-four miles away on the Tamworth road – run by a Russian chap, ex-wrestler. Oh, really? Thanks, yes, I'll bear that in mind. And now I see it's going on for eleven, so I suppose, really if I can catch my husband's eye, we ought perhaps . . .

Actually, says this nice young man, Susan and I are going to be up there for ten days as of this weekend. The parents-in-law are away for a week or so and we're combining a caretaking job for them with a spot of fishing for me. I had a bit of luck, he says – offer of a few days on the Dove by a friend of mine with a stretch of fishing.

To the chink of coffee cups, now, is added the hiss of a reel above the river's noise. One must try to look responsive, not distracted.

And so, he goes on, if there's anything we can do – about, you know, you were saying, this business of sorting out your father's house – as I say, we'll be at a bit of a loose end in the evenings, delighted to pop out some time . . .

And, thank heaven, there is Don's eye allowing itself to be caught at last so that, amid thanks and one thing and another, one can move away without having given any commitment (forgive me, I am sorry, it's just that you don't know into what you have blundered, as how could you, how can any of us?). And then there are only Joan and Jim Thwaites to negotiate and one can stumble, at last, into the passenger seat of the car.

Eleven fifteen.

* * *

There must be, she thought, some kind of seasonal peak, undetectable, at which growth gives way to decline. It can't be far off. This line of trees, on this stretch of the A446, was only just showing green two weeks ago; now, the leaves are complete. And as soon as they are complete do they move into the next stage of the cycle? Or is there a standstill period, when they do nothing, when they just are? Could a botanist, studying a leaf, tell you in which month or week it was picked? Can you pin-point that moment at which one condition slides into another?

But all that is neither here nor there. Much more to the point is the light slanting through the poplars beside the dual carriage-way; the shape of that stand of elms on the skyline; the detail of the cow-parsley on the verge as you sit here behind this commercial traveller's car (coat slung from hook on the door-pillar, samples on the back seat), waiting to turn right for Lichfield.

* * *

'I got my picture in the paper' she said to David 'I'll have you know.'

'Did you now'

'And what have you been doing?'

'Waiting'

'Me, too.'

* * *

The seedlings were an inch high; love-in-a-mist, calendula, lavatera. They flourished, defiantly different, round-leafed or long-leafed or feathered like carrots. She hung over them in admiration thinking: why have I not done this for so long? I had quite forgotten the fun of it, the triumph. She tweaked some out, regretting the waste, to give others elbow-room. There, she said to them, flowers I'll expect from you, come July.

* * *

David said, 'It hardly seems worth going back, if we're setting off at half-past nine.'

'Could you . . .?'

'No,' he said sadly, 'I couldn't really. Not tonight. Nice as it would be.'

'Not *nice*.'

'No. Quite right. But I can't think of the right word.'

'I do love you,' she said.

'I'll come back for breakfast. And we can get off good and early.'

* * *

Lying alone she thought: what if she isn't there, this woman? The sensible thing to do would be to telephone her from here in the morning, having got the number through directory enquiries, explain, ask if it is all right to come today. But of course there is no question of doing that because she is only the half of it now, and if she were not there, out or away or declining to be visited, there would no longer be good reason for going to Gloucester together, all day, just us. And I'm not going to be done out of the day – that we will have at all costs, so if she is there, she is there, and if she is not, she is not. And for the same reason, I have not done the tactful, prudent thing and written to her suggesting a visit. In case she said no.

* * *

'Down the motorway?' she said. 'Do we have to?'

'It's by far the quickest.'

'But we've got all day,' she said, 'at least most of it. And we want to see things, don't we? Motorways just whisk you there like a conveyor belt, you don't even know you've travelled.'

'All right,' said David, 'if you want. But I reckon three hours and more in that case. Let's see. . . . I suppose there's this road, by Evesham.'

'No, you're right – it would take ages. I'm sorry, I wasn't thinking. It'll give us longer there – we'll have a good look round Gloucester, after I've seen Mrs Barron, or before.'

But the motorway, as motorways go, was not so bad. It swept through and above Birmingham, aerial on its flyovers and interchanges, at a level with tower-blocks and electricity pylons, detached from the muddle of housing and factories below. Riding high, the cars streamed steadily at roof-top level; peeled off to north, south, east and west at appropriate points. The tower-blocks glittered in the sunshine, remarkable, like futuristic illustrations in an architectural magazine; beneath them, here and there, streets of red-brick terrace housing and blackened nineteenth century factories crouched in shame. 'What's the canal?' said Anne. 'The Grand Union, of course,' said David. 'Dear me, haven't you ever taught the industrial revolution?' 'I've tried not to.' 'Escapist,' he said. 'Not at all, it's just that I don't know enough about it.'

And the motorway, she thought, escaped Birmingham most competently. You hardly had to slow down at all, to go through it and beyond. A city of a million people made an interesting backdrop, a piece of scenery to be studied over the parapet of the road, sliding past at fifty miles an hour, so many acres of brick and concrete and steel, layer upon layer, topped now by the long curves of the road system, riding impervious above everything. She stared at barges, full of grass, slumped in the mud of the canal.

'There,' said David, 'that was Birmingham, that was. A clear run south now.'

Not a bad motorway at all. The Cotswolds lay now to the left, a long blue flank; to the right, the Malverns peaking sharply out of wide flat lands. Anne said, 'Elgar, on our right. Battle of Evesham coming up. Have we time for a coffee?'

'I once went to Norway,' David said, in the motorway coffee-bar. 'I don't know a thing about Scandinavia. I can't tell you how restful it was to be in a place stripped of associations.'

'Oh,' she said, 'I don't think I'd like that at all, I'd feel displaced. And I should have thought you would too. You'd start wanting to find out.'

'No, I just admired it.'

Were you alone? she wanted to ask, and could not. She sat looking at him, moved him in her mind to a picture-postcard Norway of forests and fiords, a faceless Mary at his side (tall? short? dark? fair?). 'More coffee?' he said. Or should we be getting on?'

As they drove into Gloucester Anne said, 'Have you ever been here before?', and when he replied, never so far as he could remember, felt a particular satisfaction. How nice, she thought, to spend a day together in a place that means nothing to either of us. 'Where shall we go?' she said, and he groped in the parcel shelf of the car and passed a book across. 'I thought we'd give its architectural glories a proper going over, armed with Pevsner. All we need now is a car park.'

But something seemed to have happened to the architectural glories of Gloucester. Northgate, Southgate, Eastgate and Westgate promised well but did not provide. Moving from Woolworth's to Marks and

Spencer to the British Home Stores David said, 'Presumably it was blitzed, this place. Post-war rebuilding.' 'Oh, no, I don't think so,' she said, 'why should it have been? I mean, it wasn't industrial, was it?' 'Well, it must have been. Shall we go this way?' 'There's nothing much down there,' she said, 'not according to the book, anyway.' 'It's just apparently there's this very good fishing-tackle shop here and I promised Tom some flies. I rather suspect it may be in this street.'

Bother Tom, she thought, walking the length of an undistinguished street of butchers and greengrocers. Beyond, the tower of the cathedral rose behind office buildings. 'Actually,' she said, 'it's nearly one, you know.' 'Sorry, I did promise him, that's all. Do you mind if we just have a look along here?'. 'No,' she said, 'of course not.'

'What did you say?' he shouted, over a thunderous lorry.

'I said it doesn't seem to have been blitzed. According to Pevsner it was pulled down – ". . . no less than about twenty-five buildings in Westgate Street which were listed as of architectural or historic interest under the Town and Country Planning Act after the Second World War have now been demolished." Isn't that dreadful?'

'Ah. There it is, on the corner. Sorry, Anne, I won't be a minute.'

'I thought,' she said, 'you'd like to know, that's all.' But he was gone now, into the shop. She stood on the pavement, resentfully reading of a two-storeyed eighteenth century house of red brick with stone dressings, and the National Provincial Bank which preserves a section of Roman pavement in the hall. Surely, she thought, flies could be bought anywhere, I've seen flies in Woolworth's come to that.

Over lunch she said, 'I must ring Mrs Barron.' 'Already? We shall have to cut short the cathedral. I hadn't realized it was so late.' 'We spent,' she said, 'rather a long time looking for that shop.' Their eyes met for a moment and she thought: we are irritated with each other, and I don't know what to do about it. She went to find a telephone.

'Any luck?'

'Yes. She said it would be best if I came along about three.'

'What did she seem like?'

'Hard to tell. She was a bit taken aback, I think. I should have written before.'

'I thought you had.'

'No,' she said, 'I didn't.' They sat in silence for a moment. 'David . . .'

'Mmn?'

'Have you ever thought – do you ever think – about what happens after my father dies?'

He looked at her, and quickly away again. 'Oh, but you'll be coming up, won't you, for one thing and another?'

'Will I?'

'Anne,' he said, 'look, if there's one thing I've learned about living it's not to imagine that much if anything can be planned ahead.'

'I wasn't planning. Just wondering.'

'Don't let's,' he said. 'Not today, anyway.' He put out his hand and laid it on her arm for a moment. 'Well now, what about a bit more of Gloucester before your date with Mrs B.?'

Plan? she thought, wandering around the cathedral, no, I've never planned anything much either except children which in fact is one of the most bizarre things one does. Plan another life, when one has so little control over one's own. She looked at David, standing in the rainbow light of a stained-glass window, and thought: You are unplanned, if ever anything was. A year ago you did not exist, and now I step gingerly from one day to the next. A year ago or thereabouts I took father for a jaunt one day to Ludlow and Mrs Barron did not exist either; we drove along Wenlock Edge and he enjoyed the castle and tea in a hotel. There will never, she thought in bitterness, be that again. The east walk of the cloisters, she read, has the earliest fan vaulting known. I have forgotten to give Paul the money for the deposit on the school camping holiday. All my life now I shall see David stand like that, looking at something I cannot see, sunshine on one side of his face.

* * *

Outside Mrs Barron's house he said, 'When should I pick you up, do you think?' 'I don't know. An hour? Less, maybe. Suppose it's awkward. I've got cold feet, suddenly.'

'It'll be all right.' He smiled in sudden intimacy. 'Don't worry. Look, best perhaps if we meet. Outside the cathedral – between half-past four and five?'

'Yes' she said, grateful. 'Yes, that would be better.'

The house was in a street of modest detached houses; quiet, tree-lined, secure. Anne rang the bell and thought with sudden surprise that her father, probably, had done just this, at some point, stood on this well-swept step looking at the panel of opaque glass half-concealing the someone who, on the other side, fiddled with latch and handle.

She was older than Anne had expected – nearer fifty than forty. Carefully dressed, if dully, and with a reserve, a stiffness, about her that seemed not the product of this particular occasion. Anne followed her into a tidy, somehow dispirited sitting-room as she explained that any other day she would have been at work, in the Public Library, but had had the day off to go with her daughter to the hospital that morning. Anne said, 'I hope it's nothing serious?'

'It's for her hay-fever. They give them these injections now. She's got her As coming up, so we're keeping our fingers crossed – it makes her wretched most years. So, as I say, any other day you wouldn't have caught me in.' Covertly, she returned Anne's examining look. 'I'm sorry to hear about your father. I'd been wondering how he was these days. Is it bad?'

Anne told her. Finishing, she said, 'I wondered – I have no idea when you last saw him?'

'Not for some time now. Two or three years. He used to drop in on us once in a while, when he was more active. I'd have liked to go over there – but I didn't like to intrude too much.'

Anne said, 'Look, I think I ought to say – I knew nothing about you, or – or your mother – until just recently. It's come as a bit of a shock.'

Mrs Barron was silent for a moment. When she replied there was a response in her voice that had not been there before. 'Oh, I see. I'd not imagined that. Yes, I can see you'd be taken aback – anyone would.' She looked across at Anne with, now, an awkward friendliness. 'I don't know what to say, really. Except I'm sorry he's so ill. He was always good to me – he helped me out, you know, after my husband left me. He's been very good.'

Anne said, 'What did you call him?'

'Uncle James.'

There was a pause. Mrs Barron said, 'I'd have liked to see him. But if as you say he's not really. . . . Well, there doesn't seem a lot of point.'

'I don't really think there is.'

'Here's Janice. Jan, just come in here a minute.'

The girl stared sullenly at Anne through her mother's explanations. She said 'Hello,' and then at once to her mother, 'I don't see why I should have to help with this school concert. It's always the Lower Sixth gets stuck with it and it's not bloody fair.' She blew her nose into a shredded hank of Kleenex, glaring aggressively at her mother.

'Well, what do you expect me to do?'

'Nothing. But I can't do that and come shopping, can I?'

'Nobody's asking you. And I've told you – don't wear that old skirt. I was ashamed of you in the hospital, looking like that.'

Anne turned to look at the photographs on the mantelpiece. Mrs Barron with a younger Janice; an elderly woman; Janice as a baby. Behind her, mother and daughter wrangled until suddenly Janice said 'Well, you know what I feel, anyway.' She banged out of the room, without another look at Anne.

Mrs Barron said, 'I'd have liked her to go to a private school, but that's been out of the question. She's bright, there's no doubt about that.' She seemed undisturbed by, or unaware of, her daughter's gracelessness. Without apparent interest, she sat while Anne spoke for a few moments of her own children, looking at Jan who stood in the gateway talking to another girl. As Anne paused she said, 'I don't like that Linda, she's not the right type for her.'

Anne said 'Would you mind very much if I asked you a few things – about your mother?'

'I don't see why not. It's a funny situation, isn't it? Wait, though, I'll make us a cup of coffee.' Turning at the door, she said 'You should have brought your husband in – you didn't have to send him off, I wouldn't have minded.'

Returning with a tray of coffee things, she began to talk with less restraint. 'They met, oh, in about nineteen forty it would have been. My father was killed right at the start of the war and mother was working in the Ministry then, where your father was, not the same part but they met on committees or something, and it must all have started then. I was evacuated with the school to Wales, so I didn't see all that much of mother but in the holidays she'd take cottages or whatever, where we could be together, and he used to come then. That's when I first remember him. I was an only, of course, there was just me and mother. It's funny, isn't it, the way things repeat themselves – now it's the same with me and Jan. I sometimes wonder . . .' she broke off for a moment. 'You can get a bit enclosed, but there it is, nobody can do anything about that.' She looked up at Anne. 'My husband went off with someone else when Jan was four.'

'I'm so sorry.'

'Anyway, you don't want to hear about me. I'm not much like mother. Here.' She went over to a desk and brought out a photograph. 'That was taken in the war.'

Not a pretty face, but a memorable one. Dark hair; dark, slightly heavy eyebrows; wide features; an abstracted look that might just have been a response to the camera. Anne put the photograph down and said, 'What did she . . . What was she like? I'm sorry – that's an impossible question for you to answer.'

'She was a nice person, I can tell you that. Everybody liked her – she had lots of friends. She was always busy, she had plenty of interests, she was always involved in this and that. Lively, you know. . . . And a cheerful sort of person – she'd make you laugh, even up to the end when she was so ill she'd make you laugh. She made your father laugh – she used to tease him a bit. Make fun of him – nicely, though, you know.'

Anne said, 'I can't really imagine that. How long ago did she die?'

'Nine years now. I miss her a lot. But there it is. . . . More coffee?'

'Thank you. What did they talk about?'

Mrs Barron stared for a moment. 'Oh, you mean her and your father. Goodness, it's hard to remember now. They were always talking, though, I can tell you that. They'd argue, too – she had strong opinions, mother. Politics, they'd talk about. Pictures and that kind of thing. Music – she loved music, mother, she played the piano very well when she was a girl but she rather let it go later on, and of course your father was keen on music, wasn't he?'

'No,' said Anne, 'I hadn't thought he was. But I seem to be wrong.'

Mrs Barron said, 'It's funny, talking like this brings things back. I can see them now, sitting out in the garden of the house we had in Twickenham, not long after the war, listening to a Prom on the radio. I'd just gone to training college – your father helped me a lot over that too, finding out about courses and things. That's what Jan hasn't got, and the school's not much help, I can tell you.' She stared morosely out of the window for a minute. 'Do you have a job, Mrs Linton.'

'I wish you'd call me Anne. I did teach until recently, and I expect I shall again.'

'My name's Shirley. I keep on at Jan about her As – I daresay I go on at her too much – but she's got to look after herself, it's no good thinking otherwise. They don't realize, do they, at that age?'

'I'm sure she'll be all right – if as you say she's working quite hard.'

'I hope so.'

'When did . . . You say you didn't see my father all that often, recently?'

'No, not really. We always kept in touch, after mother died – he'd ring up, every now and then, or come over for a Sunday. They were always friends, even after – well after they stopped being quite so close. I used to think that was funny, when I was older, a man and a woman staying friends like that. Do you think that's usual?'

Anne said, 'I don't know. I honestly don't know.'

'Well, it seems funny to me. But you can't help feeling kind of envious – no, not envious, admiring it in a way. Mother always had him to turn to, to talk about things to – long after, well, long after there wasn't really anything else. I think that's nice.' She looked sharply at Anne. 'I used to wonder about you sometimes. And your brother.'

'Then you knew . . .'

'Oh, yes, we knew about you. Mother never mentioned it. I think she felt – well, you know – guilty.'

'Yes, I know.'

'But I used to wonder about you. I suppose I was jealous, a bit. I was fond of your father – oh, I suppose you could say I wished he'd been mine, when I was a kid.' She went on, diffidently, 'I hadn't ever realized you didn't know about us. That's a bit hard. And you must feel badly – well, for your mother.'

There was a brief pause, awkward. Anne said 'I don't think, really, you or I having feelings about it now is very sensible – at least feelings on other people's behalf. Yes, I suppose I do. But she never knew, it seems, so that's one thing.'

Shirley Barron said, 'Well, I'm glad of that too.' After a moment she added, 'You can't judge other people, can you? You don't know what goes on.' In the hall, the girl's voice, on the telephone, kept up an almost inaudible monologue. Her mother said, 'I've told her time and again to make her calls in the evening, when it's cheaper. Excuse me a minute.' Beyond the half-open door, they argued in barely-subdued tones· 'It wouldn't take you five minutes to walk round to Hilary's, rather than waste a phone call.' 'I've got my maths to do, haven't I?.' 'There's nothing that couldn't wait till tomorrow.' 'Why shouldn't I talk to my friends – you do.' The small, lacklustre house enclosed them, setting them apart even from the life of the suburban street – small children on bicycles, women with prams and shopping-bags. It was hard to see how the allegedly extrovert, popular woman in that photograph could have produced this uneasy household. Thinking this, trying not to listen to the squabble beyond the door, bland clichés came into Anne's head: someone has to suffer, you can't make an omelette without breaking eggs. When Shirley Barron came back she said quickly, 'I mustn't take up too much of your day. And I do hope, really, that you didn't mind my coming.'

'I didn't mind. I won't say I'm not surprised – but I don't mind. There's never been anyone much I could talk about things to – she wouldn't be interested' – jerking her head towards the door – 'my husband couldn't have cared less. Mother never liked him, she always said at the time I was making a mistake. I was very young, of course, nineteen. I'm afraid sometimes she'll do the same thing – Jan – trying to show me, you know, that she's grown-up and doesn't need me.'

Anne said, embarrassed, 'I'm sure you don't need to feel that things repeat themselves quite so much.'

'Well, let's hope not.'

'How much time did they have together?'

'Mother and Uncle James? Not a lot, really, when you add it up –

over the ten years or so – just an odd night now and then that he could manage. Sometimes I suppose she didn't see him for a month or two. But I've told you, she wouldn't sit around moaning, she wasn't that type. Mind, it's funny she didn't ever marry again but I suppose in a way she didn't want to. She could have. But I think it wasn't because of him, your father. She could manage on her own and she liked it best like that.'

Anne said, 'What was her name?'

'Mother's? How odd – you not knowing. But you wouldn't, of course, would you? Mansell. Betty Mansell.'

They are all, Anne thought, either dead or beyond remembering what happened. Mother. Mrs Mansell. Father. But because of them we sit here, two people otherwise unconnected, talking about something that is only our affair at one remove, and yet, somehow, matters very much to us both. She felt suddenly dejected. Shirley Barron was scrubbing with her handkerchief at a cup-ring on the polished top of the table, talking again about her daughter; the clock on the mantelpiece chimed for half-past three; a gust of rain scudded against the window. Anne explained that she had to go, and they walked together to the door.

'I'm glad we've met,' said Shirley Barron. 'And – well, if he can take it in at all, give him my love. And look, tell his bank not to send that money any more. He's done quite enough for me and there's better uses it could be put to.'

Anne began, 'I'm sure he . . .'

'I'd rather. Please. And I would like to hear how he goes on – if, if you wouldn't mind.'

'Of course I'll let you know.'

Walking away down the street, Anne realised that she had no idea in which direction to go. Coming, she had been too preoccupied to pay attention to the place. Now, she wandered for a few minutes aimlessly from road to road until the cathedral reared suddenly beyond a break in the houses, and she was able to navigate her way towards it. Cloud filled the sky, a leaden backdrop to the wild green of trees and the cathedral's flaming stone; she felt quenched still by Shirley Barron's lifeless home. Reaching the cathedral square, she saw David standing at the porch, and for a moment the sight of him evoked no feeling, as though he were a stranger among others.

Ten

Judy sat impassive in the car. Once, she said 'I'm missing French and P.E. and two Englishes and two Maths.'

'It doesn't matter.'

'I know. Are we nearly there?'

Anne said, 'Getting on. Shall we have a break? Would you like some squash?' They pulled off the road and sat on a verge exuberant with flowers. 'Look,' she said. 'Look at all these – red campion and stitchwort and meadow crane's-bill and this little yellow thing – what's it called, Judy? Do you remember that time in the Lakes, when you were about eight or nine? You were mad about wild flowers, we collected everything and you used to look them up and make lists.'

'Did I? I've forgotten.'

'Have you honestly? You used to get cross with me because I couldn't remember the names of things. You must remember that?'

'I suppose so,' said Judy, 'sort of.' She stared at the flowers. 'Can I go youth hostelling next year, with Mary and the others, on bikes?'

Going into the nursing-home Anne said, 'I'm afraid grandfather may not know who you are – you mustn't mind about that. Or about how he looks. He isn't like he used to be.' And as they went into her father's room she saw the sudden shock on the girl's face and felt compunction at having brought her. But it was right, she thought, she should see him once more, and you cannot pretend that things are other than what they are, to children, that is wrong. And it might, too mean something to him. She said to the old man, 'Here's Judy, father – you know who Judy is. Your granddaughter.'

The old man turned his head and saw a woman with a girl coming towards him. He was worried about the girl. She was not his responsibility, and yet she was. She was not his doing, but it seemed to him that her situation might well be his doing. He said to the woman, in silence, with querying glance: trouble? And Betty with nod and quick grimace said: Yes, ructions again. 'Tell you what,' he said to the girl, 'why don't we have a jaunt together, you and I? Your mother won't mind if we abandon her for once. How about an afternoon at the coast?' And the girl glowed at him, her resentments dispelled, so that he thought: poor thing, it's not easy for her, not easy for any of us, all one can do is see the least harm's done that need be. Down at the coast, in a streaming spring wind, he swam with the girl, and after, in a smoky cafe, watched her tuck into a plateful of food and chatter, for once, he thought, like any child. Like, for instance, his Anne. I'm sorry, he wanted to say to her, I'm sorry for that part of it which is my fault – if there was anything more I could do, I would. Instead, he talked to her about the school she resented and the friend who had gone off with someone else and (obliquely) the mother she could not manage to be like. All right, he said, I'll have a word with your mum, see if you couldn't give up Latin and concentrate on science, you're better at that, aren't you? And in the evening they drove home, the girl sleepy and content, and he projecting forwards, so that already he was with Betty, first chance in weeks, delighting in her.

* * *

Judy said, 'He didn't know who I was, did he?'

'I'm afraid not. I think actually he was mixing you up with someone he knew a long time ago. That happens to old people, sometimes. It's easier to remember long ago than recent things.'

'I wish he wasn't ill. I liked grandfather.' There were tears in her eyes.

'Oh, darling. . . . Look, don't feel like that, he's not unhappy in himself, you know.'

'Isn't he? Are you sure?'

No, Anne thought, I am not at all sure, I am just saying that, like the matron and nurses offer bland and tempting reassurances. She got into the car, against that backdrop of rook and lawn mower that, like the sound of the river at Starbridge, seemed more real now in savoured recollection than when heard again. She wound the window up, clipping off the noise, and sat staring at the mutely planing birds. Judy said, 'Why are you biting your lip like that? You're always doing that lately, you've made a red mark. Where are we going now?'

'To Starbridge. Oh, and I forgot to tell you – there's someone coming in probably who used to be a friend of grandfather's. A Mr Fielding. He comes out to fish – he's got grandfather's rod. I daresay he'll have his son with him – Tom's a bit older than you.'

* * *

They walked down towards the river, flanked by their children. To five of David's questions – or proffered starting-points for conversation – Judy had said 'No,' and to two 'Yes.' Now, they were silent, except for Tom, who whistled, tunelessly, demonstrating knowledge and efficiency and, perhaps, comradeship with his father. Judy sat pulling buttercups to pieces. 'Here,' said David, 'we've got knot trouble – whoa a minute.' He stood with his head close against his son's, bent over the line, and Anne, a smile locked on her face, turned away and hunted the surface of the water for a rise. Or dippers. Or reflections.

'Wouldn't you like a go?' said Tom (a thoughtful boy – or patronizing, just a bit?) and she said, 'Yes, please – but I'm hopeless, I always was.' Standing in the cold river, ineffectually casting, she felt his silent contempt (or amusement?) and thought irritably: could your mother do any better, I wonder, or would she even try? And then she felt ashamed.

'Judy,' she called, 'your turn now. Remember how grandfather used to teach you?'

But Judy, scowling on the bank, shook her head, rubbing her leg.

'What's the matter?'

'I've got a horsefly bite. Are we going in soon?'

'Presently. Judy, you might just try to be a bit more forthcoming. Please.'

'It *hurts*. It'll probably go septic.'

Anne moved further down the bank and sat watching mist smoke up from the fields on the far side. On the river, the line hissed forward, drifted back with the current, hissed out again. She slapped midges on her ankles, thought of Graham, who had phoned and sounded depressed, watched Tom and David and noted with sad disquiet the way in which their hair grew identically at the back, making a ducktail that lay thickly on their sweaters. 'Hey, Dad' called Tom, 'there's something rising further up – see?' Moving like a spaceman in his waders, David crunched past her on the river bed, not looking her way, and vanished round a bend. Out of sight, from time to time, she heard his voice, and Tom's. The mist thickened; it got cold; ten yards away Judy sat morosely.

She got up and walked down the river towards them. 'Would some coffee be nice?' she said. 'Back at the house? It's getting a bit chilly.'

David said, 'Oh, d'you want to go in? Right you are. Tom – pack up now. We're going in.'

The boy, turning, began to say something and swung sharply back as David called out, 'There! You've got a bite!' The fish flipped the water and he struck too late, the empty hook flying back to catch in an overhanging alder. Angrily, he tugged it free and clambered up the bank to them. David said, 'Bad luck, Tommie.' 'That's the nearest I've ever been to getting one. What was it you were shouting about?'

'The ladies are getting a bit chill.'

'I'm sorry,' said Anne, 'I didn't mean . . .'

Tom said, 'It's all right. It doesn't matter.'

'Look, do let's stay out a bit longer.'

'No, honestly,' he said, 'I don't mind. Could you just hold the rod a minute, Dad.'

As they walked up the field Tom said, 'Can we come out tomorrow?' 'Yes,' said David. 'Yes, of course.'

Back in the house, getting coffee, Anne said, 'What's the matter, Judy?'

'I don't feel very well.'

She was hot and flushed, her leg, around the bite, swollen and throbbing. Anne hunted for a thermometer and took her temperature;

it was over a hundred. She saw her up to bed while David and Tom drank coffee in silence. When she came back David said, 'Best if we leave you in peace, really, I think.'

Tom, at the door, said 'Thank you very much for lending us the rod, Mrs Linton. It's very kind of you. It's a much better one than ours.'

'I'm sure my father would like to know someone's getting some fun out of it.'

'Yes,' said David. 'Well, I hope she'll be all right . . .'

'I'm sure she will.'

'Did she get a chill, do you think?'

'I don't think so. She's a bit allergic to insect bites. I'll get her to our doctor tomorrow.'

'Well, let me know how she is, anyway. Goodnight.'

'Goodnight.'

* * *

The road led back to Cuxing in known and tedious lengths. Judy said 'It's good I feel all right again because I'm riding with Susie tomorrow. Why are you driving so fast, Mum?'

* * *

There was a heat-wave. Anne moved through leaden days, agreeing with everyone on the perfection of the weather. Sun umbrellas and reclining chairs bloomed in the gardens of Cuxing; the climbing rose came out and flamed up the side of the house; Paul and Judy flopped in and out of the kitchen, drinking squash by the pint. The days were forty-eight hours long, from bird-shrieking dawns to weary clock-ticking midnights. In normal summers, around now, one was waiting for the summer holidays – anticipating, planning – and beyond that loomed, pleasantly enough, in the natural progression of things, the autumn, which is more appropriately the beginning of the cycle than the end.

This year, not so.

The trouble with the past is that it is also time transformed. There are days, in which we move around, but in them are we also moved, and moved sometimes so far from our established selves that there is no going back. The days are gone, but are never to be emptied. And neither am I, thought Anne, not ever, now. There is no going back to June of last year when I was thirty-nine, innocent, and, I believe, happy. This is the process called experience, by which it is made certain that we have about as much stability as an amoeba. We complete, we think, an opinion, an attitude, a response – only to find it blown apart by the casual and random activities of time. Of a minute, of an hour, or a day, that, apparently, shatters the calm reflection and reassembles it differently. My garden was much the same last year – give or take a few inches of growth, the odd flower – but now, looking at it, those shapes and colours repeating last year's are invested with the images of the months between. Superimposed on the impervious lawn is my father in the clutch of his hospital pillows; David's face stares from the unsympathetic leaves of the chestnut.

Don said, 'There's a letter from the Scottish hotel people confirming the reservation. And a card for you.' He turned it over. 'Doctor Johnson's birthplace.'

'Oh, is there.'

I wonder if you could give me a ring sometime, it said, I noticed a window broken at your father's house and thought maybe I could do something about it. 57698 will find me, it went on, yours David F.

'Something wrong?' said Don.

'Oh no. It's just this schoolmaster who was a neighbour of father's – he wants me to give him a ring, something about a window broken at the house. It's nothing.'

'I'll be a bit late in tonight.'

'Will you?' she said. 'What would you like for dinner? Anything special?'

'Not particularly.'

'A steak – that would be a treat.'

'Whatever you like, Annie.'

'I'll get a steak.'

* * *

David said, 'I'm sorry about that, but I was feeling a bit low, after that rather unsatisfactory evening. How's Judy?' 'She's fine. Quite all right next day. It was unsatisfactory, wasn't it?' 'When will I see you?' 'Next week. Tuesday. Tuesday evening.'

* * *

On the A46 dual carriage-way (Warwick and Kenilworth passed a few minutes ago, lurking off-stage to right and left) the car coughed explosively and the engine died. She steered onto the side and opened the bonnet, staring into it as the landscape suddenly halted and the traffic fizzed by. Lichfield became not fifty minutes away but thirty-odd miles; the car no longer an obliging certainty but an insoluble problem. When a man in a van drew up behind her she accepted gratefully his offer of help. He would stop off, he said, at the garage down the road and ask someone to come along. She sat on the road's embankment in the sunshine, wondering how long all this would take. When at last the breakdown truck arrived the mechanic glanced into the engine and said the coil had gone. He could, he said, have it done by five or so. It was now almost twelve o'clock. He towed the car to a garage in a featureless suburb while Anne debated what to do. Bus to Lichfield, and return that evening, with David? Wait in this dispiriting place? But buses to Lichfield did not offer themselves. Now if it was Coventry, said the mechanic helpfully, the Coventry buses run every half hour, and she thought: Yes, why not? There's the cathedral, and I've not been there since that time with father, years ago. I can spend four hours in Coventry, easily enough, and come back here for five o'clock.

It was nineteen sixty-three, she seemed to remember Christmas. Her mother had stayed at Starbridge, to look after Paul, aged two, and Judy, just a few months old. And she didn't, Anne thought, want to go anyway and I did; the arrangement suited everyone – she evaded an afternoon of sight-seeing, and I achieved one. And it was a good day, somehow it sticks in the mind still – set apart from the rest of that time. I didn't mind father disagreeing about the cathedral, I enjoyed arguing, I hadn't anyone to argue with, Don never would . . .

There had been Graham (bored, not managing to conceal his impatience to be back to London and real life – he'd just got his first full-scale producer's job and was restless with ambition), herself, Don (also, perhaps, bored) and her father. It had been her father's idea. Time, he said, we took a look at this creation of Spence's, not that it's going to be my cup of tea, I imagine. Coming from the car park through and out of the new shopping precinct (where, now, Anne walked past fountains palmy with trees and shrubs where then there had been rubbish-littered earth) he had said; Look at it, now! A monstrosity! Might as well be a cinema, those great bare walls, nothing spiritual about that, just a barn, plonked down there. And what a juxtaposition – with the ruins of the old one alongside. Can't the man see how it shows him up?

But that's just the point, father, she'd said, walking beside him up the steps (up which, now, she climbed, among flocks of tourists), the point is to preserve the past and add to it – respect it but at the same time contribute something of our own. And I don't agree with you – I think it's handsome. The stone's lovely. And it's the bulk that's impressive. Of course it's not like cathedrals as we're used to them – but what would be the point of mindless architectural reproduction? We've got gothic cathedrals already. This is meant to be different.

It's different all right, he'd grumbled, going into the porch and turning right under the great engraved glass screen (to which Anne, now, turned back for a moment, thinking: yes, that's fine still, I like that), but look at this, Anne – no nave to speak of, no aisles, just pillars that might as well not be there. And what's that thing at the end, may one ask? That's the Sutherland tapestry, father, she'd said, don't rush things, we'll get to that in a minute. Now you must admit there's a marvellous feeling of light and space. And the choir stalls are splendid, like a flight of birds.

And where in all this had Don and Graham been, she wondered now, pausing in front of the baptistry window, before that boulder from Bethlehem. Were the colours perhaps rather harsh? And, as she considered this, nineteen sixty-three swam back once more with Don standing at her side and her father turning to him to say: well then, Don, what do you feel about this? Anne's pro and I'm against, on the whole, though I'd agree there's a slight case to be made out for the stone itself, but how's that for a stained glass window? Where's the imagery in that? Stained glass tells a story, as far as I'm concerned. Take Canterbury.

It's abstract, father, she'd said in irritation. It's a development of a tradition, not just doing the same old thing again. It's not trying to imitate Canterbury, or anywhere else for that matter.

And turning away from the window now (yes, the colours do seem violent) to walk on down the aisle, she searched for Don's reply. What had he felt? What had he said? But there was only her father, ahead of her now, studying the tapestry with an expression of distaste, and saying he thought it garish. And it's fussy, he said, all those creatures in little boxes, and why's the figure squatting in that awkward way? and what are his hands like that for?

It's Christ in majesty, father. I think it's very impressive.

Not much majesty there as far as I'm concerned.

Turn round and look back, father. It's from here you see the windows – that's the whole point of the building – as you turn back from the altar you see them, because they're zigzag in the walls. Isn't that tremendous?

And still is, she thought now, turning with the length of the cathedral before her. Suddenly you see where the light comes from – the walls stop being solid. And in remembrance there was Graham, hands stuck in the pockets of an expensive-looking suit, staring up at a column of greens and blues, and she went to stand by him, saying: aren't they marvellous, the windows? Mmn, he'd said, spectacular – his thoughts elsewhere, she could see, just as all that Christmas they'd been for the most part elsewhere, tolerating the domesticity of it all, bored with the babies and all the fuss they engendered, teasing her from time to time, patronising Don, raring to be off back to London first thing on the twenty-seventh.

I don't know, she thought, it all seems different, not at all how I remembered. I do like the glass – but the rest, well, I can't think how I ever approved of the tapestry, it seems hideous now, and the furnishings have dated so. Very Festival of Britain. The choir stalls look like something from Heals – all that brass and teak. And yes, I see father's point – it does seem barn-like. No surprises. It doesn't unfold, as a cathedral should. It's funny, it seems quite different – this isn't what I remember at all.

She came out and over into the ruins of the old cathedral. It was a hot afternoon. She sat on a bench (where she was joined by three Indian teenagers with Birmingham accents that sounded generations deep) and watched a sparrow ferry food to its young in a nest high in the broken tracery of a perpendicular window. But of course, she thought, it's not the cathedral that has changed. Places don't change, except willy-nilly through time – or destruction, like this one. It's me that must have changed, and if the cathedral seems to be not what I remember, then it is the remembering that has gone wrong, not the cathedral. The cathedral is as it was in nineteen sixty-three but I am not, and somewhere along the way I appear to have lost my taste for it. She listened to the teenagers talking of a football team, O-levels, and the whereabouts of the station. The sparrows lifted their cargo of scraps, tirelessly, to the shattered windows. On a nearby bench two women dumped themselves down, hung about with carrier bags – Marks & Spencer, Boots, Mac Fisheries. The teenagers had turned on a transistor that muttered the commentary to a cricket match. Anne thought of her father, of her children, of David.

Presently she went into the cathedral again and bought some postcards, then wandered slowly back through the shopping precinct to the bus station. By half-past four she was back at the garage; by eight, on her bed at Starbridge, David deep within her.

* * *

'In fact,' he said, 'I could stay. The boys are away tonight and – I said I might be out.'

To Mary. I have only twice, Anne thought, heard him say her name. 'Good,' she said, 'that's lovely. What a nice surprise.'

She woke alone in bed and lay for a moment in fear, hearing a car stop and start outside. 'David. . .' she called, and when his voice answered from the bathroom, felt a flood of relief. 'What are you doing? I heard a car – I thought you'd gone.' 'No, just shaving. That was someone in the lane. Shall I make coffee?'

'No,' she said, 'come back. It's not coffee I want. Not just yet.'

* * *

'I brought you a postcard, father, of Coventry Cathedral. Do you remember going there one Christmas? I was there yesterday and it made me think of it, and how you didn't much care for it. I didn't like it so much this time, I must say.'

The hand that has been holding the cup of tea to his lips (not sweet enough, but there is no way of telling them) comes up now with a small bright rectangle of card which is put into his hand. They are talking about cathedrals. He brings the bright card closer to his eyes and now the colours sort themselves out into a pink block, and some trees. A cinema? A school? Anne, about whom he is concerned from time to time, talks of stained glass, and a tapestry, and suddenly the concern and the picture in his hands are fused and he knows where he is, walking beside her up the steps of this disagreeable building, with a sideways glance to see if that glum fellow, his son-in-law, is still with them or has chickened out of the visit.

Something has happened to Anne. The spark has gone out of her, this last year or so. The children could account for some of that, of course, but all the same. . . . She hasn't even had a good spat with her brother, this Christmas. She has allowed a number of blatantly provocative statements of his to go unchallenged. And Graham is provocative all right, as he always has been, but more so now perhaps brandishing his seedy career – though there is admittedly a chance that one could be wrong about that, not everything on the box is meretricious, after all, but one could have wished otherwise for him, all the same. He can look after himself, though, Graham, and no doubt will. Anne is another matter. Let us see, her father says to himself, if we can't stir up a bit of the old spark. And as they go into the cathedral he offers his opinion of the place. And the bait is taken, so it seems the old and vigorous Anne lurks not too far away, hibernating, perhaps, till times are better. But will times be better? Well, Don, he says to her husband, what do you think of it? But Don has no opinion, it seems. He is glancing surreptitiously at his watch, and has toured Chapel of Unity, engraved glass screen and now the Baptistry with just the same amount of time and study allotted to each. Well, Don says, I suppose you have a point about the colours being a bit strong, but it all seems quite pleasant to me. That won't do, thinks James Stanway, that won't do at all. And he walks away down the nave (or what passes for such) wondering how all this has come about, and what it might lead to. He tries to remember the name of that chap she used to bring home when she was an undergraduate – dark, garrulous young man. Why didn't she marry him? Anne is a talker, and not just a talker of nothings, and a thinker, he suspects, too – a lot more so than her brother, in fact – and old Don is as silent as the grave. You can always talk to yourself, of course. But it is better not to. It is a great deal better not to. Oh, Anne, he thinks, I could tell you a thing or two. But I can't. There isn't, unfortunately, much to be done at all.

Well, he says to the assembled party, moving again under the engraved glass screen, how about a cup of coffee somewhere? I daresay this new shopping precinct will run to a Lyons or whatever.

* * *

Graham picked the postcard up off the mat, along with something from the income tax and a brown envelope from Charing Cross hospital, and took all three into his kitchen. He read it while waiting for the coffee to percolate: Anne had broken down here while *en route* for Lichfield and spent an hour or so looking round. Remember one Christmas, she said, ages ago? 'Here,' it appeared, as he turned the card over, was Coventry Cathedral, St Michael pinned like a butterfly to its rearing wall.

I do remember, he thought, quite well, funnily enough. Early sixties, just after I got the job with Thames. The Fanny time. And as he stands with the card in his hand (the coffee percolating away now, unobserved) he returns to Coventry and Fanny's face floats for a moment, as it floated then, in the greens and blues of some great high window. Oh God, he thinks, I want her, I really do. I can't wait till next week – how am I supposed to get through three more bloody days, festering away here? Annie is on about the glass or something, and he jerks himself from Fanny's face and walks with his sister down the cathedral, thinking: but it's different this time, she's a different kind of girl, Fanny, she's not someone you mess about with.

She could walk out on me, he thinks, in cold fear. She's not the kind of girl to stand any nonsense. Perhaps that's why I want her so.

And, walking with the others across a square and into some fearful futuristic shopping place, he thinks: I could ask her to marry me.

Sitting over the buns and coffee, he looks at his sister and thinks that marriage has knocked the stuffing out of Anne, a bit. That, or the kids. You don't, of course, he reflects sagely, have to have kids, and he'd damn well see to it they didn't. And why Annie had to pick old Don, he'd never know. You wouldn't think, really, they had two words to say to each other, but maybe that doesn't matter too much. Would Fanny marry me? I don't know, he thinks wretchedly, and wonders if he dare find out. He imagines Fanny, her lovely face turned towards him on the pillow, saying kindly: no, Graham, I'm awfully sorry, but no thanks. And knows he could not really stand that. And he imagines them married, living in some two-up, two-down in Notting Hill, fettered to one another and with maybe some damn baby yelling its head off upstairs (because as observation shows that kind of thing is not quite as controllable as is made out), and wonders if he could stand that either. . . . Oh, Fanny . . . he thinks, spooning sugar into his cup, and looks across the table at Anne and his father arguing away still about the pros and cons of the cathedral.

Graham stuck the card on the kitchen shelf and took the coffee off the stove. He opened the envelope from Charing Cross hospital and read that an appointment had been arranged for him on July 18th. Would he follow carefully the enclosed instructions and attend the Out Patients Clinic at 9.30 a.m. The telephone rang (second time already that morning – first his assistant to say that the actress they wanted for the new play was holding out for half as much again as he could offer, and now the studio to announce an impending strike of scene-shifters; his stomach began to grind and would grind, now, on and off all day). He poured himself a cup of coffee, went with it to the window, and stood there thinking of Anne, of her children (a nice boy, Paul, and the girl would be pretty, given a year or two) and of his father. I'll get up to Lichfield this weekend, he thought.

* * *

'You saw her at her worst, I'm afraid,' Anne said to David. 'She really isn't like that. She's . . . oh, it's so difficult to explain one's own children.'

'Adolescence is not the most engaging period.'

I know that, she thought with a small flare of irritation. You don't have to tell me. And come to that I thought Tom . . . 'I wish you'd seen her a couple of years ago – she was such fun. So interested in everything, always chattering on. And of course this is just a phase. Surely you must have had problems with Tom?'

'Oh, on and off,' said David. 'Mind you, girl children are rather alien territory to me, not having gone in for them either professionally or privately. What did you do in Coventry?'

'I looked at the cathedral. Of course.'

'Of course,' he said, 'catch you missing out on a cathedral.' And as he put his hand on her arm, smiling, Judy and Tom were quietly relegated, or so it seemed, and the present re-asserted itself with immediate problems of where to park the car and what to do.

They had gone to Tamworth. 'We haven't quite exhausted the possibilities of the area,' David said. 'But it could happen, before too long.'

'We don't always have to go somewhere. I should have made you help me with the sorting out at Starbridge. There's still an awful lot to do.'

'Oh, come now,' he said. 'It's July. It's the summer. We're entitled to a holiday. We shall have lunch and take an intelligent interest in the history of Tamworth.'

His school term had finished the day before. The year, suddenly, was at one of its natural watersheds. From the parapets of Tamworth Castle the landscape wheeled around them in a circle of fields already bleaching and hedges darkened into the heavy greens of high summer. The grasses on the verges had flowered; the trees began to stoop; the summer was over that point when growth passes into decline.

David said, 'Well, the holidays loom. You go to Scotland on the twenty-third?'

'That's right.' And you to Wales for a week's walking with your friend Jim Hilton whom I do not know (as I know none of your friends, nor you mine). And with your sons.

'I must say I'm rather looking forward to Wales. We've got a route planned out and it looks like some fairly spectacular countryside. And then the boys thought they'd like to do some of the castles.'

'Oh, are you,' she said, 'Good.' I can't say the same of Scotland.

Silence hung for a moment. 'What does Mary do?'

'She goes to see her mother,' David said, 'in London. And she's got an old school friend down in Kent I expect she'll call in on for a day or two.'

Ah. It can't be asked, of course, at what point holidays ceased to be shared, or what Jim Hilton thinks of Mary (or any other of your friends). Or what she looks like or what you call her or if, and if so, how often, you make love to her or any of the things that would bring instantly that shuttered look I have become more than a little afraid of. I am excluded, as I have to exclude you.

David said, 'What's the nursing-home saying, if anything, about your father?'

She told him. The matron had come in that morning, while she was there, and explained that the doctor considered that he had deteriorated, though he did not seem in any way changed to Anne, drifting from moments of near-lucidity to states of semi-coma. His heart was weaker, it seemed. He must, the matron said, be very robust. She implied, gently, that most people in his condition would not have survived that long; that there could not be long to go. As she spoke the old man had suddenly turned towards them, staring, and said something about coffee. 'Four of us there are' he said, looking towards the matron. 'Coffee ıor four, we'll want.' And the matron had smiled and said to Anne, 'He's not quite with us, this morning, is he?'. And then to her patient, 'That's tea you've just had, Mr Stanway. Would you like another cup?' But he had gone again, his fingers creeping to and fro on the sheet in front of him, his eyes closed.

They spent a muted afternoon at Tamworth, as though affected by the apathy of the landscape. Anne had a slight headache; David seemed to her unresponsive. They went early back to Starbridge and found, then, that they would not meet again until after both their holidays.

'But I'd thought you'd be up again next week.'

'I did say, actually, David. You must have forgotten. Judy's got this friend staying – I can't very well leave them on their own. I didn't realize you had to go back now – I thought you were staying this evening.'

'I'm sorry, Anne. I promised the boys I'd take them in to Birmingham. I didn't realise then that you'd be here.' Kissing her, he said, 'I'm going to miss you dreadfully.'

'Have a lovely walk in Wales.'

She got up at six and drove down to Cuxing in the early morning, through alternating bands of sunshine and sombre clouded skies. Judy, when she arrived, announced with grim satisfaction ('Sandra Butterfield's in an absolute stew, rushing round ringing everyone up, she even got hold of Dad last night when she found you weren't here . . .') that Splatt's Cottage had been razed to the ground during the night. In the afternoon Anne walked down the lane to see, and found a bulldozer pottering about around a mound of plaster, lathes and bricks, far larger, it seemed, than the cottage itself had been. Splintered timbers, riddled with rot and woodworm stuck up from the rubble of shattered brick and chunks of plaster. It was as though, in its destruction, the cottage revealed the secrets of its infirmity and gained, somehow, in sheer bulk. There was an awful mess. It would take days to clear it away before the site could be prepared for building. The bulldozer picked at the foothills of the rubbish, shovelling away into the maw of a waiting lorry. Anne stood watching for a few minutes, and saw half a china sink, a smashed door, a load of roof timbers, go crashing down into the lorry. A mini was parked on the grass verge by the field. By the gate, a rose-bush had come into bloom, the flowers powdered over with dust. There was an estate agent's sign at the roadside, advertising the freehold sale of five bungalows, a select private development. At one end of the rubble mountain, a section of undestroyed walling leaned against a heap of thatch, its structure of timber, lath and plaster shown in section as though in a museum example of country crafts. Anne picked her way round to examine it while the bulldozer driver took the vehicle into the lane and switched off the engine, evidently packing up for the day. She pulled at the longest piece of timber, and the whole wall lifted towards her with surprising lightness. Plaster fell from it, showing the skeletal framework of laths, from the cracks of which trickled husks of corn. The bulldozer driver, appearing suddenly a few yards away said, 'Some nice bits of timber there – help yourself if you're looking for a bit of kindling.'

'I was just seeing how it was made. It seems to have been infested with mice.' She pointed to the corn husks.

The man laughed. 'I daresay. But that's insulation – not mice. They packed those old walls, see, to keep the heat in. Anything that was handy – peapods, straw. Chicken bones, I've seen once, in another place like this.'

Anne said 'Oh, I see.' She felt slightly foolish. The driver turned away saying, 'Mind yourself on that broken glass.'

She pulled some nails out of the timbers and put them in her pocket. Fifteenth century nails, possibly? They looked, on the other hand, extremely modern. The bulldozer driver had got into the mini and driven away, leaving the bulldozer crouched beside what remained of Splatt's Cottage. As Anne walked up the lane she turned once to look back and saw its yellow bulk blazing in the sun. She was surprised to find that she felt really quite unemotional about the whole thing. It was bound to happen, she thought. Stopping it was never really possible at all though of course they were perfectly right to try and I have probably been half-hearted about it, which was wrong. The bulldozer's claw had cast a long toothed shadow across the rubble, like some prehistoric monster. Perched on top, she now saw, and flashing in the sun, was one of those glass lampshades that had been in an upstairs bedroom. It really did make an amazingly large mound of rubbish, for one small cottage. But, trying to remember the structure of the place, she found that, irritatingly, she no longer could, although it was only a couple of months since she had been inside it. Had there been two bedrooms, or three? Doors at back and front, or only the front? One should have drawn a plan of it, she thought, or taken a photograph. One should at least have recorded it in some way before it went.

Eleven

In Scotland, the distances on the sign-posts were always in double figures: Inverness 31, Fort William 48, Edinburgh 70. Nowhere was ever close by. In some brown and purple glen, one road leading in and the same one out, a place tethered to the real world only by the string of telegraph poles marching away to the horizon, Don said, 'Well, what's the plan? Do we head north, or west?'

In the normal way of things, Anne thought, it is I who would have taken charge of all this, said today we do this or that and then wouldn't it be nice to go there, and I've always wanted to have a look at those. Instead of which I sit here like a zombie with things moving past me at either side, hills and rivers and villages and snatches of dramatic scenery which have very little impact. Anyone else but Don would wonder why, I should think. Anyone else might feel a little peeved at driving around a wife and daughter both locked in silence.

She said to Judy, 'You're very quiet. Don't you think this is lovely? Look at the colour of the heather up there.' And Judy, hunched in her corner of the back seat, nods and glowers for a moment at Glen something, and returns to her own impenetrable preoccupations.

'What are you thinking about?'

'Nothing'.

The Welsh hills are gentler than these, of course. Somewhere among them, a cheerful male party, two young, two middle-aged, is picking its way from one bit to another by ordnance survey map and consensus of opinion. Who is saying what to whom? What do they see? Is the wind, down there, cool on the face as it is here, with a faint damp brush of mist, and a smell of peat? Ahead, for them, is the prospect of some pub with beer and chat (of what?), and later in the week a look at the odd castle.

'Why don't we,' she said to Don, 'find something other than scenery to look at? You can have too much of it.'

'Scotland doesn't go in so much for stately homes.'

But the A.A. book's helpful appendix on *What To See* has suggestions to make. 'That'll do. I've never seen a broch. It says those are the best preserved, except the one in Shetland. Let's go and see them.'

The journey to the brochs took hours (or possibly, in this time-suspended state, days); hours of driving or being driven through mile after mile of landscape apparently primeval in its arrangement of scree and moorland, punctuated by the startling intrusions of petrol station or caravan site. Sometimes, in a procession of slow-moving holiday traffic a slice of loch or mountainside would hang cinematically beyond the interiors of cars – shirt-sleeved drivers, clambering children, thermoses, coats and cushions – as though devised simply as a backdrop for the more compelling affairs of travellers. Waiting in the queue for a ferry, Anne stared apathetically through the window of the car to where, a few yards away, sheep slumped on the edge of the tarmac and wild flowers grew as though in a rockery up the brilliant slope of a hill. Shut off by the glass, they had the clinical interest of a nature film. It would have been too much trouble to open the car door, get out, and inspect them. But for the observer, studying them through the glass, they had the therapeutic quality of the scene beyond the window to an invalid; interesting but undemanding. The wild flowers were visited by quantities of very small bees; the sheep had undecipherable tattooings in deep russet; the pink rocks were marbled with a grey lichen as long and webbed as seaweed. This is really quite all right, she thought, sitting here thinking of nothing at all; so long as this goes on there is no problem, absolutely none.

The brochs, when reached, were like dour stunted industrial chimneys (or cooling towers, presiding over a reach of the A446, just after the Brownhills roundabout, on the road to Lichfield. . . .) 'This is the objective, is it?' said Don. 'Do we have a guide-book or something?' But no guide-book is offered by this silent valley, locked between sea and sky and mountain. No explanations are to be had (for Anne cannot remember, now, anything about brochs – when, or who, or why) from the spread of heather on which they park the car (gingerly, for fear of getting stuck) or the pine trees grouped beyond the brochs or the large black bird circling above (which may or may not be a raven). The brochs must be inspected without guidance; anyone's guess is as good as anyone else's. Judy, sitting on a rock a hundred yards away, reading the book she bought in Oban, has no guess. Anne has one or two, but does not make them. Don supposes they must be medieval or possibly earlier. He returns to the car to prop up the bonnet and cool the engine; the hills have been steep.

From the top of the broch you could see right down the valley to the sea. Which, Anne thought, is of course why they are where they are. She stood for a moment, looking down, slightly dizzy, and saw Judy, foreshortened, turn over the page of her book. Don, hands in pockets, looked up and called, 'Be careful.' 'Yes,' she said, 'I'm being careful.' He watched her come down and met her at the bottom. 'All right?' he said.

'Yes. Fine.'

'Rather a nice spot.'

'Yes, lovely.'

'Anne?' he said.

'Mmn. . .'

'There's something I've been wanting to talk about.'

You can see down the valley from the foot of the broch also, and to the sea, a grey-blue curve between the purple mountain flanks. A very nice spot, yes. Except that the mountains, hitherto such tranquil presences, give a disconcerting lurch. And there is a cloud that seems to threaten rain.

'Yes?'

'If this is a good moment.'

'Oh, I think this is as good a moment as any.'

'You've been a bit detached these last few days.'

'Yes,' she said. 'I'm afraid I have. I'm sorry, Don, you see I . . .'

'Did you give the nursing-home a ring last night?'

'No,' she said. 'I thought I'd leave it till tomorrow, I thought it might be . . .'

'This summer,' said Don, 'has been a bit of a strain, hasn't it?'

Don, of course, is not given to emotion. The remark is made in as cool and level a tone as he might, not to promote undue alarm or anxiety, point out that the neighbouring house is on fire, or that war appears to be imminent. It might mean anything, or nothing. The distant mountain quivers still, and one feels out of breath, which might of course be because the climb up to the top of the broch was moderately energetic.

'A bit.'

'Things just have to take their course, you know, Annie.'

And that, she thought, is what my shrinking stomach supposes that they are doing. Several courses, for several different things. And all of a sudden, staring distractedly at a clump of bee-hung heather, she remembered her seeds planted down at Starbridge, in her father's garden – 'flowering period July–Aug.' – and pictured love-in-a-mist, calendula and lavatera, obediently blazing away there with no one to take note.

'What I really wanted to talk about,' Don was saying now, 'is this question of a house. I haven't mentioned it before, but in fact Jim Thwaites has decided to retire early, which means that my senior partnership comes up rather sooner than we'd expected, so that we could think of a move to something rather bigger, outside the village maybe, now instead of in a couple of years' time. How do you feel about that, Annie?'

'Oh,' she said, 'I think that would be a good idea. Yes, do let's, darling, if that's what you'd like. Yes, of course.'

The mountain, now, is quite steady, and that black cloud the size of a man's fist which had certainly threatened rain had dispersed. The weather is back to what it was, neither one thing nor the other; indifferent.

Don now sounded, for him, surprised. 'I'd thought you might not be so keen. You weren't too enthusiastic once before – but if that's all right by you then we'll go ahead with looking out for something when we get back. Around, I thought, the thirty-five thousand mark. If you're sure that's what you'd like.'

'I'd like that very much,' she said. 'Really I would.'

'It might be a good thing, just now, to look ahead.'

And what does that mean? Anything, or nothing? Is the glance that accompanies it simply because they are moving now towards the car and Anne stands between Don and the driving-seat, so that he must turn to her because she is in the way, or does it pry out a response? 'Yes,' she says, 'I'm sure you're right,' and gets into the car, turning to open the back door for Judy, who has marked the place in her book with a sprig of heather (which will fall out, years later, and snatch back for an instant the afternoon of the brochs, to which she did not pay much attention). 'I'm sure you're right,' Anne says. 'I've always been bad at remembering that things go in two directions – forwards as well as backwards. I don't think history's ever done me much good.' And Don, sensing a joke, pats her knee and says, 'Come on, you've had a lot out of it, one way and another.'

They drive back down the valley, leaving the brochs, which have served a purpose, of a kind, to their own inscrutable affairs, both past and yet to come.

* * *

Graham lay on a plastic-covered table in a darkened room and stared up at a ceiling swagged with flexes and pulleys and tracks for this and that. A white-coated man said, 'Quite still, now, please, Mr Stanway. Deep breath in and hold it.' Machines whirred and clicked. 'Breathe out now,' said the doctor. 'Relax,' and Graham, obediently, relaxed and took a furtive glance at his watch. Just past twelve, back in the studio by two, with any luck. 'I'm just going to tilt the table a bit,' said the doctor. 'If you turn your head to the right, you'll see the picture on the screen; the fluid picks out the intestines.' And Graham, swooping gently forward and then back, stared with fascination at his own incandescent stomach, displayed on a ten-inch television screen. Christ, he thought, not a pretty sight, good thing we keep that to ourselves, in the normal way of things. 'Quite still for a moment,' said the doctor, and the table swooped again, the screen in a merry glow now, packed with pulsating coils. 'Nearly finished, Mr Stanway, we've got some nice clear pictures.' 'Fine,' mumbled Graham, feeling sick and wondering if that too would be apparent on the screen. And now what? he wondered. Off to the cutting-room with the picture for a nice bit of editing? The captions should be interesting. The inner world of Graham Stanway, our Play for Today. Or maybe they'd do better to use it in a documentary. We took our cameras deep into Stanway and brought back some amazing film of the secret rituals and bizarre customs of an unknown region. Not actually all that bloody funny, he thought, what was that black bit at the top right, for instance? And the doctor, bringing the table gently back to horizontal said, 'That's all, Mr Stanway. Thank you very much. The nurse will show you back to the changing-room and Mr Hicks will see you again before you go.'

* * *

Scotland had much to offer. It seemed, like all places in which holidays are taken, to have been thoughtfully devised to please and divert the spectator. When you tired of scenery, there were beaches on which to sit, and a chilly sea for Judy to sample and ungraciously reject. In Edinburgh, there were art galleries and museums, concerts and plays. History had been most obliging in its range and dramatic content. Even though, as Don complained, the entrance fees were exorbitant nowadays, a few pounds was little enough to pay for painless inspection of other people's catastrophic lives. And if eighty pence each seemed rather much for castle or abbey, then you could always move on to Glencoe, which was free and made a convenient picnic spot into the bargain. Edwardian hotels, bristling with tartan and antler, were agreeably of another world; only the intrusion of newspapers and television insisted on the march of time. And the events of which they spoke were also not quite real, as though taking place elsewhere. Glasgow, of course, was to be avoided, as indeed it was possible to avoid most suggestions that people live and work in this place, have personal concerns and make biscuits, ships or car components. In ten days, you can move serenely from place to place and feel nothing but appreciation at so well-constructed a playground. One should never take holidays in real places.

Once, Anne thought, we went to some European country, when I was just about the age Judy is now, and no doubt as uncompanionable, and truth to tell I don't even know which one it was. There were mountains and lakes, which doesn't reduce the possibilities much. Switzerland? Austria? Italy? I don't remember a word anyone said, so language provides no clue. There was a goat, in a field beside a road, with the most appealing pair of white kids; I knitted, intently, with multi-coloured wool that changed from pink to purple to blue; in the huge restaurant of a hotel, crisp with white napery and polished glasses, my parents spoke only of the food, and plans for tomorrow.

They say travel broadens the mind.

I was waiting, as presumably is Judy, to grow up. What were mother and father doing? Mother, in her way, enjoyed holidays as occasions for family unity (where was Graham on that occasion? Off somewhere I suppose, half-fledged by then, as Paul is now, released to camp with the school in Snowdonia). And so, I had thought, did father, but now I am not so sure. That placid figure in the mind's eye, sitting on a rock ledge beside a mountain path, apparently contemplating the view, may have been contemplating quite other things. There's no knowing, now.

She walked on the pebbly shores of a loch. It was a long, thin loch – on the map a clean and satisfying shape, like a boomerang, and now, arrived at in late afternoon, seen to lie in perfect symmetry among the hills, its curve apparently planned to lead the eye away to meet the focal point of a promontory with wind-bent tree and mountain peak beyond. The water lapped its beaches in small, regular waves which contributed just the right amount of movement to a still, reflective scene. The pieces of driftwood on the shoreline were bleached pale as bone and stood like sculptures beside clumps of rushes or heaped, glistening stones. From time to time a gull flew slowly down the loch, bright and clean against the pale, even grey of sky and water. There was no litter and no noise except for the cries of sheep and birds; this was an unfrequented place, not recommended for its beauty or interest. Anne sat on a slab of rock (of convenient sitting-height, and placed just right to command the most agreeable view) and thought that this must be the ultimate in romantic landscape. Don, wandering down there at the water's edge, should pose to left of centre, in nineteenth century costume and with appropriate gesture of appreciation towards the scenery. 'Don,' she called, 'could you be a romantic figure. . . .' But Don, too far to hear, grinned and waved and was removing shoes and socks, now, and stepping gingerly into the cold waters of the loch.

Mother wouldn't have liked this, she thought. Sad, she would have called it. She liked places to be cheerful – trim flowery suburbs or smiling beaches quick with children or the ordered white gleam of Regency spa towns. She was conditioned by scenery as by weather. A gloomy place; a gloomy day. Let's go somewhere else; hope tomorrow will be better. She once wanted them to retire to the sun – Spain or somewhere. She thought they'd feel so much better; a friend of hers went to live in Malta and felt an entirely different person.

I don't feel different, she thought. None of this does anything for me. I look out at it, and observe what it is like, and go on with what I am doing. Go on notching up the days, one by one, examining what has happened and what has not, what he said and what he did not say, cringing every time I look at Don. Every two or three nights I telephone the nursing-home, and they say there is no change. Tomorrow it will be August.

* * *

'What time is it?' said James Stanway to the person who bent over him, doing something irritating to his clothing. He brushed petulantly at her hands, but she put his aside, firmly. 'Late, dear. Are you going to settle down for the night, now? Would you like a drink?'

'I don't drink much,' he said to Betty, 'as you well know. But yes, after that I think I will, if you don't mind. A whisky. Why?' he said. 'Why after all this time? Why now?'

She moved from chair to side-board, Betty, in her blue and white dress, seeing to glass, bottle, soda-water, with her quick, neat hands. She had had her hair cut since last he saw her, so that she looked suddenly younger, nearer to the woman he first knew – fifteen years ago. Fifteen years. 'Why now?'

And she sat there, smoothing the chintz flowers on the arm of the chair, and talking about change. 'I haven't changed,' he said. 'Neither have you, I think. And yes, things are a muddle, I am with you there, but they always have been. That has not changed either.' And, pleating her hair with her fingers as she always did, smiling as she spoke, she was talking now of friendship. 'Ah, Betty,' he said, 'what has got into you? Friendship. . . .' But even as he said it, she seemed to go a little further away, to slide from intimacy to familiarity, from a person known to a person one knew. 'You may be right,' he said, 'about things taking their course, but by God I wish they didn't.'

The whisky tasted of milk, hot milk. He pushed it aside and voices talked across and above him of someone who was restless tonight, and to whom a sedative would do no harm. He turned his head sideways on the pillow and watched fish swim to and fro across a curtain, or in the shallows of a river.

* * *

Somewhere around the Sheffield turn-off Don said again, 'Sure you don't want to go back by Lichfield? Save yourself a trip next week?'

And again Anne said well no, I think not really, we've left it a bit late in the day now and Paul will be back by six, and I'd have to go up anyway, there are things I've got to see to, I ought to have a word with the bank manager and there's a man coming about the leaky pipe at Starbridge . . .

'All right,' he said, 'all right, suit yourself. I just thought it might be an idea.'

Is he insisting? Is he angry? Or is it just a long drive, with much traffic on the motorway and the office looming at nine-thirty tomorrow?

* * *

In the garden at Cuxing the grass was long and the flowers seeding. Anne walked round after breakfast on Monday morning, nipping the dead heads off some pansies and noticing that the old shrub rose against the wall had died right back through the summer and should come out. A lilac might be nice instead. But of course, she thought, we're not going to live here much longer, are we. I'd almost forgotten. Someone else will have to decide what to do with the rose. I'll have to start turning out cupboards here, soon, throwing things away, deciding what to keep and what is of no importance. I wonder what I'll find?

Her bedroom window opened and Paul shouted from it, 'Sandra's on the phone.'

'Coming' she said, and went inside, thinking of all those cupboards, hugging their menace of old clothes, exercise books, dolls, bricks, small cars, machine guns, postcards, photographs. When I'm ready I'll take them on, she thought, and not before. When it suits me, and only then.

'Hello,' said Sandra. 'You're back. I imagine you had a marvellous time. Look, I mustn't talk long – I'm terribly tied up with this hospital thing now, we're forming a local Patients' Association, things are by no means all they should be at the General, I suppose in a way it's been a blessing having those few days in there with my leg, at least one saw for oneself – but anyway, I had to get in touch to say there's a winding-up committee for the Splatt's Cottage campaign on Thursday. At the Pickerings. Do you want a lift?'

'Winding-up?'

'Well, that's all we can do, isn't it? There's a bit of money left in the kitty, that's the thing – you know, from the whip-round we had for the banners and the ads in the paper and all that – so we'll have to sort things out. Actually Hugh Sidey's awfully busy with me on the hospital business. I must say he is going to be a great asset locally.'

'Thursday's all right, I think,' said Anne. 'Yes, please, I would like a lift. Have they finished knocking it down?'

'Yes, of course. Though naturally I suppose they won't build actually on the site now. I mean I can't imagine anyone wanting to live there, can you?'

'Why not?'

Sandra said, 'Oh, of course you won't have heard. The thing is that it all turned out to be rather horrid. They started digging trenches in the garden – for drains and whatnot I suppose – and they found these skeletons. Right outside the kitchen door. Skeletons of children – two. Anyway, the police took them off and they had them looked at and they thought they were early nineteenth century, probably, but the nasty thing was one of them had been ill-treated, there were broken bones or something. And they were terribly undernourished, sort of half-starved apparently. There was a thing in the paper about it, about how they could tell about diet from bones and all that, and one of the historians from the university did a piece and said it might have been infanticide when the price of corn was awfully high or something and lots of country people were starving and couldn't cope with feeding their kids and that sort of thing. It was a rather complicated article with a lot of stuff about fluctuating bread prices and business about the Poor Laws, I didn't read it properly I must admit – most of it was rather boring, actually. But it does seem so creepy, doesn't it? The cottage was frightfully attractive, or at least it would have been if it had been looked after properly and then when you think. . . . Well, anyway, after that of course nobody's going to fancy living actually on the spot, are they, or at least not anyone local because of course everyone heard about it. In fact people are saying old Pym's going to have to knock a bit off the price of his wretched bungalows as a result, so I suppose some good's come out of it. Serves him right. I'll see you on Thursday, then, I must rush.'

Well, thought Anne, fancy that now. How clever of Splatt's Cottage. I suppose it could be said to have won, in the end. I must get hold of this article. 'Have you heard?' she said to Judy, who appeared suddenly in the kitchen doorway, 'about Splatt's Cottage?'

'The skeletons? Yeah – Susie told me. I was right, wasn't I?'

'I thought it was eels you said it had.'

'Something nasty – same thing. Where are you going?'

'Into the village. I shan't be long.'

Anne walked down Cuxing High Street, past the market cross imprisoned behind its iron railing and the impeccably restored timber-frame façade of Barclays Bank and the less-cherished eighteenth century brick front of the green-grocers, where she stopped to buy vegetables. At the War Memorial, where Cuxing's better-remembered dead were listed in order of social rank, she met Mary Pickering, who paused for a moment to give a gay account of a camping holiday in France. 'See you on Thursday,' she said. 'Do bring your husband if he'd like to come – we thought we'd make a bit of a party of it since there's not all that much business to discuss.'

Anne continued down the street. The old-fashioned draper's on the corner, whose closing-down sale had lingered on month after month, was now an Antique Emporium, she saw. She stopped in the entrance, and saw droves of stripped pine chests of drawers, corner cupboards, Victorian kitchen tables. At the sides of the room were shelves of the copper hunting horns and ewers and warming pans and horse-brasses that would be slung from the beams of pubs and restaurants. New brass handles, in eighteenth century designs, had been clapped onto old deal chests or tough functional little dressers; the painted carcase of a nineteenth century pram had been made into a plant-stand; an oak butter churn, polished up, stood as an ornament upon a marble washstand which had itself been stripped and given new china handles to its drawers. Each object was wrenched from its own past. It was as though by displaying what had gone before and making an ornament of it, you destroyed its potency. Less sophisticated societies propitiate their ancestors; this one makes a display of them and renders them harmless, like parents whose warnings may safely be ignored for we see now that wet feet do not in fact give you a cold in the head.

She felt a presence beside her and turned to see Mr Jewkes, of the County Planning Office. He said, 'Pricey, I imagine.'

'I expect so. I used to like Hapgood's – the old shop. It was the last place I know to have cotton reels and things in tiers of little drawers with glass fronts.'

'And lady assistants in black frocks,' said Mr Jewkes unexpectedly. They smiled at each other. 'We last met, of course,' he went on, 'over Splatt's Cottage. Now that's a coincidence – I had that case in mind only yesterday. There was this interesting article in the paper, apropos of the burials found there.'

Anne said, 'I missed that. We were on holiday.'

'I must see if I still have it. You would have been interested.' They moved away together down the street, Mr Jewkes explaining that he was in Cuxing to inspect a site for which planning permission had been applied for an estate of forty houses.

'Will you grant it?' Anne said.

'Confidentially, Mrs Linton, I doubt it. The proposed development is not in sympathy with the rest of the village and I don't like the idea of much more infilling on the Reading road. I must say,' he went on, 'I like Cuxing. It always seems to me one of the more fortunate Berkshire villages – fortunate in that it escaped too much twenties and thirties building. I know you may feel that from time to time the planning laws are misapplied – but I'm sure you wouldn't want to go back to the anarchy of the pre-war years.' He looked at her over his gold-rimmed spectacles, with a teasing smile.

'No,' she said, 'I certainly wouldn't.' She smiled back; there was no getting away from it, he was rather nice, Mr Jewkes. 'As a matter of fact,' she went on, 'we're probably leaving it. My husband wants to buy a bigger house somewhere.'

'Well now,' said Mr Jewkes, 'I wonder what kind of thing he has in mind. . . . I've just come from a place that might possibly be of interest. Pym's of Wallingford – brother, you know, of your Pym here – have applied to convert an old coach-house just down the river. I had a look at it on the way here and could see no reason why not. Unused for donkey's years – lovely site, views across the Downs. Quite a nice tasteful outline plan they've produced – keeping the exterior much as it is. Your husband might like to get in touch with the builders before they advertise – that's the kind of thing that tends to get snapped up rather quickly these days.'

'Yes. I expect it does. I'll tell him. Thank you, Mr Jewkes.'

'Don't mention it. By the way – I put two and two together after we last met and realised you taught my eldest at some point, in the comprehensive. He enjoyed your classes, he said – he's rather keen on history.'

Anne said, 'Good. In fact I don't teach there any more.' She explained the circumstances of her dismissal. Mr Jewkes made sounds of disapproval and regret. 'And does that mean you'll be on the look-out for a job, Mrs Linton?'

'I suppose so. I hadn't thought, really. I've been a bit taken up with other things lately. My father is very ill – until that's over it's a bit difficult to concentrate on anything else.' What a euphemism, she thought. What a stupid, self-deceiving euphemism, in every way.

'Quite,' said Mr Jewkes crisply. 'May I offer my sympathies. I take it your father is of a considerable age?'

'Yes. He's quite old.'

They paused now by the turning to the car park. 'Very nice to have met you again,' said Mr Jewkes, and hesitated for a moment, as though not knowing how to break away, jingling the car keys in his pocket. 'I imagine you studied history at some point, Mrs Linton? Excuse me – I don't mean to sound impertinent.'

'Well, yes,' she said, surprised. 'I took a degree in it.' Something made her add, 'Ages ago, of course,' which sounded foolish. Mr Jewkes nodded. They shook hands, with awkward formality, and he walked away to his car.

Anne went home. At the corner of the street she saw the postman, bringing the second delivery, pause at her gate, flick through the pile in his hand, and go up to the front door. She walked very slowly the rest of the way, stopping to examine a notice on a lamp-post, to talk to the small boy next door. Inside the house, on the mat, was the glitter of a scenic postcard. She picked it up without looking at it and carried it into the kitchen. There, she read that Don's mother was in Devon, having a few days by the sea, and looked forward to seeing them in a few weeks' time, in September.

She was filled at the same time with yearning and a deep sense of oppression. She stood at the table, the postcard in her hand, and thought of the immeasurable distances from Cuxing to Lichfield. She could hear David's voice, but could not remember what he looked like.

Twelve

In the fourth week of August Anne took the road to Lichfield. It was twenty-seven days since she had last driven it, in the opposite direction. The fields had been harvested now; there were apples on orchard trees; front gardens were full of michaelmas daisies and chrysanthemums. She stopped for petrol at the garage she had used on the first trip of all and which had then become her usual one (thus unwittingly are habits formed) and the attendant, handing change through the window said, 'Things starting up again, now, after the holidays. You're busy, I daresay?' 'What?' she said, bewildered, and he went on, 'Aren't you in business?' 'Oh, no' she said. 'It's just I'd noticed you going up and down regularly this year – I imagined you had business bringing you up here.' 'No,' she said. 'It's my father I go to see. He's been ill.' 'Ah. Sorry to hear that. Hope it's nothing much. Four ninety that was, thank you.'

Her father lay with his eyes closed, breathing noisily. The nurse, moving from bed to basin, said 'I don't think we'll get him to wake, dear.' She leaned over and spoke to him, and shook her head. 'Matron wanted a word with you on your way out.'

The matron said, 'The doctor saw him this morning and thinks he's picked up again a bit. He had a crisis in the night and we thought he'd go then. I would have rung you, Mrs Linton, but there seemed little point. He wouldn't have known you, and since you were coming up today anyway . . . It's astonishing the way he holds on I'm afraid all this has been a strain on you, but I really cannot think it will be for much longer, poor old man.'

Anne walked out through the gardens, past the old people arranged on chairs and benches as they had been in the April sunshine when she first came here. One woman she recognized, and smiled at. Most of them were anonymous; they might always have been there, or have just arrived. I am unobservant, she thought, unobservant and unperceptive. That matron was exhausted, there were grooves under her eyes, perhaps she had been up all night, while I lay awake in Cuxing. He nearly went last night. . . . How much does he know? Anything? Nothing at all?

She wandered in the Starbridge garden, waiting for David. There had been a dry period and her flowers had withered and almost died, so that the imagined profusion of colours was a brown and wilting muddle. All that and in the end I never saw them, she thought. The car stopped outside the gate and she went chill with expectation and walked towards him with a stiff smile so that he said 'What's the matter? Aren't I welcome any more?'. 'Oh, David . . .' she said, and felt herself near tears, turning aside so that he wouldn't see.

They went to bed in the afternoon, as on that earlier afternoon in May, and lay with sunshine slanting across Anne's bare thigh, across David's arm. She saw his hair dappled with it, as she looked down the length of her body, and thought, even at that moment: September sun is different, quite different, you couldn't mistake it for any other, you can tell the time of year by the sun. Later, she said this to David and he answered that it wasn't September.

'Nearly. On Sunday.'

'Well, don't let's have it sooner than we must. School, and everything else. How was Scotland?'

'I'm not sure,' she said. 'I hardly noticed it.'

He sat on the edge of the bed, pulling on his shirt. 'The boys had a good time in Wales. I must say, they walk me into the ground these days. Tom did over twenty miles on one occasion.' He looked down, and saw her face, and put his hand on her arm. 'I missed you. I thought of you in – oh, in all sorts of funny places – I wished you were with us.' He stared out of the window, and then said suddenly 'I don't know, I don't know, Anne, do you. . . ?'

'Don't know what, David?'

'Nothing. I've felt a bit low, lately, I suppose. But I'm not going to inflict it on you. Have you been to the nursing-home yet?'

'They said it can't be much longer.'

He nodded, staring again out of the window.

* * *

I tell lies, he thought. I distort. I evade. First to my sons. Now to Anne. I cannot, somehow, be honest. Lying – evading – is always just that much easier, that much less painful, than telling the truth. And I have always been craven in my personal life. Not in the public one – the school, the boys – I'm efficient enough there. But the rest, no.

He drove the car onto the strip of concrete in front of the garage and sat in it, in front of his darkened house, not wanting to go in. I hate this house, he thought, always have done. I've slept in it and eaten in it for five years or so, and never looked at it closely enough to be quite certain which it is without checking the number first. Only Tom's bike by the hedge tells me now. I suppose she's back, he thought, back and gone to bed. Tomorrow at the breakfast table she'll look across at me to see if I've taken everything in properly. If I've read, marked, learned and inwardly digested it all.

He sat in misery, phrases from her letter marching through his head: '. . . better I think to get this down in writing before I come back. I want to make myself quite clear, and that doesn't always happen face to face . . . imagine that this is not the first time, you were luckier other times in that no one was kind enough (or unkind enough) to inform me . . . found out a bit, mainly that she has children too . . . don't want a divorce, for reasons of my own, we've managed for eighteen years and can go on doing so.'

Eighteen and a half, actually, he thought, nineteen in December. But no matter.

'. . . apparently can't stop you, under this new law, if that's what you intend . . . might as well warn you now, once and for all . . . Tom and Alan . . . her children too . . . her husband . . . contempt . . . unlikely to have much respect . . . make things as unpleasant as possible, and I think you know . . .'

Yes, I know.

'. . . owed something for eighteen years work, and a lot else besides . . . not always a great success but don't see why I should take all the blame for that . . . possible to exaggerate the physical side, and personally I . . . and furthermore I don't see why I should put up with the humiliation of . . . perfectly frank with Tom and Alan, and have no doubt they'll feel as I do that you . . . so I would feel free and indeed under a certain obligation to contact her husband . . . don't see why he should be left in blissful ignorance . . . their children too . . . if, on the other hand . . . prepared to wipe the sheet clean and go on as we were . . . make up your mind within the next few weeks which you want.'

As we were. How were we? he thought. Because since April I haven't known, having been in a state of disturbance. I can't remember now how I was before. How it felt. Was I unhappy? I don't think so. One got on with things: work, things with which one is involved, the boys. One day was much the same as another; there were few extremes of temperature. Was it so bad?

Surely not, he told himself, surely not. He stared at the dark windows of his house, behind two of which his sons slept. I don't know, he thought, I don't know . . .

* * *

'Oh, Graham,' Anne said, 'I *am* sorry. You poor old thing. But at least you know now what it is. And it could have been worse. Much. And it doesn't mean an operation, does it?'

Graham, down in London, said that a special diet of bloody baby food as far as he could make out and no alcohol at all sounded to him considerably worse than an operation.

'Come to us this weekend – please do.'

But there was this filming in Suffolk, apparently, and then he had to go to Berlin for three days for some European television jamboree, and then he had to be in London non-stop for some new series. 'Come up and have lunch with me, Annie,' he said. 'I'll buy you a slap-up meal. I wish you would – I'd like that.'

'Right,' she said. 'Right, I will. Week after next. And look after yourself, Graham. Be sensible about food and things.'

'Yes, auntie' he said, and she put the receiver down thinking: that's a bit more like it, he sounds a bit more himself now.

Poor Graham. It's not fun being ill all on your own.

She had come back from Lichfield the day before. David had telephoned to say he would not be able to meet her in Lichfield for lunch, as arranged. 'I'm sorry,' he said. 'Someone has to take Tom and Alan to Birmingham and Mary can't manage it. Sorry, Anne.' 'It doesn't matter a bit' she said, and after a fractional pause he went on, 'When will you be up again?' 'I'm not too sure,' she said. 'I'll let you know – I'll give you a ring at school, or leave a message.' She drove back fast, seeing little or nothing, surprised to find herself suddenly in Cuxing, outside her own gate.

When Sandra called for her that evening, to take her to the Pickerings, Anne said, 'Someone seems to have got it in for us, this year – for my family. Graham's got an ulcer – my brother Graham.'

Sandra said, 'What awfully bad luck. I wouldn't have thought he'd be the type to get ill, I must say.'

'Does it go in types?'

'Well, I mean with some people you just aren't all that surprised to hear they've gone down with something – it seems somehow in character. Like poor little Mrs Hedges' husband having a heart attack at forty, when she'd just had a new baby and he'd lost his job – I mean, it all fitted. And the kind of child that's accident-prone. Actually,' she went on, 'I'd have thought you'd be the type, more than your brother, if you don't mind me saying.'

'I don't think there's anything wrong with me,' said Anne. 'Nothing to speak of, anyway.'

'Oh, I don't mean you look unhealthy. It's just there's always something a bit kind of unrevealed about you. I mean, you're just not as obvious as most people, somehow. Actually, I don't mind telling you now, but when I first knew you I was a bit frightened of you. You seemed awfully clever.'

'I'm sorry,' said Anne, 'I didn't mean to be. I hope I don't still.'

Sandra said 'Oh, no. And of course one changes oneself in how one kind of reacts to people. Goodness, I hope I'm not seeming frightfully rude.'

'Not a bit,' said Anne. 'I rather like the idea of being unrevealed – so long as we're sure it's not unrevealed disease.'

Sandra said 'Oh, I shouldn't honestly think so.' She turned into the Pickerings' drive, gravel spraying up from under the car. 'Look, they've got their engine up, isn't that fun!'

Spot-lit from a lamp mounted on the side of the house was a massive piece of industrial machinery. It had been sunk onto a base of concrete which was carefully masked with pots and tubs of summer flowers. The white-washed wall of an outbuilding made a background to the shining, oiled, polished and painted machine, its pistons and wheels projecting sharp black shadows in the spot-light. Brian Pickering came out of the open front door as they got out of the car and Sandra said, 'I must say it's awfully effective, Brian – I do think you were clever.'

'It is rather nice, isn't it?' he said.

Anne said, 'What is it?'

'A beam-engine. Early industrial revolution. They were dismantling this factory somewhere in the Black Country and a mate of mine heard about it and went up to poke around for bits and pieces of stuff for sculpture, and told me about this. So of course I beetled up there and they let me have it for a hundred quid. It's got a few parts missing or it would have been worth a lot more, for a museum or collection or something.'

'How did it work?'

'Ah,' said Brian. 'Now there you have me rather. Engineering's not my strong point. Those things go up and down, of course, and turn that. I'm a bit vague about what that bit's for. The inside of my own car's a mystery to me, frankly. But I couldn't resist it.' He ran his hand affectionately over the shiny surface of the machine.

'I don't blame you,' said Sandra. 'Well, I suppose we'd better get started. Is everyone here?'

They went inside. Mary Pickering said, 'I thought your husband was coming, Anne?'

'He couldn't make it, I'm afraid.'

'Miss Standish isn't coming either. She said she thought there wasn't anything more she could be useful about and sent apologies.'

'Of course one really only had her on the committee to be tactful,' said Sandra. 'She is a bit out of touch, poor old dear. Still, we'd better let her know what we do with the money. Hugh, are you going to just run through things?'

The Splatt's Cottage Preservation Committee heard, over some rather nice home-brewed beer of Brian Pickering's, that there were four pounds seventy-five pence left in the fund, which it decided, without argument, to donate to the Council for the Preservation of Rural England. The professor, in his capacity as secretary, deplored the fact that the committee must be said to have been unsuccessful in its aims. Nevertheless, he felt that it could congratulate itself on having made a firm stand in defence of a principle in which its members profoundly believed. We've shown, he said, that certain people in Cuxing are not going to sit by and see the past tampered with or destroyed without putting up a fight (there was a murmur of agreement, around the room) and even if, in a sense, we lost this time, we've shown our muscle, as it were, ready for the next occasion. ('Absolutely,' said Mary Pickering sternly, her head bent over her patchwork.) We didn't perhaps, in this case, rally our forces quite early enough: next time we must be in a position to go into the offensive almost before the enemy make a move, as it were. He would like to suggest that, rather than disband itself, the committee should be re-formed, or metamorphosed, or however anyone liked to put it, into a watchdog group for Cuxing and the surrounding area: it would list and record everything that was old and might at some point be endangered, and stand by for action. 'Super idea,' murmured Sandra, 'but aren't we going to overlap with the C.P.R.E.? One doesn't want to tread on toes.' But no, the professor thought not: what he had in mind was something frankly rather more militant than what some people might feel to be perhaps from time to time a rather lack-lustre organization (here Sandra nodded sagely). Perhaps on second thoughts they might hang onto that four pounds seventy-five (Sandra nodded again). And, he said, I think we should assume an altogether more educative role, too. I suspect that ignorance lies behind a great deal of indifference and vandalism. That chap Pym, for instance – local boy made good, plenty of drive and initiative there. We need people like that on our side, we don't want to be fighting them. It's a question of opening people's eyes – showing them the world they live in. Teaching them how to appreciate their own past instead of just ignoring it. We must have lectures and exhibitions. We must bring history into the market place. We must make people feel its relevance to their own lives. ('More drink, anyone?' said Brian Pickering, *sotto voce*, opening the glass front of the bread oven to reveal bottles and glasses. 'There's whisky, if anyone would rather?') We must make Cuxing a bit more *au fait* with modern sensibility.

'The modern sensibility I've come across,' said Anne, 'finds history an outdated concept.'

'You agree with that?' said Hugh Sidey sharply.

'No, of course not. It's just that there seems to be a bit of confusion about what it should do, or shouldn't do. Or how to take it.'

'I don't quite follow.'

'Well,' said Anne, 'I lost my job at the comprehensive because apparently my way of teaching history isn't acceptable any more. Looking at it chronologically won't do – children can't grasp it. So you don't teach it to them at all, or you give it to them in nice digestible chunks, as themes or projects. You teach them about revolutions, or civil wars, or whatever.'

'Of course,' said Sandra, 'the old way of teaching was deadly boring, dates and all that. I mean, that's why I'm so jolly ignorant, I'm sure – if I'd been taught the way my kids are one would have been able to get interested.' She looked round the room for support.

Anne said irritably, 'I'm not talking about tables of dates, or the rights and wrongs of different ways of teaching. I'm talking about paying attention to what actually happened.'

'I think perhaps we're straying just a bit from the matter in hand,' said Hugh Sidey. 'Anyway, I imagine you're with us in all this, Mrs Linton?'

Anne looked round the room, from Brian Pickering fiddling with drinks beside the blacksmith's anvil, to his wife sitting cross-legged on a cushion, sewing, to the professor (it was English he had professed, it seemed), to Sandra. She noticed again the collection of Victorian portrait photographs, other people's relatives as agreeable decoration, and the display of agricultural implements and the collection of china mugs and plates with A Present from somewhere or other on them, in sloping nineteenth century script. She said, 'What are you going to do with the buildings you save?'

'Well, obviously it depends,' said the professor. 'Presumably most things can be adapted to contemporary use of some kind. One will have to see. What would you suggest?'

They were all looking at her now. Oh dear, she thought, I've brought dissension into their nice comfortable evening. Not really what I meant. She said, half apologetically, 'I don't think I have any strong opinions about that. I'm fairly muddled about it myself. It's just I feel worried about indiscriminate hanging onto the past – in the form of buildings, or – or anything else. Sometimes I think we're not too sure why we're doing it – and we may not even be quite clear what it is we're hanging onto. But at the same time I think it's very important to know about it – but to know properly, not just to have a vague idea or even to adapt it to suit your own purposes.' Oh Lord, she thought, I shouldn't have said that last bit, she glanced guiltily at Brian Pickering, but he was looking puzzled rather than annoyed.

'I must say you're being frightfully solemn tonight, Anne,' said Sandra.

'I daresay I am. Sorry. And I hope you won't feel too badly of me if in fact I don't stay on the committee. Truth to tell, we may be moving in any case so I'm not sure I'd be eligible.' She got up, and smiled placatingly. 'And if you don't mind, I think I'll get back – I told Don I wouldn't be out long. Don't worry, Sandra – I'll walk back, it's no distance and I'd rather like some fresh air.'

It was not quite dark, the lanes murky in the half-light of an almost-full moon, eroded at one side (it had been whole, five days ago in Starbridge, seen though her bedroom window there . . .). She walked fast, dodging puddles and stepping back into the hedge once or twice as cars passed. Approaching Cuxing, the unappealing but undeniably old frontage of a nineteenth century warehouse loomed alongside, the windows smashed and boarded up, surely a vulnerable subject. They'd better start here, she thought, that can be item one on their list; warehouse, circa 1840, of brick, three stories, with slate roof and twentieth century addition in concrete and corrugated iron on the west side. And then there's the Baptist Chapel, all locked up and unused, there can't be any Baptists in the village now, that should convert nicely into something more relevant for here and now. Coming round the corner into the main street, she passed the Victorian school, its high windows ablaze with light; there would be no need to save that, it had been snapped up during the property boom for some amazing figure. Now an architect lived there with many children; through an uncurtained window she could see the blue glimmer of a television, and their dark contented shapes in front of it. Perhaps those less contented children of Splatt's Cottage had attended the school, once upon a time (or had they been too young for that?). Oh, the past is disagreeable all right, she thought, no wonder we'd rather not know. And it has this way of jumping out at you from behind corners when you're least expecting it, so that you have to spend time and energy readjusting to it, re-digesting it. Or it hangs around your neck like an albatross, so that there is no putting it aside ever, even if you wanted to. Even if you knew if you wanted to, or if David did? Does he? Did he ever? I won't go to Lichfield for a while, she thought, not unless things change with father. I'll stay here. Or try to.

She came into her house, and Don was in the kitchen, stoking the boiler, and turned to say 'Oh, Annie, I'm afraid they phoned from the nursing-home, things aren't too good, they wanted you to ring back.'

* * *

The river was high today, in flood. It roared in James Stanway's ears as he cast, like some tropical torrent, not a quiet English trout-stream, and the rush of water carried his line away till he could no longer see it, further and further, unreeling and vanishing so that surely there could be none left, the reel must be empty. . . . And now he had dropped reel and rod and was clambering up the bank to get away from that noise, and from the water grabbing at his knees that was going to sweep him away with it if he was not careful, knock him down and take him spinning downstream like that bit of driftwood. But he'd beaten it, got out of it and up on the bank, and there was his wife, sitting there with a book on her lap, which was surprising because he had never made her a fishing widow, never planted her out for long waiting days like some men do. So he sat beside her and took out his pipe and began to talk, trying to explain. Look, he said, I don't expect you to forgive me or even, probably, to understand. But just to get things straight or as straight as I have any right ever to expect they might be, I want to tell you why. It's not, he said, that I don't love you. Or that I love her more. I suppose that I've enjoyed going to bed with her more, but that is not the whole of it, not by any means, not even the most important part, perhaps. I have been able to talk more with her than ever I have with you, but I don't think I have ever told her anything I have not told you, or would not have told you, had you asked. It is not your fault, he said, in no way at all. It is not that you are inadequate, or that I have been unhappy with you. You see, he said, I have led a rather ordinary life: my job has been interesting, stimulating even, but I have sometimes felt unused by it. Oh, it is not that I imagine myself some undeveloped genius. I know my limitations. I have been quite satisfied, on the whole, with the way things were. But let me try to explain.

Once, when I was a boy, I rescued a dog from a river. I have never mentioned this to anyone, because it seemed to me at the time, and still does, a stupid thing to do. The river was deep and fast and I was not a strong swimmer; the risk of drowning was considerable and my life was more valuable than the dog's. I was not particularly fond of animals. I just thought it would be interesting to take the risk, that I might be missing something if I did not. Some people would call that courage: I don't think I would. I tell you this, he said, because it seems to illustrate an aspect of me that you have probably never recognized. I don't expect I have ever seemed anything other than a moderate and cautious man to you. And on the whole I am. Just once or twice in my life that part of me has taken over, has insisted on going as far as there is to be gone, on having what there is to be had. The dog is not perhaps a very good analogy for Betty; there was neither risking nor saving being done there. But the incident will do to illustrate what I mean about myself, Betty and the dog being both in a sense irrelevant.

He turned and looked at his wife, sitting there reading on the river bank, saying nothing. I am so sorry, he said, that I seem to have kept something of myself back from you; that is perhaps the shabbiest betrayal of all.

Thirteen

Anne thought, once, that he said something. She leaned forward and spoke to him, but the mutter, if it had been that, died away. His mouth fell open and he breathed noisily. It was nearly eleven o'clock; she had got up at six, had driven along empty early-morning roads. Now, she sat by her father's bedside, holding his hand, watching the rooks glide above the gardens beyond the window. The trees were patched with autumn colour.

She fell asleep, sitting upright in the wicker chair, and dreamed that she and her father walked together, hand in hand, on a huge, sea-rimmed beach. She was ten. They came to a breakwater and she wanted to jump off it, but was afraid. She stood skipping from one foot to another on its shingly top, and her father down below on the sand said, 'Come on, Anne, now, make up your mind – either do it or don't.' 'Will you catch me?' she cried. 'Promise you'll catch me!', and he said in his sensible matter-of-fact voice that he couldn't promise that, now could he? If she wanted to jump, she must jump, it must be her choice and she must either do it or not, it was up to her. She dithered there on the breakwater, while gulls leered at her from the clear salty sky and far away the waves curled white at the edge of the shining sand.

Waking, she did not know if she had dreamed or remembered. The door opened and the matron came in, with a doctor. Anne went and stood by the window while the doctor examined her father, and then said that the pulse was stronger, but his breathing very poor now. The matron said, 'Why don't you go off and get a bit of rest, Mrs Linton, and come back later? We have your phone number at Starbridge, haven't we?' Yes, she said, yes I think I will.

There was a note from David at the house, undated. Could you ring me, it said, at the school – leave a message if I'm not there.

He was there. 'Oh, Anne,' he said, 'you've come. . . . I wondered – you didn't say. I thought maybe you mightn't get up till next week.' She began to explain. In the background a door opened and closed; there were voices; David in an aside told someone he wouldn't be a moment. He returned to her and said, 'I'll come out to the house tonight – around eight. Is that all right, Anne?' 'I expect so,' she said. 'If I can't be there I'll leave a note.'

She sat in the garden at Starbridge, outside the study window, within earshot of the telephone. She had intended to spend an hour or so on some of her father's files, but the boxes lay beside her, untouched. There'll be time enough for that, she thought, later. Or perhaps in the end I'll do what Graham said we should do in the first place – throw the lot away.

The grass of the lawn had grown tall, and seeded, and was now the fawn of uncut hay. The roses had flowered, and flowered again, and thrown up huge juicy suckers. The outlines of the beds were blurred by weed and grass; it would be hard to recover them now. Bindweed, pouring down the bank at one side, had half-filled the small concrete chasm beside the coal bunker, submerging a dustbin and creeping into the back yard. How much grows, Anne thought, in a summer. So many pounds of grass and leaf and flower and seed, all gushing out, come what may. She saw for a moment her mother, moving among the dahlias in that bed at the end there, staking and tying: the dahlias flowered still, flopping across an undergrowth of weed. A garden is an unresponsive thing, its anarchic temperament re-asserting itself as soon as the back is turned. We invent gardens, she thought, picturing the gardens of medieval Books of Hours, stiff formal Elizabethan gardens, herb gardens, oriental gardens. A garden is a fantasy – an arrangement of plants as we think they should be, not as they really are. And time of course puts everything back into place. She wondered if she would ever make another garden. I don't think I've got the heart for it, she thought, not again.

Later, she returned to Lichfield. There was a nurse sitting by her father's bedside. 'He's had a little stroke, Mrs Linton,' she said. 'The doctor feels it must be a matter of hours now.' The old man's face was dark; he seemed barely to breathe. Anne said, 'I suppose there's no chance he might – know anything now?' The nurse said, 'Oh no, dear, not now. I'm afraid he won't know you're here at all.'

She sat for a while in the wicker chair, in a strange peace, beyond time or suffering. She believed, now, the nurse's claim that her father knew nothing. When the nursing-home began to clatter into its evening routine of food-trolleys and bed-pans she returned to Starbridge.

* * *

They walked down to the river. David said, 'I've put the rod in your father's cloakroom, by the way.'

'Fishing's over?'

'For this year.'

Standing beside him on the bank, as once before, Anne saw his reflection in the water, alongside those of trees suspended head-down like recollections of nineteenth century trees in a darkened oil-painting. David was tethered by a rim of grass and reeds to another, dimmer David falling away into the river, his face and expression indistinct, fractured by tiny shiftings of the river's surface. He had turned to her and was smiling, but when her eyes travelled downwards to the reflection again his smile had been shattered by some distortion. He scowled from far down in the water, rejecting her, a stranger she could never have known.

She said, 'Sorry – what did you say?'

'I said have you done anything about a new job?'

'Not so far. I haven't felt much like it.'

'Did the nursing-home ring again?'

'Not yet.'

They followed the river bank, past the place where, once, they had sat drinking tea from David's flask, had seen a dipper. 'I don't think I'm going to go on teaching,' she said. 'Not history, anyway '

'Oh, come,' he said, 'you can't rat on it now. What's wrong with it?'

'There's nothing wrong with it. If anything's wrong it's with me.' She stopped and stripped leaves off a willow (yellow-mottled, September leaves), dropping them into the water one by one. 'I really don't know any more,' she went on, 'if I have anything straight about the past at all. How I feel about it. I certainly don't feel competent to lecture children. I don't know if it's something people carry around like a mill-stone, or if it's what they prop themselves up with. Sometimes I think that perhaps it's only buildings that successfully digest the past. Cathedrals. People like you and me seem to drag it around with them, in many ways.'

'I thought we were talking about history, not us in particular.'

'I'd rather talk about people. Us, maybe.'

'Look, Anne,' he said, 'I'm sure this isn't the right time. . . .'

'With my father dying? My father's been dying since we first met.'

'Yes, I suppose that's true.'

'And after he dies,' she said, 'to put it brutally, because one might as well be brutal, just about everything else is – after he dies, we aren't going to see each other any more, are we, David?'

He said, after a moment, 'Do you think anything else was ever possible?'

'I have no idea.'

'I told you I was craven.'

'You're not craven,' she said. 'Not more than most.'

They walked back to the house across the field. David said 'There was a boy here last week with an air-gun, blasting off at the lapwings, which I imagine is illegal.'

'I imagine so.'

'I told him not to.'

'Good.'

'Look' he said, at the garden fence, 'I'll see you . . . When?'

'That rather depends.'

'Will you let me know about your father?'

'Probably.'

'Anne,' he said, 'I don't really want to go into it – it does no good to anyone – Mary knows about it, somehow.'

'I imagined there was something like that. Don't go into it, David – I don't really want to hear.' She put her hand on his arm, and took it off again at once. 'I'll let you know how he is.'

Presently, while she was heating herself a tin of soup for supper, the matron rang to say that her father had died, quite peacefully, without regaining consciousness, a few minutes before.

She sat beside the cooling soup for a while, and then went back to the telephone to dial Graham's number.

* * *

The road reached back to Cuxing in orderly lengths; from Staffordshire through Warwickshire into Oxfordshire. No surprises there, no unsuspected town popping up to right or left, no shifting hills or wandering rivers. The landscape at least is constant. Places don't change. There, she saw, were the cooling towers, and there the traffic light in Banbury where once one hummed *The Marriage of Figaro* between lorries, and there the spot where poppies had blazed, suddenly, in the middle of June. You must know that road like the back of your hand, Don had remarked once, and oh yes, she thought, I do indeed. One is never going to get rid of it now, along with a great deal else. It has its associations now, come what may, as Lichfield is associated forever with Samuel Johnson. Places aren't quite as detached as they're made out to be.

Blanched of feeling, observing without seeing, she drove from the A446 to the A41 to the A423.

* * *

Come up to London, Graham had said. Don't sit around feeling low, Annie, I should think you're a bit whacked, one way and another. He wouldn't have wanted that, you know. Let's not have any fuss now – remember? That's what he would have said. Tell you what – come up and meet me at the studio and we'll go out and have a nice lunch and cheer ourselves up. He'd have approved of that. How about it?

And so she walked now through glass doors into this large reception hall where people dressed as Graham dressed sat around on leather-upholstered chairs or vanished through swinging doors with lights above them into unseen hinterlands where, presumably, work was done. Graham Stanway? said the girl behind the desk, is he expecting you? They've got a studio day, you know – oh, I see, I'll ask the porter to take you up then. Studio One it is, The Tower of London. The what? said Anne, confused. Tower of London, said the girl – series title. Jim, could you take this lady to Graham Stanway in One?

What an unreal place, Anne thought, following the man down corridors, up staircases, past flashing lights, over cables. How odd to come and work in a place like this, to come and spend the day making things up, inventing a world that isn't. Behind a closed door a typewriter clacked, tethering the place for a moment to the real world of letters and figures. This way, miss, said the man, and now they were in some cavernous place where lights blazed onto a set with cardboard-painted stone walls, *trompe l'oeil* barred window, historical-seeming furnishings, man in jeans and T-shirt doing something to a candle-stick; beyond, the room vanished into dusk, wires coiling down from an invisible ceiling, people milling about among cameras and cables. He's not on the floor, someone said, better take her up to the control room, and now suddenly here was Graham at the bottom of a spiral staircase, saying hello, Annie, sorry, I've been on the look-out for you but I couldn't get along to Reception. And suddenly she felt like crying.

Come up and watch, he said, we break in half an hour or so and then we can go and have some lunch. How are you, Annie, are you O.K.? I'm all right, she said, what about you, how are your insides? A bloody nuisance, he said, we don't talk about them – oh, they're under control, not to worry.

And now they were in this cool dark goldfish bowl of a room with banked rows of monitors and a line of people on swivel chairs in front of dials and switches, more people glassed-off to right and left, jeans and shirt-sleeves everywhere, voices crackling out of the darkness. Here, said Graham, you sit down here, mind the step, that's the operative monitor, for your information, the one in the middle, that's the picture that goes on the screen, the rest are the different camera shots. You'll hear us behind you talking to the studio floor, at least Maggie does most of the talking – she's the director, I'll introduce you later but I'll have to go now. O.K., love? It won't be for long – anyway I'm told it's quite amusing when you don't see it day in day out.

What is it? she said, what's the film? Historical soap-opera, said Graham, life and times of the Tower of London in eight episodes. We've got to the sixteenth century in this one, there's Sir Walter Raleigh coming up on Camera Two now – actually it's turning out quite nice, we've got some good film in the can, super stuff we did in Epping Forest last week. It's not all in the Tower, then? she said. Oh, Lord, no – we move around, the Tower's just handy as a central theme – you know, take something solid like a place and watch history seething around it and all that, it's a good device, gives us scope to bring in just about everything. Good old bread-and-butter costume drama, everybody loves it. See you in half an hour or so, Annie, O.K.?

Fine, she said, and indeed this curving leather sofa thing was very comfortable after trains and tubes, and the darkness was soothing, one could sit here and feel nothing, just watch this fantasy world displayed from one point of view and then another on the numbered screens there in front of you. Like Rashomon, she thought, the same event from different points of view, several-dimensional, very symbolic. Or the past itself, if you want to push the point a bit, which on the whole I think we won't. I just want to sit, she thought, and think about nothing at all. This will do very well for half an hour, longer wouldn't matter, all day for all I care, and tomorrow too.

Monitor 1 is filled now with a blue-jeaned bum. Monitor 2 lingers on two huge men trolleying a slice of cardboard staircase across the studio floor. Elsewhere are framed the corner of a deal table, the top of a curtain with a microphone peering in top right like an inquisitive insect, Sir Walter Raleigh talking to a man with clipboard in hand, earphones clamped to his head. There is ceaseless chatter from the row of chairs behind. Graham's voice says this is fourteen, take one, right? I've got a bit lost, and another voice says can I see them in shot for a second, please, fine, no, there's a slight shoot-off through that open door, O.K. that's nice. Are we going for a take? another voice is saying. Right, says the woman's voice, we're going for one, boys, mind that boom, Ken, O.K., then. And now someone is counting: going in twenty seconds, fifteen, ten, nine, eight, seven. . . . On the big central monitor we have Sir Walter Raleigh now, sitting writing at a table, and then a close-up of what he is writing or has written, authentic curly Elizabethan script, and now we cut to Camera One's shot of the opening door, with gaoler coming in. The actors' voices are loud and clear above the chat from behind – shot twenty-eight on three, twenty-nine on one, thirty on two, I don't like that turn, I don't like that at all, he's too far out, thirty-one on one, the boom's in trouble, the boom's in a lot of trouble, all right, that's it, we'll have to go again, cut. The central screen blacks out, at either side are seen again those fretful sections of some hidden larger scene – man with clipboard instructing a costumed actor, the back of someone's head, a still-life of jacket slung across the arm of a chair.

A note for Lady Agnes, says the woman's voice from behind, could she take another half pace forward after her entrance or she's out of shot. And I want a close-up in there for reaction – have you got that, Liz? Graham's voice says we had some flare there didn't we? just a bit? and other voices ask each other if there was flare, did anyone see any flare? And so the chat goes on in the darkness, like the dead squeaking and gibbering in the streets or however it goes, Anne thinks. Except that that's a fallacy too, pathetic or otherwise, the dead don't squeak or gibber, they are dead and that's all there is to it.

In the central monitor now is her father, sitting on the side of an Alp with pipe-smoke streaming in the wind, and alongside but a size smaller on Camera Three is her mother but what she is doing is not at all clear, there is some fuzziness there, perhaps that is what is meant by flare. Camera One has Betty Mansell, as in the photograph on her daughter's mantelpiece in Gloucester, a strong-featured woman staring thoughtful from the screen. And there are Graham and Anne herself, on bikes, pedalling away down a road, plump-thighed teenagers, and to their right is Shirley Barron, but she is middle-aged, not young, glumly wiping cup-rings from her coffee-table. And at either end there are blank screens, several. What are they for? Anne wonders, and seems to remember Graham saying something about not using all the cameras today.

Something has been going on that she has missed. O.K., says the voice behind, I'll buy that. Thank you, studio, that was a good take. We're going over to the bedroom scene now, right? Get ready to block, please. And there is a wild whirling and flashing on the monitors, a world of uncertainty until everything settles down again and we have now a four-poster bed around which people swarm on ladders, and a girl in a nightdress sits on the edge while cameras consider her from different angles.

A number of girls in nightdresses, in fact, both in and out of them, and women too. There is the claustrophobic attic bedroom in which she loved and fought with Patrick, and there is the Leckford road room, with Don naked bending to take off shoes and socks which brings a remembered gush not of desire but of irritation. He does not know, and one cannot say, that it should be done the other way round. And there is the Langdale Villas bedroom, in London, and beside it the Cuxing one, but Don is not to be seen in them, or perhaps he is blotted out by boom or flare or one of these other problems they have around here. And now, despite all her resistance, there is David on the bed at Starbridge, turning towards her. He is on all the screens now, one after another, there are two banks of his face, row upon row, black and white and full colour. She sits with tears streaming until suddenly Graham is leaning over her saying well that's it, Annie, we knock off now, hope you haven't been too bored.

* * *

He ordered wine. 'Graham . . . I thought you weren't supposed to drink.' 'One glass won't hurt. Anyway, I can't let you get sloshed alone, it's not gentlemanly.' 'I'm not going to get sloshed.' 'You might as well, Annie – you've been sitting there weeping, haven't you – you might as well go the whole way. Come on,' he said, reaching out suddenly, patting her hand. 'Come on, cheer up, let's not have a performance, he wouldn't have cared for that at all, would he?'

'You know something?' she said, half an hour later. 'You're really quite nice. I never used to think that. But you really are.'

'Well, thanks a lot. It's good to know one's appreciated at last.' He grinned across the debris of the meal. 'Or is it that I've improved with time, do you imagine?'

'I don't think people do. Or at least – oh, I don't know one way or the other. Tell me something – tell me what mother was like.'

'Mother? Heavens, Annie, you knew her as well as I did.'

'I'm wondering,' she said, 'If I ever noticed her. I suppose that seems an extraordinary thing to say.'

'Not entirely.' He was silent for a moment. 'I see what you mean. You were always very busy, weren't you – as a kid, wrapped up in the things you were doing, and then bustling off at eighteen to get educated, working, getting married, all that . . .'

'Oh,' she said, 'that's not fair. I always . . .'

'. . . Popped back to see they were O.K.? Of course you did – I'm not criticising, Annie, you did a lot better by them than I did.'

'You were always mother's favourite.'

'Probably she felt there was more to worry about there. She was a bit scared of you – you were as sharp as a pin.'

'Was I? I never felt like that.'

'People never feel like they are,' Graham said. 'Or so I'm told. Come on, we'll have another half bottle.'

'What did she and father talk to each other about? That's what I don't seem to have any idea of. I can't even see them,' she said, 'when I look back. Talking.'

'The house? Holidays? You and me? Isn't that the kind of thing husbands and wives talk to each other about?'

'No.'

'Ah. Well, that's something you know more about than I do. My information is a bit stereotyped – picked up from scripts mostly, plus the odd bit of observation most of which I daresay one interprets quite wrongly. That's not what's talked about, then?'

'It's maybe what's talked. It's not what's talked about.'

'Ah.' He re-filled both their glasses, took the last cigarette from his packet and sat looking at her across the table.

'Mother . . .' she said, 'Go on.'

'I'll tell you one thing. I think she was happy, insofar as people are.'

'Was she? Yes, perhaps. I remember her being up, or down, but not as though it went very deep.'

'I think perhaps it didn't. She kind of absorbed things, mother. Backgrounds, people. Maybe that's why you feel you didn't know her. She had a habit of disappearing, as it were.'

'Yes, she did, didn't she? You're right. She was always there, but not determining things. Being determined by. Depressed if it was a nasty day; cheerful in nice places.'

'Negative,' said Graham. 'Dad, on the other hand, was positive.'

'Was he happy, do you imagine?'

'That I don't know. That's where I dry up. I don't think *I* ever noticed *him* enough. What do you think?'

'I'm glad he had this Betty Mansell person.'

'Glad?' he was startled now. 'I thought you were rather upset about all that.'

'I was at first. I've come to see it a bit differently, somehow.'

'Why, Annie?'

'Oh, I don't know. One thing and another. I went to see the daughter, by the way, I never told you, Shirley Barron.'

'What was she like?'

'Quite nice. A bit depressing. I think she'd want to come to the funeral. Or at least be told about it.'

'Oh Lord,' said Graham. 'Would she?' He sat fiddling with his glass, frowning a bit.

'We've got away from mother again.'

'Yes, we have, haven't we? Something else I'll tell you – she didn't ever know about Dad's lady, and she couldn't have done, either.'

'Couldn't have done?'

'She couldn't for one moment have believed it. That sort of thing wasn't inside her world; it was what went on in books, or in other people's lives. And Dad was very much inside her world. So he needn't have worried, really, if he did. He wasted a lot of feeling guilty, if he did feel guilty, which being the kind of bloke he was, I imagine he did.'

'Can you waste feelings?'

'Oh Lord, you're being as intense as when you were seventeen, Annie. I can't go through all that again – have a heart. It was wearing enough at the time.'

'I was quite wrong,' she said. 'You're not nice at all.'

'Well, it was worth waiting for. You've smiled. First time today.'

'Oh, Graham . . .'

'For God's sake – don't get all weepy again now. Here, have some more wine.'

'I've had quite enough. Sorry. There, I'm organized again.'

'Talking of which, I suppose we have to organize for Friday. Don'll go up with you, presumably.'

'Yes.'

'I'll meet you out at the house, then, shall I? I'll be driving up first thing. Is there anything else we have to fix – things in the paper, letting people know, all that?'

'No,' she said. 'I've done all that.'

'And we've got to think about the house at some point. Do we sell it or what. Or do you want to hang onto it for the time being, Annie?'

'No. We'd better sell it.'

'Sure? I just thought maybe . . .'

'No,' she said, 'there's nothing I want it for.'

The restaurant was empty. In a corner, the waiter totted up figures, glanced across at them from time to time. Graham said, 'I'll have to go – it's past three. Not that things won't grind on without me. Will you be all right?'

'Yes,' she said. 'I'll be all right.'

'See you on Friday.' He hesitated, then went on, 'You're quite sure about the house? I wondered if perhaps . . .'

'Then don't. Please, Graham.'

'O.K., Annie, enough said. You know best, I imagine. See you on Friday.'

'Look after yourself,' she said. 'And thanks for the lunch.'

She watched him pad away down the street on rubber-soled shoes, hands in the pockets of faded blue cotton trousers, his hair a little thin behind, very slightly stooped. He walks like father, she thought, just a bit, I've never noticed that before. The thought warmed her a little, sustained her on the journey back to Cuxing.

Fourteen

There is an element of mercy about the afterlude to death. Like the ritual mourning of primitive societies, the official requirements take up time and energy and place what has happened in a context. Anne, absorbed in the formula of letters, telephone calls, notification of this person and that, found herself carried almost painlessly through to Friday morning, seven o'clock, breakfast in the kitchen at Cuxing, rain coursing down the windows, Don in unfamiliar black suit checking the map.

'We shan't need that. I know the way.'

'Just thought there might be a possibility of dodging Banbury. Shall we get off, then?'

She walked out of the house, wearing an uncomfortable, unbecoming grey dress that had seemed the only appropriate garment, lurking unworn at the back of the wardrobe for years as though balefully awaiting just this occasion. The day reached ahead like a ladder to be climbed. There should be some drug, she thought, for days like this; a prescription that knocked you out so that you could do what has to be done and feel nothing, wake up twelve hours later with it all over, like an operation, kindly faces looking down at you saying, there, it's done with now, out of the way.

'Are you coming?' Don called from the car. 'It's past eight, Annie.' She picked up a brown envelope from the mat, addressed to herself, and stuffed it unopened into her bag.

Rain pelted the windscreen. Somewhere to the left of Oxford Don said, 'The weather's not doing much to lighten the occasion.' 'No,' she said, 'it all fits.' 'I've booked dinner for us at a place in Warwick this evening on the way back. I thought it might cheer you up.' 'Have you, darling?' she said, touched. 'That was nice, thank you.' She looked sideways at him, leaning a little forward to peer through the clogged windscreen, intent upon the road, and felt shrivelled with guilt, as though to toothache were added a sharp bout of arthritis. Is there any limit, she wondered, to the feelings that can be piled one upon another? Does nothing blunt anything else? Oxfordshire gave way to Warwickshire and rain to high winds that set the landscape heaving.

At Starbridge they waited for Graham in the sitting-room, awkward as though distanced from each other by the oddity of the day and their own appearance. Anne said, 'Goodness, when did you last wear that suit? It's not the one you had at Oxford, is it?' And Don replied no, not since London, as far as he could remember, it was never one he cared for. And as she thought of Graham and wondered how he would have seen fit to appear for today, there suddenly was his car and Graham getting out of it wearing a dark green suit with all the unease of a small boy rigged out for the first time in school uniform. 'I say,' she said, 'you do look peculiar.' And Graham wrenching at the too-tight waistband muttered something about having to borrow it from a friend and she began to laugh. 'Oh dear,' she said, 'how idiotic, why do we feel we have to dress like this. . . ?' They stood there, the three of them, outside the front door, with Don saying something about all going in his car rather than taking two, and for an instant she saw this same group seventeen years ago, in the same place, again costumed for the occasion, but bridal then, festive, and with her parents at either side, her father with grey top hat in his hand, looking (in recollection, at least) thoughtfully at Don. Weddings and funerals, she thought, (and christenings, except that we never paid too much attention to those), why compound the business by making people wear fancy dress? Or is it so that people forget the enormity of what has happened . . . She was gripped with the knowledge that she would never talk to her father again, person to person, daughter to father, as somehow she had never been during the weeks of his illness and senility. She got into the car beside Don and sat bleakly silent, staring out at the wind-ravaged trees and hedges. Graham had gone into the house to telephone the funeral parlour. They were to meet the hearse at the church.

'Who exactly,' Don had asked the night before, 'will be there?' And she had said, well, hardly anyone except us three. We knew he wouldn't have wanted a fuss, a big affair, you know . . . So I've written to cousin Edward and he's coming over from Stafford, and then there are a few local people who were friends, I got in touch with Mr Hammond, he's someone father saw a lot of over the last few years and he's told anyone else who ought to know. Mrs Ransome who used to work at the house sent flowers, apparently, that was nice, wasn't it? That's all, really – oh, except a Mrs Barron, she's someone whose mother was a family friend, she's dead now, though, the mother. And a man called David Fielding – a schoolmaster father used to go fishing with.

And Don had said 'Yes, I see,' and turned once more to the crossword.

The hearse stood in fat black prosperity in the lane that led to the church. 'If you're ready, sir,' said the man to Don (so obviously the responsible, head-of-family figure . . .) 'perhaps you'd like to lead into the church behind us.' And Don nods and says to Graham, I think you two should go ahead, and now Anne sees the others standing about uneasily by the porch, cousin Edward and the rest, and Shirley Barron in a dark blue dress and hat. And David. 'Right' says Graham, and takes her arm, and they walk together up the churchyard path behind the coffin (like the wedding, she thinks again, absurdly, I've done this before . . .) and into the church, past cousin Edward and the rest, without looking or speaking.

The church is Dec., with Perp. window on the north aisle and traces of Norman arch at the crossing, intruded upon by Victorian restoration work and alterations to the height of the nave at some point unspecified. The font, which Anne can see as she turns to walk down the aisle, is fifteenth century, carved with the seven sacraments, the figures ritually defaced in Cromwellian times. The hassock upon which she should kneel to pray, if she were in the habit of praying, has been embroidered in rather unpleasing colours by a member of the Mothers'

Union, and the screen at which she sits staring, so as to look ahead and not at the pews to the right, into which the rest of the congregation now quietly file, is another nineteenth century intrusion, of heavy oak.

The coffin has been placed at the top of the nave, just below the choir stalls. It looks lonely there, and smaller, somehow, than one would expect. There are flowers on it.

They have all been given little leaflets with the order of the funeral service. You are not expected to know that, as you should know Mattins or Evensong. She and Graham, in worried collaboration, have chosen the hymns, trying to remember what father liked. It was not easy. Since, as Graham pointed out, they had both been lapsed C. of E. since an early age, they had not been to church with him nor discussed his tastes. He had accepted their abandonment of religion without comment or apparent distress. He went to church himself more or less regularly, but without fuss, as one might visit the public library or attend meetings of a local society: it was not possible to know what he felt about it. There had been a paragraph in the Will expressing his wish to be buried in this churchyard.

They stand to sing, and sit to listen to the vicar, and stand again. The service is orderly, and tranquil, and although not lengthy somehow takes a long time: long enough for thoughts to roam from what the vicar is saying ('. . . whose neighbourly presence here in Starbridge so many of us are going to miss, a man whose natural modesty and reticence kept from many of us his past record as . . .') to the incongruity of the War Memorial window in the chapel (bayonets and tin helmets in khaki-coloured glass) to the coffin under its canopy of dahlias and chrysanthemums, whose shape becomes less disturbing as the half hour passes. It is not possible to see the non-family part of the congregation, segregated on the other side of the aisle, without turning the head, which Anne does not do.

It isn't really sad at all, she thinks, not just at this moment, anyway. It is like time suspended, as though here and now had no precedent nor sequence but existed all on its own, for its own sake, which is quite painless.

The sun shafts down through the Perp. north window (it must have stopped raining) and the congregation, uncertain in its small size which allows individual voices to be heard, sings and answers the vicar and sits and stands. Shirley Barron has a rather nice contralto; other voices are difficult to pin to persons. I understand, for once, Anne thinks, the solace of religion, not I think that it would ever have done me any good. And she wonders about her father: what did he find here, just a suspension of time and bother, or something larger?

But the suspension of time, like much else, is illusory. All of a sudden the vicar is turning to the altar to say the final prayer and the frock-coated men who have sat so unobtrusively in a side pew have moved forward to take up the coffin. Graham looks at her to see that she is ready and again they walk after the coffin down the aisle, with Don a tactful step or two behind, and out into the sunny churchyard and up through the long grass among the graves to a place at the far corner where a canvas-covered hole is ready. There is purple vetch in the grass, and a foam of old-man's-beard over the hedge at the end, and a robin singing in a bush. The vicar is already at the grave-side, and arranges them all with smile and gesture on the turf beyond, Anne and Graham in front, the rest somewhere about. A clump of blue crane's-bill, profusely flowering, has been sliced in two by the spade when the grave was dug, which seems a pity. The vicar folds his hands on his surplice and prays, and while he prays the frock-coated men do what has to be done with long canvas straps, quietly and competently, and the coffin has gone almost before one realizes it. The sun is very warm on the back, like an affectionate hand, and the wind shaking the line of poplars beyond the churchyard wall creates a blink of green and silver that is almost distracting. The men are pulling up their straps now, and stooping to roll them, and the vicar is strewing some earth upon the coffin.

Anne is amazed: she has never seen a burial before, except in films (Hamlet springs ridiculously to mind), and is surprised to find reality so close to pretence. This is how it is done, just as they said. The vicar stands for a moment in silent prayer, and then moves away over the grass, and after they have all stood for a moment or two they turn and move after him. The robin is still singing in the bush, and the wind ruffles the ivy on the older gravestones over there by the wall, the ones whose inscriptions are all but obliterated.

It is finished. That is that. They are all by the church porch again now and the vicar is shaking them by the hand, but it is Don who murmurs thanks and appreciation, not Anne or Graham who seem as yet unequal to the moment. And then the local friends come up and say a few words before discreetly leaving. And Shirley Barron. Anne says, 'It was very nice of you to come. This is my brother Graham,' and Shirley and Graham smile at one another and talk for a moment, until there is an awkward pause and Shirley Barron says well, she must be getting along, she supposes, and does so.

And now there is only David left. 'Oh,' Anne says, 'this is David Fielding, Don, who used to live here near father. You've met Graham, haven't you, David?' And David says, yes, he has indeed, and they all four stand there and agree that the service was very nicely done. The churchyard is quiet now, quite still except for a blackbird rummaging among the leaves; one feels the place would prefer to be left to itself now. David is saying something about one of the neighbours who came to the funeral and as he puts his hand up to shade his eyes from the sun Anne sees that healed scar on his thumb, from the day he cut himself pulling out the rose-bush. The rose-bush, she noticed last week, has produced two very vigorous new shoots; the roots must have survived underground. She feels suddenly very tired, and wishes everyone would go away. They walk together to the churchyard gate, and say goodbye, and David gets into his car and drives off, and Anne, Don and Graham get into Don's car. Don says he thinks they could all do with some lunch now, and what about that hotel in Lichfield?

* * *

'You never told me you were moving, Annie?' said Graham over lunch, and she replied guiltily that she must have forgotten, with everything else that had been going on.

'Nice house?' said Graham, and Don described the converted coach house with its two acres and its view of the downs and its scope for extension, should one want that. 'I was a bit lucky there,' he said. 'Anne got a tip-off from someone she knows in the local planning office and I was able to buy it before it came properly on the market.' And as he spoke Anne remembered that brown envelope she picked up off the mat as they left the house, stamped on the outside "Berkshire County

Council", she now saw, taking it from her bag, which accounted for the association of ideas.

'Excuse me,' she said. 'I never read my letter this morning.'

Reading, she began to smile. Oh no, she thought, this is absurd really, whatever will Sandra say . . . 'What's the joke?' said Don.

'I'm being offered a job. Would you believe it! By Mr Jewkes. They're appointing someone called an adviser to the planning officer, apparently, whose job is to go round looking at buildings from a historical point of view – finding out about their origins and so forth – supplementing their information on listed buildings – so that the local planning office can keep one jump ahead, as it were, and have information ready on old buildings that aren't listed but may become vulnerable to development or whatever.'

'It sounds just up your street,' said Don.

'It's a nice letter. Yes – yes, it does.'

'Local government – much more lucrative than teaching.'

'I'd get Grade III' she said, looking again at the letter. 'Whatever that may be.'

'Never mind the money,' said Graham. 'It's the job satisfaction that counts. You take it – next thing you know you'll be Town Clerk.'

'I think I will,' she said. 'You know I rather think I will take it.'

They went back to Starbridge, after calling in at the town's main estate agent. 'Are you sure,' Graham had said once more, coming out of the hotel, 'sure we shouldn't leave it for a few months?', and she replied no, we might as well get it over with, no point in the house standing empty through the winter. And if we haven't anything to make us we'll never get on with clearing things up there, will we? You'd better come out there now, if you've time, and decide what you want. We're not going home till later, Don and I.

She felt better. They were over now, both things; the funeral, seeing David. Time was on the move again. It will be all right, she thought, if it's no worse than this. Let's get on now, and do things. And I have a job; fancy that.

They toured the house. 'Oh Lord,' said Graham helplessly. 'What do we do with all this?' 'We see what we would like to keep,' she said, 'and give the rest away. Jumble sales and that.' Graham opened a wardrobe, and they fell silent at the row of suits, shoes, shirts. 'Look,' said Don, 'why don't you two leave me to put all this in boxes and take it down to Oxfam or somewhere – then you could get on looking through the china and things.' How tactful, she thought, how considerate. We seem all to be on our best behaviour today; perhaps it is the clothes that do it.

It did not take long, disposing of objects; this for him, that for me. But I don't need anything, Graham kept saying, the flat's stuffed with rubbish I don't use, anyway.

'It's not a case of needing. Here, I think you should have his desk. Do you remember how fascinating it used to seem, when one was a child – all those little drawers.'

'That ink-stain was your doing, wasn't it? I remember the commotion.'

They stood side by side, watching Don through the window, getting out of the car after his excursion to Oxfam. He came back into the house and went into the cloakroom. Anne said, 'We'd better get on – there's all the china yet.'

'It occurred to me,' said Don, coming into the room, the fishing-rod in his hand, 'that maybe this should go to that chap we were talking to this morning – didn't you say he was a fishing friend of your father's? And I suppose none of us has any use for it.'

Her father's desk, once before associated with the nauseous creep of guilt, heaves and plunges; the room is unstable for several seconds before she is able to say, 'Oh, I don't know . . . Maybe, but I expect he's got one of his own and I believe they're worth quite a bit.'

'Just as you like,' says Don, putting the rod in a corner, and Graham says, 'How about I make us all a cup of tea?'

'Lovely,' Anne says in gratitude. 'Yes, that's just what we need.'

* * *

'Haven't we been here before once?' she said, going into the hotel. 'Or is it that all Red Lions and Black Swans or whatever look the same?' The bar was lavishly beamed, aglow with brass and copper, the walls energetic with Regency hunting prints and racing scenes, unseasonal flowers spilling from the stone fireplace.

'Come to think of it,' said Don, 'you may be right. I seem to remember some jaunt to Stratford – years ago. But we didn't eat here; we tried to but it was full up. We bought stuff in the end and ate it by the river. Sherry?'

'Of course' she said, when he came back from the bar. 'It was the time we went to *Much Ado*. And yes, you're right, they turned us away and we had this picnic.'

'Nice that we've made it at last, then. Hungry?'

'So so. That was when we decided to have Judy.'

'Well, that I don't remember. I don't have your kind of total recall when it comes to some things. How about fish? Trout with almonds?'

'Fine,' she said. 'Imagine if we'd decided differently. No Judy.'

'Well, we didn't, did we? So there she is, take it or leave it. I think I'm going to try the duck.'

'Don't you ever think,' she said, 'about things being otherwise? Or having been otherwise?'

'It seems an unproductive line of thought.'

'Oh, it's unproductive all right, I suppose. But interesting. Anyway, I'm glad we decided to produce Judy. Aren't you?'

'Of course. She's not so bad, by and large. Which reminds me, are we to allow this request for a pony? One trout,' he said to the waiter, 'and one duck. What about a starter, Anne?'

'Melon. Or something. All right, a pony, I suppose. Remember I'm going to be working, though.'

'So you are. And could you,' he went on to the waiter, 'ask them to hurry it a bit. We've got a longish drive ahead.'

'Wasn't it nice of my Mr Jewkes,' she said, over the melon, 'to think of asking. And I thought we'd crossed swords, in a way, at the start.'

'Very nice.'

'I'd like to think it was a kind of beginning. Like the new house – I'm really feeling quite keen on that, darling. I can't think why I forgot to tell Graham about it. Beginning a different bit of life – I know you'll think that sounds silly, but well, I just feel that would be a good idea. It fits in, somehow, with father dying. And it being autumn.'

'Spring,' said Don, 'is surely the conventional time for new beginnings. But I daresay you're right. Change never did anyone any harm.'

'And you too. Taking over from Jim Thwaites. It's a beginning for you, too.'

'I suppose it is. Talking of which' – he paused, studying, apparently, the layout of the cutlery – 'talking of which, I ran into that young accountant we met with them that evening. Waiter . . . I think we could do with some rolls or something.'

'Oh, yes, I remember vaguely.'

'He seemed to remember you rather better than that. In fact he'd been out to your father's house to see if you were there, on the off-chance you could do with some help clearing things out.'

'Oh. I suppose I wasn't there.'

'You were there. But he didn't, in the end, ring the bell. It was first thing in the morning, apparently – he was on his way to Derbyshire for a day's fishing – he saw a car, two, in fact, he said, and . . .'

The trout and duck, arriving, interrupted for a moment. '. . . No, the fish is for my wife. And we asked for some salad, I think . . . Yes, we were somewhat at cross purposes at that point, he seemed to have been under the impression that I was up there, saw me, apparently, shaving at the bathroom window and decided that it was too early to intrude so . . .'

'But,' she said stupidly, 'you weren't.'

'Quite.'

The shock, the downward plummet of the stomach, is like, insofar as it is like anything, the realization that there is already another car on the crest of the road, coming hard at one. But there is no recession of the feeling as one brakes and swings back out of danger. Instead it lies there in the gullet, like a cold hard stone, and the hotel dining-room becomes very sharp and intense, like a dream landscape, and other people's voices unnaturally loud. The man at the next table is saying that given the present situation he cannot but feel one should draw in one's horns a bit, and a woman across the room thinks it is a mistake to use dahlias and michaelmas daisies together. The trout, which should be eaten, looks like plaster food, stage food on a set.

'Quite,' said Don. 'Which put me in a slightly awkward position. But fortunately someone turned up at that point – it was a pub, one lunch-time – and the thing was dropped.'

'Don,' she said, 'I . . .'

'It was, I take it, that schoolmaster?'

She nodded.

'Everything all right, sir?' said the dark presence looming behind Don's right shoulder, and Don, taking an exploratory mouthful of duck, said everything seemed to be fine, thank you.

'Madam?'

She nodded.

I feel sick, she thought, I can't eat this. Opposite, Don ate steadily. The man at the next table thought a lot depended on the next election; the woman across the room did not much care for antirrhinums, herself.

'How long?' said Don. 'If I may ask.'

'Since April.'

'And is he,' he said, 'married?'

'Yes.'

'Children?'

'Two.'

'Ah,' said Don. He glanced across the table at her. 'You haven't had any salad.'

She took salad, arranged it on her plate, looked at it. 'Don,' she said, 'I am so sorry.'

Don said again 'Ah . . .' The waiter, pausing in flight between the tables, swooped up their bottle of wine, filled both glasses, passed on.

'How long,' she said, 'have you . . .? No, I've no right to ask.'

'Let me see. It must have been about June I met Sheldon in that pub. End of.'

June. July. Scotland.

Nothing said.

All that time.

'Aren't you,' said Don, 'going to eat that trout?'

She picked up the knife and fork.

'Sheldon,' said Don, 'does a bit of work for us now and then, which made it the more potentially embarrassing.'

Embarrassing?

In former times, in some circles, the price of betrayal has been death, which seems reasonable enough.

Embarrassing.

'Why didn't you,' she said, 'say?'

'Say?'

'Say you knew.'

He looked at her now, over his plate, which was empty, and hers, which was not. 'I assumed,' he said, 'That it would blow over.'

Blow over?

'And am I,' he said after a minute or so, 'right?'

'Yes,' she said. 'Yes. It's blown over.'

The waiter, hovering for plates, looked pointedly at the quarter-eaten trout.

'I'm sorry,' she said. 'I'm not very hungry.'

'A sweet, sir? Cheese?'

'I think we'll just have coffee.'

They walk, Anne in front, Don behind, to the bar, which is also where coffee is taken. The other diners do not give them so much as a glance. They sit in the bar, amid the brass and copper and hounds in full cry, and drink coffee. Don scrutinizes the bill. There is an item which puzzles him, and which he queries with the waiter, but it is satisfactorily explained: Don takes ten pounds from his wallet, and the bill is paid. That was an expensive trout. 'Perhaps,' he says, 'we should be on our way?'

She said, 'Do you want to talk about it any more?'

'I don't see much point. Do you?'

'If I were you,' she said, 'I'd want . . . I'd feel . . .'

'But you aren't,' said Don. 'And as far as I am concerned, unpleasant as it is, the best thing now for both of us is to let things be. I take your word for it that it's blown over. I don't see the point in harping on what's done with. I'm not saying it doesn't make a difference, because of course it does. I think,' he said, 'you've been under rather a strain, this year, with your father's illness; I'd prefer to put this down, in part at least, to that, and regard the matter as closed. I don't want to make a meal of it, which I suppose some men might.'

Anne said, 'Yes. I think they might.'

'I assume it isn't going to become a habit?'

Is this a joke? She scans his face, but Don is not, on the whole, in the habit of making jokes, though sarcasm is not unknown. No, he is asking a question, because presumably he wishes to know the answer, and she replies that she is not planning to make a habit of it. Don nods and stares across the table at her; for an instant their eyes meet, before they both look away. The waiter brings change for Don's ten pounds, at which he quickly glances before he puts it in his pocket, leaving the appropriate tip in the saucer. 'Ready?' he says, and gets up. He goes towards the door, and Anne, taking her coat and following, finds that she is shaking all over, so convulsively that she cannot cope with putting on the coat, and has to carry it over her arm.

* * *

The road to Cuxing unreeled before the car, the headlights stripping away the darkness length by length – as far as the next corner, the top of the hill, the end of that line of trees. The road-signs, briefly illuminated, were according to expectation; Edgehill, Aynho, Abingdon. The landscape itself, diminished to the patch of light before the car, kept throwing up surprises; a bridge, a house, a tree, un-noticed on other journeys. The night both concealed and revealed. Anne thought: I knew this road, or imagined I did, but now it seems different – of course I've not done it at night before. She had stopped shaking. Don drove in silence except to remark once, at the Deddington traffic-lights, that he preferred driving by night. 'Do you?' she said dully. 'I don't. You see nothing but the road.' 'That's the point. It's the road you need to see. Quicker, too. Though I must admit this seems further than I'd thought.' Yes, she wanted to say, places have this way of being unreliable, never quite as constant as you think they are going to be. You think you have them under control, and then find that you have not. But there was a road-sign now, swimming into view at the Oxford roundabout, and Don, slowing for the junction, said 'Thirty-two miles now, give or take a bit, so we know where we are.' 'Yes. We shan't be too late back.' The car swept on, channelled as though by tramlines, and she sat looking ahead, seeing nothing, thinking backwards through the day, the year.